T0149318

Every Rogue Has His Charm

Also by Susanna Craig

Every Rogue Has His Charm

A Love & Let Spy Romance

By Susanna Craig

LYRICAL PRESS
Kensington Publishing Corp.
www.kensingtonbooks.com

LYRICAL PRESS BOOKS are published by

Kensington Publishing Corp.
119 West 40th Street
New York, NY 10018

All Kensington titles, imprints, and distributed lines are available at special quantity discounts for bulk purchases for sales promotion, premiums, fund-raising, educational, or institutional use.

Special book excerpts or customized printings can also be created to fit specific needs. For details, write or phone the office of the Kensington Sales Manager: Kensington Publishing Corp., 119 West 40th Street, New York, NY 10018. Attn. Sales Department. Phone: 1-800-221-2647.

Lyrical Press and Lyrical Press logo Reg. U.S. Pat. & TM Off.

First Electronic Edition: August 2022
ISBN: 978-1-5161-1130-5 (ebook)

First Print Edition: August 2022
ISBN: 978-1-5161-1131-2

Printed in the United States of America

Acknowledgments

My family's, and especially my husband's, support for my writing continues to amaze me; I am truly blessed. Many thanks to my agent Jill Marsal, my editor Esi Sogah, and the whole Kensington team for their patience, persistence, and perseverance in the face of extraordinary challenges. The authors of The Drawing Room have been exceptionally generous with their time and knowledge. I'm also grateful to my friend and colleague Randi Polk, who put into (French) words what I could not. Finally, to the readers whose enthusiasm for the Love & Let Spy series made this story possible, thank you. I hope you'll love what comes next, too.

To Amy,
for helping me through this—and every—book.
I can't thank you enough.

Chapter 1

September 1802

On the rare occasions when his conscience troubled him, Maximilien Grant reminded himself that all noblemen were thieves.

A man did not become a duke or an earl without claiming a right to things that were not truly his: land, the labor of those who worked the land, even the very bodies of those who labored. Distance—a few thousand miles, a few generations—made the provenance of their extraordinary wealth murky, allowed mere bandits to call themselves gentlemen. Some, he felt certain, had even persuaded themselves that their hands truly were clean. Nevertheless, every nobleman Maxim had ever met had something in his possession he ought not to have. Including Lord Earnshaw.

Otherwise, why would the man keep his library door locked?

Maxim had tested the door whenever he passed down the corridor—a dozen times at least. Never once had it been open. Strange behavior indeed, especially when at least a few of the guests at this infernal house party must be in want of something to read. It had been raining steadily for more than three days, and surely billiards and whist and even gossip could not stretch to fill eighty-two hours and some odd minutes.

Of course, several of the guests were content to while away the time in a supine position, either asleep, or—if the groans and giggles he had heard as he'd slipped from his chamber and passed silently through the west wing were any indication—awake and with a willing partner.

He'd not graced a house party in so long, he had forgotten the favored pastime: sex.

If he had remembered it, it would have been another excuse for turning down Earnshaw's invitation. Not that he objected to the occasional tumble, something to work off his frustrations and clear his head. But the sort of ladies one met at a house party were not his sort at all—which was to say, they were *ladies*, with expectations of gentlemanly behavior and the power to compel entanglements. He had no intention of being caught in either trap.

Good God, why had he listened to General Scott and come to Hertfordshire?

Two reasons, if he were honest. First, the damned Treaty of Amiens had somehow managed to bring about peace between Britain and France after nearly a decade of war, and Maxim had forgotten what to do with himself when he wasn't on assignment for the Crown. He'd hoped the party would offer something to counter his boredom.

(It hadn't. Perhaps because the boredom that plagued him was no ordinary sort. Perhaps it was not boredom at all, that deep pit inside him that nothing could fill. The war at least had been a distraction from it. The companionship and coziness on display at the house party had only made matters worse, providing a vivid reminder of what he lacked, of something he would never have.)

Second, he'd felt certain Scott had pressed him to accept the invitation to Earnshaw's estate for reasons that had nothing to do with a fortnight's leisure and everything to do with a suspicion that the earl was hiding something.

(He was. He must be. What other reason did Maxim have for being here? Why else was the damned library door always locked?)

The corridor was dim, the single sconce that had been left burning too far from the entrance to the library to provide either assistance or exposure as Maxim slipped a hand into his breast pocket and withdrew a set of lock picks in a worn leather case.

The thin metal implements had become old friends, having secured both his survival and his reputation at various points of his life. He could open a door or a drawer swifter than a rake could divest a virgin of her honor—and with fewer scruples. Other people's secrets were never safe with him. With practiced fingers, blunt and bold, he reached out to trace the keyhole. Earnshaw would regret—

At the slightest touch, the door swung inward a few inches, the only sound the catch of shock in Maxim's throat. Confronted with the unexpected liberty to search, he was suddenly no longer sure what he really sought. After sending a glance over his shoulder, he sidled through the narrow opening into the library and shut the door behind him.

For half a moment, he fancied he was alone in the pitch-black room.

Then he caught a whiff of smoke, the acrid hint of a recently snuffed candle.

"Who's there?"

The voice—a young woman's—came from across the room and to his left. He turned toward her automatically. "You'd have your answer already, ma'am, if you'd kept your candle lit."

She laughed, a low, genuine sound he had not expected.

Over the past week and a half—eleven days, to be precise—he had become well acquainted with the species of feminine laughter known as a giggle. From what he had been able to make out, giggling was intended to attract the gentlemen's notice, an effort in which it nominally succeeded, for such a grating noise proved difficult to ignore. A pity that no one seemed to have explained to the young women that what they really sought was a gentleman's unwavering *attention*.

Well, this young woman had his attention now. Her throaty laugh shot through him, accompanied by a bolt of lust.

"An excellent point, sir," she conceded, her voice closer now. The room must be familiar enough to her that she could navigate around its furnishings without benefit of sight. She had the advantage of him, then; he still could make out nothing. Only a trio of tall windows on the opposite wall hinted at anything less than utter blackness. "I put out the light because I thought you were my father, come to order me back to bed."

He'd been introduced to every one of Earnshaw's guests. But in his mind, the half dozen or so young women were still an undifferentiated huddle of silliness. In the drawing room and at dinner, clad in pale gowns, their feathered headdresses tipped together, they reminded him of nothing so much as an unruly brood of clucking hens.

Now, he found himself wishing he had looked closer. Or listened more carefully. Then he might have been able to recognize this one, despite the darkness.

"I'm not your father." He spoke low, his gravelly voice little more than a growl.

He bit back the temptation to make some remark about ordering her to bed anyway.

Another laugh, this one a shade less confident. Almost a giggle. Perhaps she'd begun to consider the risks of being a young woman alone, in the dark, with a stranger.

Good.

"I'll just...go," she whispered, brushing past him on her way to the door, close enough that he smelled her rosewater perfume. Her hand must have trembled when it at last found the doorknob. It rattled loudly in the quiet room as she fumbled to open it, not once, but three times. The final attempt was accompanied by a low moan of something very like terror. "You—you've locked us in, sir."

"Nonsense." He too reached for the doorknob and caught her hand instead. She jerked away as if scalded. Grasping the brass oval, he twisted hard—foolishly; he of all people should know that opening a lock was rarely a matter of strength—and felt the knob come loose in his hand. He swore.

She did not, as he'd half expected, suck in a sharp breath or scold him or faint. Instead, her sigh was thick with exasperation. "You've broken it entirely, haven't you?" And then she swore too—a more delicate epithet, rather than an oath, but still outside the bounds of ladylike behavior. "Can I trust you not to do any further damage if I leave you and try to find the tinderbox to light another candle?"

Before he could warn her never to trust him, or any man, a whisper of fabric told him she had already walked away, presumably in the direction of the hearth. A few moments later, he heard the telltale rattle and scratch of a flame being struck, followed by a flare of light, and finally the steady glow of first one and then a pair of candles on the mantel.

She'd had to stand on tiptoe to reach them, and the long dark braid running down her back swayed gently as she dropped back onto her heels. Her feet were bare beneath a pale gown that he knew without having to investigate was her nightgown, not even a dressing gown to cover it. The thin fabric—muslin, cambric, something—did shockingly little to disguise her pleasantly round arse.

If he'd needed further proof that he was cursed, he'd found it: alone, in a locked room, with a young woman in a shocking state of dishabille. He'd be fortunate if he didn't find himself paying for this mistake with the rest of his life. "*Merde*," he muttered beneath his breath.

Slowly she turned, giving him more than a glimpse of her lush curves—thighs, belly, breasts—along with their equally tempting shadows. Above the nightgown's high neckline, her face was that of a debutante, fresh from her first season, still youthfully round. Even her lips were plump, soft...though presently set in a prim line, an expression he suspected she'd borrowed from some matron, probably her mother.

"Lord Chesleigh," she said, and sighed again. "I might have known it would be you."

* * * *

Caro hadn't schemed to get caught in a compromising position. But if she'd thought of it, she certainly would have chosen to be trapped after midnight in the library with some other of the eight eligible gentlemen in the house. Most anyone but the Marquess of Chesleigh.

A man of thirty or thereabouts, heir to a dukedom, ought to have been the party prize every marriage-minded young lady and her parents were angling to win. But not one of them had pushed their daughter in Lord Chesleigh's direction.

The man was…well, *daunting* she supposed was the politest word to describe him. Six feet tall and then some, with broad shoulders. Dark hair and eyes, and a faintly Mediterranean tint to his complexion. A severe expression, even at the best of times—which this most assuredly was not.

At the moment, however, she could not see his expression. He had turned his entire attention back to the door, dropping heavily to one knee, the better to fiddle with the broken knob. She slipped back to the window seat to collect her woolen shawl, draped it around her shoulders, and then obliged him by bringing the light closer.

He grunted his acknowledgment—no one would have called it a sound of gratitude—never glancing her way. Even in profile, his scowl was ominous. "How the devil did you get in here to begin with?" he demanded as he worked. "The door's always locked."

"It isn't," she countered. "The latch sticks. I had one of the footmen show me the trick—you have to jiggle the handle just so to get it to cooperate," she explained, miming the movement. The motion made the light dance, earning her a hard glare. She dropped her free hand to her side. "But he warned me never to shut the door once I was inside, or I'd be here until the parlor maid came—the bell pull is broken, and she only dusts the library every third day."

Lord Chesleigh answered with a single word, one she did not recognize and which she felt certain no lady ought. She wasn't even sure it was English. He tossed the knob onto the carpet, where it landed with a soft thud, then pushed himself to standing. Her eyes were level with his chest. "Well, what now, Miss—?"

"C-Caro." The polished buttons of his waistcoat shone; she fought the urge to adjust the topmost one, still caught partly in its buttonhole. Either he had dressed hurriedly, or his valet was unobservant. "Lady Caroline Brent. Lord Laughton is my father. And I suppose we might as well sit down and wait."

He did not sit down. He strode past her, threading his way among the groupings of tables and chairs with ease, despite a noticeable limp. At the center window, he stopped. She had spent enough time in those deep window wells over the past week to know that the drop to the ground below must be nearly twenty feet. Nevertheless, he stood for some time, watching the rain lash the glass, staring out into the bleak darkness as if contemplating the leap.

At long last, he dragged a hand through his hair and turned away from the window, though not to face her.

"Have you read *The Highwayman's Hostage*?" she asked. "It's by a new author, Robin Ratliff. I must say, you bear an uncanny resemblance to one of the characters."

It was the scars that did it, the worst of them a jagged seam down the left side of his face, running from temple to jaw, over a cheek that was slightly concave. Rumor had it, there were still more scars beneath his hair, which he let grow overlong expressly for the purpose of disguising them. But nothing could hide his nose, which no doubt had been prominent even before it had been broken, its aquiline shape rendered crooked and distinctive. He'd been injured in a brawl, a brothel, a duel—or so the rumors went.

Where Lord Chesleigh was concerned, there were no end of rumors.

One corner of his mouth lifted, though she could by no stretch of the imagination consider the expression a smile. Perhaps the injury to the opposite side of his face meant he never smiled. "The villain, I presume?"

When it had first been announced that he was to be among the guests at Lord Earnshaw's house party, whispers had buzzed around the drawing room like so many bees. A marquess. Grandson of the Duke of Hartwell. Wealthy. And despite his evident injuries, still in possession of all his faculties and most of his limbs.

But mysterious, too. Secretive. No one had seen him for years. Rumor had it he'd run away to India. Or perhaps it was the West Indies.

Rumor had it, he'd done scandalous things.

And here she was, wearing only her nightgown, trapped alone in a room with him for heaven knew how long. The clock on the mantel chimed one. What would happen when they were found?

What might happen if they weren't?

"I cannot say, my lord. I'm only halfway through volume one."

Lord Chesleigh's chest rose and fell—not a laugh, precisely, but something like it. "You're a great reader, I take it?" He gestured her toward a chair, not waiting until she had seated herself before sprawling in the one opposite.

She perched on the edge of the seat, curling her toes into the carpet to keep herself from sliding forward, conscious of the prickle of horsehair beneath her bottom. "I am."

"Gothic tales, romances—I daresay those are your favorites." The words were accompanied by another smile that wasn't. Lord Chesleigh was not a handsome man. But striking, compelling. A man obviously accustomed to being found intimidating.

Her chin popped up, almost of its own volition. "Yes."

"Your father approves of his daughter filling her head with such notions?" He tipped his head to one side, studying her. "No. If he did, you would not be sneaking out after bedtime. Hmm." She could not decide whether she liked the way his black eyes glittered as they swept over her. "What will he do if he catches you?"

"I am not a child, Lord Chesleigh."

"In some ways, certainly not. But in others?" He punctuated the words with a Gallic shrug. "You are evidently child enough not to have considered the ramifications of the predicament in which you find yourself."

"In which I—? But you—do you mean to suggest that people will think we—?" Her cheeks heated. Hadn't she just been thinking along those same lines herself? "Well, then, why aren't you working to get the door open?"

"Why aren't *you*?" He steepled his fingers over his chest and leaned his head against the chair's high back, as if preparing to take a nap. "Some of us haven't a reputation left to guard."

"How dare you—!" She jumped to her feet and hustled to the door, stooping to gather the pieces of the broken door latch and then kneeling as she tried to fit them back into their places. It was no use, of course, since her hands were trembling with fury and she had no idea what she was doing.

He left her to fuss over it for perhaps five minutes, though it felt an eternity, before striding once more across the room and thrusting out his hand. With a choked noise, she laid the assorted pieces of metal on his palm.

He tumbled them over with his thumb, then once more tossed them aside before holding out his hand to her again. It took her a long moment to realize that he meant to help her rise. As soon as she was on her feet, he ordered her to fetch a light and knelt stiffly in her place. When she returned with the candle, he was trailing a fingertip over a set of thin metal implements in a leather case, a notch of concentration in his brow. Once he'd made his choice of tools, he tucked the case into his breast pocket and set to his task.

She held up the candlestick with determinedly steady hands and watched him work out of the corner of her eye. Surely he could get them free before anyone discovered her foolish mistake?

…Surely a gentleman shouldn't know how to pick a lock?

He muttered under his breath all the while; she didn't try to sort out the words. After a few minutes, he paused to shrug out of his coat and tossed the garment aside to join the broken pieces of the lock. If there were rumors that his tailor padded his shoulders to make them appear broader, Caro now knew enough to deny them.

At long last, she heard a soft click, and he rocked back slightly as the door sprang inward an inch or two. The breath that shuddered from her lungs nearly extinguished the candle.

He hoisted himself to his feet. "You sound relieved. Has my company grown tiresome, ma'am?"

She avoided his sardonic gaze. "I'm quite sure, my lord, that you must be equally pleased to be at liberty. You did not come to the library tonight expecting to have to break out."

She'd spoken lightly, thoughtlessly. But hard on the heels of her words came a more somber truth, one that would have been obvious sooner if she hadn't been so distracted. He'd come after midnight to a room he believed to be locked...prepared to break in.

Why?

Swiftly looking up, she saw the reflection of her belated realization in his eyes, and for the first time, she felt a frisson of fear. The candlestick began to slip from her suddenly sweat-dampened hand. He curled his fingers around hers to keep it from tumbling from her grasp, but just as he opened his mouth to speak, she heard footsteps in the corridor.

Without thinking, she reached out with her free hand to shut the library door again. Lord Chesleigh caught her other wrist in an implacable grip. One dark eyebrow arched skyward. "Once is enough for me, ma'am."

"There's a light in the library." *Oh, God. Papa's voice. No hope of escape now.*

"Caro?" Her mother that time, sounding worried.

With surprising gentleness, Lord Chesleigh nudged her toward the door as he opened it wider, so that as she stepped into the corridor, he remained invisible to the arrivals.

Among the search party were Lord and Lady Earnshaw and Miss Shelley, with whom Caro had struck up a friendship over the past week. Mama and Papa must have knocked at her door first, in hopes of finding their daughter, and gone next to alert their hosts.

"What are you doing here?" Papa demanded, leaning toward her with such a ferocious gleam in his eye that she had no choice but to take half a step backward.

"I couldn't sleep. I came to fetch something to read, but then the d-door—" A shiver passed through her.

"I thought you told Wilson to see to that broken latch," said Lady Earnshaw to her husband. Mama tutted and reached out to draw the woolen shawl more tightly around Caro's shoulders.

But Papa would hear nothing of the excuse. "And what if word of this little escapade gets about?" he hissed, looking her up and down, his disgust plainly written on his face. "What will become of you—your sister—all of us—if the gossips learn you were running about Earnshaw's house after midnight, half-naked? People will say you were meeting a lover. And who will want to marry you then?"

"Who indeed, Laughton?"

Lord Chesleigh's voice was impossibly deep. It made her feel as tremulous as the plucked strings of a harp. And that faint accent...hadn't someone said his mother was French? Or was that merely another rumor?

Still clad in his shirtsleeves, he stepped out of the shadows to stand close behind her, and she had the satisfaction—brief and bleak though it might be—of watching the color leach from her father's face.

Miss Shelley, in contrast, turned brightest pink, and Lady Earnshaw laid a consoling hand on Mama's shoulder as she sobbed a single, quiet word: "R-ruined."

In spite of his pallor, something strange glittered in Papa's eyes. "You'll regret this, Chesleigh."

"I daresay," the marquess drawled.

And then, to Caro's shock—she'd never before known that the word comprised such a welter of emotions: surprise, uncertainty, and a surge of anticipation—he dropped to his knee for the third time that night and, with an ironic twist to his lips, asked her to make him the happiest of men.

Chapter 2

If he lived to be one hundred years old—and he wouldn't; thirty had been challenge enough—Maxim would never know why he'd done it. Despite his brawn, he wasn't the protecting sort. And despite—or perhaps because of—his title, he certainly wasn't the honorable sort.

But Lady Caroline Brent, who'd shown no fear of him, had flinched at the sound of her father's voice, and he'd been forcibly reminded of what it was to feel helpless and to long for a way to escape.

Was it escape he'd offered her?

Perhaps there was no escape, just moving from one prison to another.

In any case, she'd accepted him, and with only a moment's hesitation. And he had left Earnshaw's house a few hours later, the steely dawn sky presaging another day of rain, bound for London to arrange for a special license and to meet with his solicitors.

His last night as a bachelor he spent alone in his study on Curzon Street; he'd won the house in a hand of cards from some fool who'd promptly blown out his own brains—thankfully somewhere other than in the study. Since coming into its possession in June, Maxim had done nothing at all to make the house his, except to improve the quality of the brandy in the decanter on the corner of the desk.

Now, he splashed a swallow of rich amber into a glass as he sat down to write a letter to his grandfather, scratching out a few lines in French— *qu'il aille se faire foutre, ce vieux*—to be sent only after the fateful deed was done.

The morning of his wedding dawned bright and fair. A good omen—at least until the moment Lady Caroline Brent had stood beside him before the chancel and a shaft of sunlight had fallen across her veiled face. Her hair—he'd thought it brown—gleamed auburn, fierce and fiery, reminding him of her show of boldness in Earnshaw's library.

But an innocent girl of twenty could have no notion of what she'd gotten herself into by agreeing to marry a man like him. The void in his soul would smother the flame of her spirit. The certainty of it left him breathless.

What another, wiser man might have recognized as feelings of pity or dread, he could only call anger. And the sight of a familiar older gentleman near the rear of the church, smiling at him and his bride, further ratcheted up Maxim's fury. If he hadn't agreed to go to Earnshaw's bloody party, he would never have—

"Allow me to be the first to offer you felicitations, Lady Chesleigh," the man said, bowing over her hand.

Before she could reply, they were surrounded, or so it seemed. The mother of the bride and a maiden aunt on her father's side, both sniveling; Caro's weak-chinned young brother offering to shake his hand; beside him, another dowerless sister, no doubt eager for her coming-out in another year or two. All of them, burbling their well wishes and exclaiming over Caro's good fortune. And then, above the din, Laughton's voice, proclaiming his hearty appetite for the wedding breakfast.

On his way out of the house that morning, Maxim had passed by the dining room, vaguely astonished that his few words to Mrs. Horn, the housekeeper, had resulted in such a transformation: china and silver and glassware for a dozen guests, polished and laid out on pristine linens; flowers and dainties, both abundant; a row of chafing dishes at the ready; a pair of footmen—did he employ them?—in spotless livery, standing guard.

"I hope Lady Chesleigh will be pleased," Mrs. Horn had said, watching him survey her preparations.

Now, Maxim blinked away the memory and laid a heavy hand on his father-in-law's shoulder. With the proper pressure, the man would crumple to his knees.

"Perhaps, Laughton, you did not read the marriage settlements with sufficient care." If he had, the terms Maxim's solicitors had set out would have dulled the avaricious gleam in the man's eye. "You and your family must expect nothing further from me." He tightened his grip and had the pleasure of watching Laughton grimace. "Not even if you are starving."

Not sparing a glance for his wife, Maxim caught her by the elbow and led her from the church and into his waiting carriage, blessedly unsullied by trailing streamers, old boots, and the like. He'd ordered his groom to shoot vandals on sight.

To his immense relief, she neither wept nor cowered. She sat, ramrod straight, as the horses began to move and the scenery of Mayfair began to slide past. In the relative dimness of the carriage, her hair was once more merely brown. But her eyes, which were fixed on him with a remarkably steady gaze, he now knew to be hazel, a mixture of gold and brown and green that intrigued him in spite of himself.

They were halfway to Curzon Street before she spoke. "Why did you propose this marriage, my lord? To punish me, or yourself?"

The question earned her a smile, his first of the day and the sincerest in months. "Mostly, I think, to punish your father."

At his answer, the corners of her mouth curved upward slightly and the set of her spine relaxed. "What a remarkable coincidence, my lord. I accepted you for the same reason."

Maxim's shoulders eased too. Spite, he understood. As a motive, he could appreciate it.

Perhaps there was hope for his new wife after all.

* * * *

Caro felt quite certain that any young woman in her right mind would be afraid of Lord Chesleigh. What did it say of her that she was not?

Not that her new husband was not intimidating. But given the choice between her father's familiar cruelties and the temperament of a perfect stranger, she'd been more than ready to take her chances.

"Did he strike you?"

Was it her imagination or had Lord Chesleigh's already dark eyes darkened a shade further?

"With words," she answered after a moment, "more often than his hand. I have been a grave disappointment to him, you see. I was expected to marry well to save the family fortunes, but alas, until a few days past, my charms had proved insufficient to overcome my lack of dowry."

Skepticism flashed across his features. "And your sister?"

Would he relent on his vow never to help her family, if she pleaded on their behalf? But the truth was, her father's wrath had never been meted out equally. And in spite of a proper Christian upbringing, she was not quite ready to forgive. "Catherine is clever enough not to displease him." A wicked, humorless laugh tugged at her lips before she could chase it away. "She is not, for example, a great reader."

He folded his arms across his chest and muttered a few words she did not catch.

They rode the rest of the way in silence. The house before which the carriage stopped was large and grand, befitting a man of Lord Chesleigh's station. His family's townhome, she assumed.

But once inside, he surrendered her to the care of the housekeeper, Mrs. Horn, who explained in the most delicate terms possible that his lordship, who had lived abroad for many years, had only recently acquired the property, following the previous proprietor's unfortunate accident.

"I do believe," Mrs. Horn told her in a low voice, her matronly cheeks a surprising shade of pink, "that his lordship has held off on any redecorating, in order to give his bride the pleasure."

For her part, Caro saw little need for great changes. The public rooms were not done up in the latest fashion, it was true, but neither were they shabby. Her own chambers were airy and bright, with pale blue walls and draperies framing wide windows through which she could just glimpse the green expanse of Hyde Park. She could imagine any number of ways to better use her time than looking at swatch books and wrangling with decorators and tradesmen.

After promising to send up a tray, Mrs. Horn left her to rest. In the dressing room, Caro discovered that her things had already been unpacked—hardly a daunting task, for there had been neither funds nor time to order a lavish trousseau. Would Lord Chesleigh be displeased tonight to find her wearing the same nightgown in which he had first seen her?

Despite a sudden flush of nervousness, she mustered a laugh. He did not strike her as the sort of man who noticed such things at all.

By the time she had removed her gloves and unpinned her hat, the breakfast tray had come. Afterward, she lay down on the bed, as Mrs. Horn had urged. She had slept little enough the last few nights that when she awoke, it was midafternoon. After writing a letter to Miss Shelley, she made her way downstairs and asked one of the servants where she might find her husband.

"His lordship's gone out, ma'am, and begs you not to wait for him to dine."

At seven, then, she dined alone, at one end of a vast table, in a room that smelled of flowers, though there were none. At eight, restless, she peered into the drawing room and two sitting rooms, but finding nothing with which to amuse herself, she asked whether there was a library in the house.

"Only his lordship's study, ma'am." And though the footman's eyes directed her to the proper door, she demurred, curious but reluctant to trespass, and retired to her chambers instead, to bathe and ready herself for bed.

At half past nine, clad in her high-necked cambric nightgown, both the hem on one sleeve and her nerves beginning to fray, she answered the diffident tap at her door—Mrs. Horn, or one of the maids—with a rather testy-sounding, "Come."

The door swung open to reveal Lord Chesleigh, wearing a brocaded silk dressing gown over his shirt and trousers and carrying a paper-wrapped parcel. "Should I take it from that rather insincere invitation that you do not wish to be disturbed?"

When she'd gone to bed, she'd left three candles burning, two on the mantelpiece, their flames doubled by a gilt-framed mirror hanging above the hearth, and one on the bedside table. Their combined light was insufficient to make out the expression in his hooded eyes, but enough to silver the wicked scar along the side of his face. Her heart began to hammer against her ribs—though what drove its rhythm still was not fear.

"Is that for me?" She pushed herself more upright against the pillows and nodded toward the package.

He stepped into the room and closed the door behind him. "A wedding gift, you might say." He laid the parcel on the bed beside her.

She tugged at the bow of twine, and the paper fell away to reveal three duodecimo volumes, neatly bound in claret-colored leather. With one fingertip, she lifted the topmost cover. "*The Highwayman's Hostage*," she breathed, surprise nearly robbing her of breath. The book she'd mentioned in Lord Earnshaw's library. He'd remembered. "Thank you. But I haven't anyth—"

I haven't anything for you.

Foolish, foolish words. She knew why he had come, of course.

Just as he knew what she had been about to say. A sardonic smile twisted his features. "If you would rather read, I can leave you in peace," he said.

Words stuck in her throat. Methodically, she wrapped the books again and laid them on the table. When the place beside her on the bed was free, he took it, settling just on the edge of the mattress, not touching her, though she had never in her life been so aware of another person's presence.

"I waited until it was dark." He was looking not at her, but at the candle, as if mesmerized by its flickering light. "To spare you as much unpleasantness as I could."

As if to confirm that he referred to his scars, a muscle ticked along his jaw and the mark on his cheek leaped into prominence.

"I'm not afraid," she insisted, reaching for his hand.

He jerked away before she could touch him, rising to his feet. "I hope to God this show of bravery isn't due to ignorance." As he spoke, he stumped to the mantel and extinguished the candles there. "Perhaps no one has explained the rudiments of marital relations to you?"

Her cheeks burned brighter than the single taper that remained lit. "I know enough. You—your"—she circled her wrist in the air, hoping to grasp the proper words—"manly affair gets stiff and in order to p-plant your seed, you push it inside me, and I must bear up under the discomfort of it, because that is how heirs are made."

He coughed—to disguise a laugh, she felt sure. "That is...*rudimentary* knowledge, indeed. But enough to be going on with, I suppose." He shed his dressing gown, revealing the deep V of his open shirt, filled by a forest of dark, curling hair.

As he moved to snuff the wick of the last candle between his forefinger and thumb, she said, "Wait."

His hand hovered there, barely out of reach of the flame.

"Mama also hinted..." Mortification flooded her veins, but she had to know. "Rumor has it your injuries are so extensive that you might not be able to perform your, um, husbandly duties."

She had no word for the emotion that flared to life in the depths of his black eyes. "No such luck, I'm afraid." And with a snap of his fingers, the room went dark.

"I'm glad," she whispered into night. "Then Papa will not be able to have this marriage annulled."

The bitter ghost of a laugh skated across her scalp. He'd stepped closer— how did he move so silently with that limp? "Let him try."

She felt the coverlet lift away. "I want you bare, Caro. Every inch."

"But you cannot *see* me," she protested feebly, even as she reached for the hem of her nightgown to draw it off.

"I can touch you. Taste you. That must be enough."

"Oh." The nightgown whispered to the floor. "And will you be bare too?"

The answering silence was loud, broken only by the creak of the bed as the mattress sank a few inches beneath his weight. His featherlight touch along her arm made the fine hairs there rise, but when she turned toward him, he swiftly caught her wrists in one hand, the room's darkness evidently no impediment to him. "The sight of my scars would repulse you; the sensation of you probing them would be agony to me." Stretching her arms above her head, he pinned them there with inexorable, but not uncomfortable, pressure. "I will tie your hands to the bedpost if I must."

"I—I won't touch you. You have my word."

But he did not release her, only set his lips unerringly to hers.

Everything was new and strange to her: the softness of his mouth, the flick of his tongue, the sandy scrape of his freshly shaven jaw against her cheek. She found a paradoxical freedom in being his prisoner, free to let the rest of her senses run wild.

From her mother's scant description, she could not have expected that he would be slow about his business, or gentle. She could not have known how her skin would respond to his calloused fingertips as he traced the shell of her ear, the turn of her throat, the valley between her breasts, learning her body—every inch of it, as he'd vowed. And when his mouth followed his fingers down her neck to her breast, she could not disguise her whimper of need.

"Please, my lord," she whispered against his hair, uncertain for what she begged.

"When I'm in your bed, you may call me Maxim."

She'd spoken his name—a long string of names, some French, some English—in church, of course, though she'd been too nervous to commit them to memory. But she recalled now that *Maximilien* had been among them. "Maxim," she repeated. She would not forget again.

His hand moved lower, to the joining of her thighs. *This is it*, she thought, steeling herself. But he continued his unhurried exploration, brushing softly over her crisp curls, stroking the delicate skin of her inner thighs, and finally circling his fingertip around a place so sensitive, she bit her lip to keep from crying out. When he discovered what she had done, he first chided her, then covered her mouth with his, greedily swallowing her moans as he ruthlessly built her pleasure, driving her toward something that sparkled and shone just out of reach.

The crisis, when it came, brought tears to her eyes, and rippling waves of delight that unspooled from deep within her. Hardly had she released a sigh of satisfaction when he began to kiss the tears away. "Again," he murmured, his breath hot at her ear, his touch insistent—almost too much, at first, but then, just what she needed.

Twice more he brought her to climax, until she was boneless, floating above herself. As she listened to him shuck his clothes, she realized he must have released her hands, though she didn't move them, wasn't even sure she had the strength to lift her arms.

Maxim, however, had strength enough for both of them. With ease, he rolled her onto her belly. "Lift your hips," he coaxed.

She'd nearly forgotten what was yet to come. But Mama's description of the marital bed had been nothing like this. He positioned himself behind her, his member hot against the backs of her thighs. "This is how beasts mate," she exclaimed, not exactly protesting. She could feel him at the entrance to her body.

"And does not rumor have it that I'm a beast?"

His voice rumbled through her as he nudged his pelvis forward, one hand holding her hip, the other stroking soothingly up her spine. Still pliant from his earlier efforts, her body was ready to welcome him, and a momentary pinch of discomfort soon gave way to the pleasure of being stretched by him, filled by him.

As he began to thrust, she instinctively pushed back to meet him, arching her back, the better to feel the fur of his chest against her skin. "Yes, a beast," she gasped when at last he drove into her with a grunt and held himself deep. A rush of heat flooded her core.

His weight bore her down to the mattress, and his body covered hers. Though in this position it was still impossible for her to touch him, she no longer cared. He was touching her, inside and out, everywhere at once.

She wasn't sure if she dozed, but the next thing she remembered, the weight and warmth of his body had lifted, leaving her chilled. The darkness of her bedchamber was not as absolute as the darkness of Lord Earnshaw's library. She watched the shadowy outline of his figure as he slipped into his dressing gown, a few feet from the bed.

"Must you go?" she murmured drowsily.

Startled by the sound of her voice—or by the question she posed—he paused. "You wish me to stay?"

"Yes."

He returned to the bedside and dropped a soft kiss on her shoulder. *"Et c'est pour ça que je dois partir."*

And that is why I must leave.

In her present state, she could just manage the translation. What he meant by those words was beyond her.

"Bonne nuit, Lady Chesleigh."

Good night, my lord.

The words never left her lips. She was asleep before the door closed behind him.

* * * *

Maxim made it his business not to be taken by surprise. He had known the character of his father-in-law, well before his wife's description of the man. Knew his brother-in-law to be an imbecile and his sister-in-law a flirt; knew too that his mother-in-law muted her sorrows with laudanum.

Poor form, perhaps, to use his vaunted investigative skills to gather such paltry information, but since the peace, what else was he to do with them?

What he had not known, what he could never have expected, was that his innocent English bride would show no sign of fear or repulsion when he'd come to her bed. That his rough touch would make her sigh and plead and mewl with pleasure. That when she had rightly called him a beast as he'd ridden her with animal abandon, there would be both hunger and satisfaction in her voice.

The discovery had alarmed him enough that he had been unable to sleep, despite his own satiation. He'd prowled the house until dawn, then taken to the streets, walking until Mayfair was far behind him, eventually picking a fight with his fists—and not at one of those posh clubs where so-called gentlemen liked to box.

He returned to Curzon Street not quite an hour before dinner and rang for bathwater. Only after the footmen left did he strip off his clothes. As he stepped toward the tub, he prodded a tender spot on his side, where his opponent had landed a single blow before Maxim had pummeled him into mincemeat. The large cheval glass caught the reflection of his movement, drawing his eye. Steam rising from the bath softened the image, but evidence of his myriad injuries was still plainly visible: the innumerable scars, the knobby protrusions of once-broken ribs, the twisted sinews stretched taut over the withered muscles of his thigh.

He'd lied to her.

The old wounds no longer pained him, much—leastways, not the visible ones.

She was waiting for him in the dining room, dressed in a gown she had probably worn at least once at Earnshaw's. And perhaps last season as well.

Much like her thin, worn nightdress.

"Go to the best modiste on Bond Street," he said. "Buy whatever your heart desires. Have the bills sent to me."

She blinked up at him, her eyes more gold than green in the candlelight. "Thank you, my lord."

He could tell she had been more pleased with the gift of books.

As the footman laid plates of soup before them, she reached for her spoon. "My lord, who was the gentleman at the church yesterday? The one seated in the very back?"

Maxim dismissed the servants with an imperious look. "General Zebadiah Scott."

"Oh. A military man." The spoon hovered over the dish for a long moment before breaking the surface of the creamy soup. "A friend of yours, I take it?"

He pondered how Scott would have answered the question. Friendship required trust, after all. A willingness to trust others. The ability to trust oneself.

Then, just as he started to shake his head, he thought again of the fact that Scott had sent him to Earnshaw's, where he had met Caro. An act of friendship?

"In a manner of speaking," he conceded, pushing away his untouched plate.

Over fish, she asked whether it was true that he had been away from England for many years.

"More rumors?"

His fiercest scowl did not deter her. "Yes."

"I've traveled on the Continent and...elsewhere," he answered her, after a moment. *Egypt, the West Indies. But what were countries, continents, to a man without a home?*

"What fascinating stories you must have to tell."

"Yes," he agreed, thinking for a moment of what relief a man might enjoy, at last having someone to whom he could tell his tales.

But he did not offer to tell them.

Despite his warning, she was testing, prodding, probing. Too clever by half, his lady wife.

And far too tempting.

He had foreseen no difficulty in keeping a safe, respectable distance between them; instead, after dessert, he found himself following her into her chambers, snuffing the candles, and joining her in her bed.

"Maxim." She sighed into his mouth as he pinned her wrists again, and he let himself stay with her nearly until dawn, pouring sweet words into her ears, driving her to peak after peak, seeking something from her that had no name in any language he knew.

The next morning, in the breakfast parlor, as she buttered a piece of toast, she asked, "Is it true you have cut off all communication with your grandfather, the duke?"

"Of course not," he said, thinking of the terse letter at present wending its way to Northumberland and hoping that the rattle of his coffee cup in its saucer did not betray his agitation.

He stole secrets. He did not surrender them.

Nevertheless, that night, he contemplated leaving the candles lit. How he wanted to watch her peach plump arse quiver as he took her, to know the color of her areolas and whether the crisp curls that guarded her mound were the same rich auburn as her hair. To gaze deep into her whisky-warm eyes and—

He unwound his cravat, wondering what she would say if he offered to blindfold her with it. She had denied him nothing thus far.

Letting the strip of linen slip from his hand to the floor, he pinched the candle wick between thumb and forefinger, relishing both the sting and the darkness, and ordered her onto her belly.

"Rumor has it your mother was French," she said afterward as she lay beneath him.

He made no reply.

"It is French, isn't it? The language you speak to me when you—when we..." Even without the benefit of candlelight, he knew that she blushed.

"Some of it," he conceded. "French is, after all, *le langage de l'amour.*"

She laughed, the same throaty sound that had drawn him in Earnshaw's library. "Not on the tongue of an English governess."

He didn't doubt it, though he'd never had an English governess. His mother—his first teacher—had in fact been Breton. All his life her language had risen naturally to his lips in moments of passion. She'd taught him French too, of course, little anticipating the uses to which he would eventually put such knowledge. His extraordinary fluency had made him a boon to the Crown over the last decade.

The lock-picking he had taught himself.

Midmorning, on the fourth day following their wedding, he was reading over some papers in his study when she appeared in the doorway, a leather-bound volume in her hands.

"I finished it. *The Highwayman's Hostage.*" Her eyes shone, today a rich, luminous brown.

He gave a wry smile. "I assume the ugly fellow—the one who reminded you of me—met a suitably sticky end?"

"Oh, no. Mr. Ratliff is far too clever for that," she insisted, clutching the book to her chest as she stepped closer. "The man with the scars, the one everyone assumes to be the villain, proves himself a hero at the last."

A hero? Oh, God.

Surely, this bright, beautiful woman hadn't persuaded herself that she wanted him, didn't imagine him capable of...

Maxim dropped his gaze to his desktop, his eyes unseeing. His ability to scent a threat had kept him alive all these years. But at present, he could not say who was in greater danger: Caro, or himself.

"I must finish packing," he announced, pushing to his feet.

"P-packing?"

"Yes." He stacked the papers and tucked them into a drawer. "I'm for Paris, as soon as I can make myself ready."

Hope radiated from her posture, piercing him with its rays. "Surely not alone. It's our honeymoon."

"Too risky. You're staying here."

"But..." she protested, deflating slightly. "I know of many families that have made the journey in perfect safety, now that Britain and France have sworn peace."

On the threshold, he brushed past, careful not to touch her. "Peace?" he scoffed beneath his breath. "We'll just see about that."

Chapter 3

September 1808

"And *that*, Mrs. Scott," General Zebadiah Scott said, leaning back against the squabs as the carriage rumbled toward Whitehall, "is the unfortunate tale of the Chesleigh marriage."

"He left her?" Helen's eyes were round, and the flush of anger on her cheeks was quite becoming. "After only four days? And he's never been back since?"

Scott shook his head.

Now her eyes narrowed accusatorily. "And *you* made the match."

"It's not as if I tampered with the lock on the library door! I wasn't even in Hertfordshire," he defended himself. "But," he conceded after a moment, "I did encourage him to attend Earnshaw's house party, in hopes that if he met a suitable young lady, she might help him..." He shook his head again. "Chesleigh was—is—a deeply scarred man, inside and out. I should have known that some wounds never heal."

She reached out and patted his hand consolingly. "Was he injured in the war?"

"No, an accident. When he was not quite eleven. His father had suffered an apoplexy, and Chesleigh—though of course he wasn't Chesleigh then—was dispatched in the rain for the physician. There was a thunderclap. His horse threw him, dragged him for half a mile by the stirrup, and then trampled him. Cracked ribs, a badly broken leg, and his face..." Scott paused, reluctant to distress his wife further. "His father was already gone by the time they found the lad, and he wasn't expected to survive either. Frankly, I'm not sure how he did. When he finally came to, it appeared that either the fall or the kick to the head had scrambled his brains besides. He woke up speaking only a mixture of French and Breton."

"Breton?"

"His mother's tongue. When I first heard of it, I wondered whether the boy was merely putting it on, to anger his grandfather. Hartwell had made no secret of his displeasure at his son's choice of wife. I'm still not sure, but if such was Chesleigh's aim, he succeeded."

Traffic had slowed their progress across town. Helen peered out the window, as if hoping to guess their destination. "I suppose that was your interest in him—the Breton, I mean."

"How so?"

"It's a rare language, isn't it? Might make a useful code."

Scott smiled, more than usually impressed by his wife's perspicacity. "It might at that, my dear. But no, I first met Chesleigh on a visit to Eton, where he had embarked on a career as a first-rate thief."

"A thief?" Her fingers fluttered to her chest. "What did he steal?"

"Back then, mostly food—or the means to purchase it."

"The heir to the Duke of Hartwell was driven to steal food?" she echoed, incredulous.

"The board at our fine public schools is often insufficient for growing lads. The thinking seems to be that cruelty and deprivation will somehow make the pupils manly and strong. Of course, most of the boys can simply spend from their allowances to supplement their diets. But Chesleigh's grandfather was ever a miserly man—not content merely to starve the lad of affection."

His softhearted wife paled and appeared to blink back a tear. "And it was that," she asked after a moment, "his thievery, which made him useful to you?"

Scott grabbed his hat, which had been resting on his knee, and turned it thrice around by the brim. The ground on which they tread had been growing increasingly thin all afternoon. He had heretofore always abided by the principle that the less Helen knew of his work, the happier and safer she would be.

Thankfully, she moved on without waiting for an answer. "But he is not an officer?"

"At the time, I rather thought he might accept a commission merely for the chance to drive his grandfather mad. But in the end he laughed and said he didn't fancy the way he looked in scarlet. Nevertheless, he's proved very useful to me—to the Crown. He can pass for French, you see."

"So, when he left his wife, he actually did go to Paris?"

"Eventually—though not on any official assignment, you understand. Officially, Britain and France had declared a truce, though it was always an uneasy peace. Fraying already when winter came, and dissolved into nothing by the spring of '03. I was glad enough to have Chesleigh firmly ensconced when war broke out again."

The carriage jerked into motion once more. Helen dropped her voice to a confidential whisper, hardly to be heard above the rattle of the wheels. "At the house, you said you can't be sure that he's...one of yours. Do you mean to tell me, he's gone over to their side?"

"He's been embedded in French intelligence for years—that was his mission." Scott spun his hat again. "The question, I suppose, is whether he's now keeping our secrets, or theirs."

"His grandfather is dying?"

"If my information can be trusted, and I believe it can, he won't last a fortnight."

"And you're certain Lord Chesleigh will come home when his grandfather is gone?"

"Yes. If only to dance on the man's grave."

A shuddering sigh escaped his wife's lips. "Poor Lady Chesleigh."

"Poor Lady Chesleigh, indeed. But your suggestion to send her a companion was a stroke of genius, my dear."

"And this...Mrs. Drummond, I believe you said—what can you tell me of her?"

Scott craned his neck, the better to assess their location. "In another moment, you'll be able to make your own assessment of her character. We're nearly there."

A few minutes later the carriage rolled to a stop. Helen peered through the window, then abruptly drew down the shade and leaned back against her seat. "Zebby? I believe there's been some mistake."

He chuckled. "Rest assured, ma'am, Mrs. Drummond has naught to do with *that* sort of house—at least, not that I know of," he added with a wink. "We'll find her here." He tapped on the opposite window to direct her attention to the other side of the street and the swaying shingle that read *W. Millrose, fine tobacco.*

Inside the shop, the bell jingled merrily to signal their arrival, and Scott drew a deep breath of the warmly spiced air. "You promised," Helen said, watching him with one eyebrow raised, "to give up the habit."

"On my honor, my dear," he said, laying his hand over his heart. "Now, Mr. Millrose," he called to the proprietor, a portly Black man whose silvering head was at present bent over a small brass scale.

"Sir," Millrose answered, his spine stiffening almost imperceptibly as he looked up from his measurements. "To what do I owe the pleasure?"

"We're here to see a Mrs. Drummond," his wife answered for him, a frown flickering across her brow as she glanced around the glass-fronted shop, which was otherwise empty of customers. Millrose looked from her to Scott and back again, his expression a mixture of surprise and disapproval. "If it's not too much trouble."

Scott laughed. "You heard the lady."

"Yes, sir." Millrose set aside the scale and reached beneath the counter behind which he stood. A section of the countertop lifted on a hinge, forming a passageway between the customers' side and the proprietor's. Once both the general and his wife had passed through, Millrose gestured toward a door at the back of the shop. "She's just below, sir."

"Thank you, Colonel," Scott said, opening the door to reveal a steeply pitched stairwell that descended into darkness. "I'll go first, shall I, my dear? I have not been down these stairs in years."

At the bottom of the steps, a long, dimly lit corridor stretched before them, with closed doors lining either side. "Some time ago," he explained to his wife, "I purchased this building with the intent of creating a place where my best domestic agents could work and live, somewhere their comings and goings wouldn't attract too much notice. The men call it the 'Underground'—quite smart, don't you think?"

"The cellar beneath a tobacco shop?" she asked, not bothering to hide her skepticism. He began to wonder if her brows were ever going to settle to their normal positions.

"Better that than a gaming hell."

"Zeb—!" she began, her brows now diving low. But she swallowed the rest of her reprimand as the door to their left swung open and a young man with ginger hair appeared.

Though out of uniform, he snapped to attention. "General Scott, sir!"

Scott recognized him immediately as Fitzwilliam Hopkins, the field agent who, late last spring, had retrieved a valuable codebook, only to find himself soon thereafter held captive and tortured by ruthless French agents who had come all the way to London looking for it. Despite the intervening months, the young man still looked harrowed by the experience.

"Lieutenant Hopkins, would you do me the kindness of informing Mrs. Drummond that Mrs. Scott and I are here to see her?"

"Yes, sir," Hopkins said and disappeared down the narrow corridor. Though he was gone no more than a minute or two, by the time he returned,

Colonel Millrose had joined them at the bottom of the stairs, and so it was as a party of four that they entered Mrs. Drummond's sitting room.

"I do beg your pardon for the intrusion, Mrs. Drummond," Scott said with a bow.

For a moment, she only stared at him. A pretty widow, about thirty years of age, she was possessed of remarkably fair hair and remarkably pale blue eyes, the combination lending her a perpetually icy appearance. Coming to herself with a start, she dipped into a low curtsy, the skirts of her black crape gown rustling noisily in the otherwise quiet room.

Her quarters, considerably more generous than the men's, were nonetheless modest: a single room, in which a pair of upholstered chairs and a tea table were divided from her bed by a painted silk screen. Five people filled the room to overflowing.

"Well, Mrs. Drummond," he began, "how would you like a sojourn in Brighton?"

"Sir?" She looked among her guests, her expression just shy of total bewilderment.

"I believe it might be best if Mrs. Scott explains the particulars to you, one lady to another, while Millrose, Hopkins, and I adjourn to another room."

"An excellent notion," agreed his wife, stepping to Mrs. Drummond's side and linking their arms.

Once again, he let Hopkins lead the party, this time to a plainly furnished workroom with whitewashed walls. Once he had opened the door to the general and the colonel, Lieutenant Hopkins bowed and reached to shut it after them, with the obvious intention of leaving his superior officers to their affairs.

"One moment, please. Do sit down. Both of you." Scott did not wait to see whether either man followed his affable order, as he turned to study a map on one wall, strategically marked with pins.

Colonel Millrose spoke first. "I take it you aren't sending Mrs. Drummond on holiday."

"I certainly do hope she finds the seaside pleasant," Scott said, moving to the next map. "But there is a particular task I would like her to undertake while she is there."

"And that is?"

"You needn't sound so concerned, Millrose."

"You placed her under my protection when Drummond was killed. Or had you forgotten?"

Scott turned to discover both men still on their feet, the young lieutenant standing by the door, glancing between him and Millrose, very little less bewildered than Mrs. Drummond had been. "I have not forgotten," Scott replied, with a deceptively mild smile. "But Mrs. Drummond cannot wish to stay here forever."

"She's *safe* here."

For just a moment, he considered whether it was possible that Colonel Millrose had developed an attachment to Frances Drummond. But he suspected it was more in the nature of a paternal affection for the much younger woman; besides, though he doubted Millrose realized it, Scott knew all there was to know about the, er, *flirtation* the man had been carrying on for years with the Jamaican-born missionary who considered this sin-riddled street her battleground.

"It is not my intention to put her in danger, Billy," he reassured the colonel. "But the situation requires a woman's touch." Briefly he explained his concerns about Lord Chesleigh and the man's impending return. "He will call on his wife in Brighton, I am sure of it. Having Mrs. Drummond installed as her friend and companion will not only provide the poor marchioness—the duchess, she will be by then—with proper feminine support through the ordeal, but also give us the opportunity to observe Chesleigh at close range, yet undetected. He will not suspect a lady spy."

"Spy," Millrose echoed, the taste of the word evidently unpleasant in his mouth.

"I cannot very well offer her a commission as an intelligence officer, can I?"

"And is there any cause to believe that Chesleigh may pose a danger to his wife—or her companion?"

"Oh, I think not. But if you are worried, Mrs. Drummond need not travel alone. We can send a field agent to accompany her. Why,"—he smiled toward the lieutenant—"how about this young man? You look as if you could do with some sea air, Hopkins."

Hopkins choked and was still stumbling for a reply when the door opened again to admit Helen and Mrs. Drummond.

"I'm honored by the faith you've put in me, sir," Mrs. Drummond said, dipping into another curtsy. "I can be ready to leave for Brighton the day after tomorrow."

"Excellent, excellent," Scott said, stepping forward to take her hand, and favoring his wife with a wink. "Mrs. Scott can be very persuasive. Now, Colonel Millrose and I have been discussing the matter, and we've decided that it would be best if Lieutenant Hopkins goes with you. For your protection. You may say he is your cousin, your manservant—anything you like."

Color suffused Mrs. Drummond's face—the first he'd seen there since he'd arrived. She glanced surreptitiously toward Lieutenant Hopkins. "That won't be necessary, sir."

Hopkins had recovered from his coughing fit to stand ramrod straight, but his cheeks were still flushed and turned pinker yet as Scott pretended to give the matter more thought. Whether the pair were well suited to one another remained to be seen. And Scott had learned some details about Captain Drummond that might mean Mrs. Drummond would be reluctant ever to remarry. But both she and Hopkins would benefit from some time away from this musty cellar. "Perhaps," he suggested to Mrs. Drummond, "you would rather not go at all...."

Her spine stiffened too. "Of course not, sir. I will defer to your judgment in the matter."

"Thank you, Mrs. Drummond. Mrs. Scott has given you all the particulars, yes? Lady Chesleigh's direction in Brighton and a letter of introduction? Good, good. Then we shall leave the two of you to pack. And I expect the colonel also has work to do," he added, with a pointed look at Millrose.

"Always, sir. Let me see you out."

They made their way up the narrow staircase and through the shop, where Scott paused to perform the niceties of an ordinary customer, even going so far as to purchase a packet of his favorite tobacco—"all part of the ruse," he assured his wife as she wagged a chiding finger.

Afterward, as he handed her into their waiting carriage, she favored him with a gentler, knowing look. "I can guess what you're up to, Zebby, sending Lieutenant Hopkins with Mrs. Drummond. I do believe you're the very definition of an incurable romantic. But do you really think it's wise to go on matchmaking, after the fiasco with Lord and Lady Chesleigh?"

"Fiasco? Let us wait and see, my dear," he said, pressing his lips to the back of her gloved hand. "Let us wait and see."

Chapter 4

Caro made a point of rising early enough that she could walk along the Marine Parade alone without incurring too many raised eyebrows.

Society had never settled the matter of how Lady Chesleigh was to be treated: like a lovelorn woman (which she did not appear to be), like a widow (which, as far as anyone had been able to determine, she wasn't), or like a curiosity and a scandal (which she most certainly was).

In six years' time, she had almost persuaded herself not to care.

Here, her surroundings were ever changing. Buildings seemed to spring up overnight. At the assemblies and private parties, one was forever glimpsing fresh faces, from season to season and year to year. Even the beach was new each morning, scraped and sculpted by the power of the sea.

A gust of wind off the channel tugged at the veil pinned to her bonnet, and she turned to face the salt-sharp air. As always, the tide pulled her, drew her in, tempting her to become one with its wild heartbeat.

In six years' time, she had never approached closer than the promenade that ran along the cliff's edge, set back twenty yards or more from the sea.

Certainly, she had never set foot in the water.

She did not intend to let herself be swept away again.

Even before it had become clear that her husband did not mean to return to her, she had known she could not stay in the house in London. Could not go on sleeping in that bed.

When I'm in your bed, you may call me Maxim.

Away from those memories, he would be nothing more (or less) to her than Lord Chesleigh. Even in the privacy of her thoughts.

So she had met with Lord Chesleigh's chief solicitor, Mr. Sellers, who had agreed to find a tenant for the house on Curzon Street.

"But where will you go?" he had asked.

"The seaside," she had answered.

Not because she had ever been, but precisely because she had not.

And when she had recalled her father's frequent remarks about "the Prince of Wales and his whore," she had known precisely which stretch of the seaside would suit her best.

If Brighton was good enough for the scandalous Mrs. Fitzherbert, it was good enough for Lady Chesleigh.

Once she had reached the bottom of the inviting garden known as the Steyne, she turned back and let her footman escort her home. The newly completed Royal Crescent, a curved row of black-tiled houses facing the water, was entirely without history, set apart from the ancient village of Brighthelmstone. In the drawing room of Number 2, Mrs. Horn greeted her with black coffee, toast dabbed with gooseberry preserves, and the day's correspondence.

The stack of invitations had been growing steadily smaller since Michaelmas, as the high season drew to a close. Brighton would not be truly abandoned until the bleakest winter months, but the strand in October was a different world from the strand in July.

Beneath the invitations lay two letters. The first contained her quarterly allowance, which Mr. Sellers had sent for years without fail, always accompanied by a brief note expressing his hope that she was well and his regret that he knew no other news that would interest her. No news of Lord Chesleigh, in other words. She laid the letter aside, unread.

The contents of the second letter were equally familiar, equally unwelcome.

Papa's hand, this time.

Things must be desperate indeed.

Nearly as desperate as she had been, in the early weeks, and months, when she would have done almost anything—even gone back to her family—in order not to be alone with her thoughts. Tears had sprung to her eyes when her sister Catherine's first ill-spelled note had arrived, though it did little more than repeat their father's claim that if she could afford to live among the fashionable set on perpetual holiday, then the Marchioness of Chesleigh must want for nothing.

By return post, she had sent her sister five pounds for a new gown, finding that her past eagerness to spite her father had been replaced by a new eagerness to spite her husband. Lord Chesleigh had said her family must expect nothing from him, but surely, a lady might spend her pin money as she liked.

Then, the onslaught had begun.

The latest bills from Aunt Brent's physician were unexpectedly large, but I'm sure it would be no trouble to you....

Remember, your little brother is an Oxford man now—and an Oxford man must honor his vowels. A mere fifty guineas would put things right again....

...and when he learned the charming details of my own dear niece's establishment, Dr. Cardew quite concurred that a little sea bathing would set me up for life....

I've heard that Lady Ainsley plans to summer in Brighton, and since you will surely move in the same circles, it will be no trouble for you to drop a word in her ear about the matter....

...but the cards must sometime turn in my favor. Just another hundred, my sweet sister. A hundred fifty, if you could spare it...

Spare such shocking sums from her pin money? Occasionally she wondered whether her family—her father in particular, for as often as not, the notes revealed that *he* had suggested writing to her for help—had forgotten that her husband was not rumored to be a generous man.

Doubtless Mr. Sellers would have been willing to advise her on the matter. How little it would cost her to confess to him that she was nothing more to her own flesh and blood than a purse with loose strings. After all, the man already knew that she was nothing to her husband.

Nothing at all.

Perhaps that was precisely why she had instead chosen to cling to what remained of her dignity, determined to manage on her own.

She weighed Papa's unopened letter against Mr. Sellers's, wondering whether the contents of one could hope to meet the other's demands. With a sigh, she broke the seal.

"My dear daughter," she read and choked back a skeptical laugh. *Dear*, indeed.

I write to say we intend to settle in London this winter. Your mama and aunt cannot be expected to suffer the draftiness of Springhallow. The workmen came to repair the roof, but they refused to begin until I have paid them in advance, as well as the balance due on last year's improvements. Outrageous to treat a gentleman so, is it not?

In any case, one hopes we will not still find the town ablaze with rumors about why Chesleigh left you. After six years, surely the flames of gossip have moved on to devour some other poor soul. Nevertheless, I fear it would be easy enough to fan them in your direction once more. I sincerely hope no one will be tempted to do anything of the sort. If Chesleigh ever

*returns, I should not like to see his expression if he were to hear—for
instance—that you had been playing him false.*

*Now that I think on it, it would have been wise of you to set aside a little
fund—two thousand should do it—to guard against such unscrupulousness.
You always were a clever child, so I'm certain this advice will not fall on
deaf ears.*

The letter fluttered from Caro's nerveless fingers and drifted down to
the desktop. *Two thousand pounds.* Her family's previous requests were
nothing to this demand. Even if Chesleigh had left her with a cache of
jewels to hock, she wouldn't have known how to raise half that sum.

And her husband had entrusted her with nothing of the sort.

She wanted to laugh at her father's outrageous demand. But never before
had one of her family's wheedling notes included a threat.

Not that she was afraid of her husband. She never had been, and she
did not intend to start now, after so long and with such a distance between
them. But she had scrupulously guarded her reputation, perhaps the last
item of value she possessed.

Now to think she might lose even that?

In her mind she heard the echo of her mother's trembling voice when
they'd found her in Lord Earnshaw's library, saw the relief in her eyes
when Lord Chesleigh had made his astounding offer.

"Yes, indeed, Mama," Caro whispered, crumpling her father's note and
preparing to toss it onto the empty hearth, "thank God I was not *ruined.*"

At a tap on the door, she hurriedly smoothed the letter, set it aside, and
turned to see Mrs. Horn, wearing a curious expression.

"A Mrs. Drummond to see you, ma'am. She bade me give you this,"
the housekeeper said, proffering a third letter.

Caro's first thought was that her family had hit upon yet another way
to distress her. Reluctantly, she took the note, broke the seal, and unfolded
the square of hot-pressed paper, only to find it filled with the delightfully
expressive scrawl of Helen Scott.

When General and Mrs. Zebadiah Scott had first arrived in Brighton
more than a month ago, Caro's heart had caught in her throat. The mere
sight of the general had been enough to make her recall her wedding day.

A friend of yours?

In a manner of speaking.

Might that ostensible friend know what had become of her husband?

But the general had given no sign of recollecting their previous encounter,
and the more she knew of him, the less she could imagine such a genial,
grandfatherly gentleman capable of keeping secrets. And though Mrs.

Scott was more than twice Caro's age, she was a lady of such good humor, remarkably disinclined to gossip, that when summer had drawn to a close, Caro had felt the loss of her company keenly and had even written to tell her as much.

Now Mrs. Scott wrote "to beg a favor," she said. But Caro was only too familiar with begging. What this letter offered was a gift—the gift of a new acquaintance. Mrs. Scott's note described Mrs. Drummond as "a widowed lady, near in age to yourself," sent to Brighton to recover her spirits and in need of a friend.

A friend.

The very word was balm to Caro's tortured, lonely soul. She laid it atop her escritoire, covering her father's note. "Please," she said to Mrs. Horn, "send her in."

* * * *

Though it was only late afternoon, in the shadows of the Pyrenees dusk had already fallen. Rather than pause to light a candle, Maxim shifted his papers across the rough-hewn table, chasing the fading sunlight, and continued to write.

The seriousness of the communiqué, and the need to encrypt it as he wrote, left no room for niceties. Napoleon had turned on his Spanish allies and meant to take Madrid. Already engaged in defending Portugal, British forces were about to find themselves in a new phase of the war.

Maxim's work had never felt more urgent. Or more futile.

In the silence of the room, broken only by the scratch of his pen, he jumped at a tap on the door as if it were the crack of a rifle.

"*Entrez,*" he snarled, folding the paper on which he'd been writing even as he pushed away from the table and to his feet.

"I'm sorry to disturb you, sir," came the reply, in French. Pierre Leclerc stepped into the room and made an apologetic bow.

Maxim had hired him as a manservant upon his arrival in the South of France more than a year ago, to help give cover to his assignment. Leclerc, who knew no more than a few words of English, had told him his sister had been assaulted by French soldiers, which he considered ample excuse for his willingness to work for an Englishman.

To explain his own seemingly aimless wandering through the area, Maxim had claimed—in French that belied his own fluency—to be conducting a survey of agricultural practices. Leclerc frequently served as his unwitting courier, ferrying packets of papers to London—to Maxim's demanding publisher, or so he explained—via the port of Marseille or occasionally even further afield.

Tonight, he would order Leclerc to begin the journey north, to Paris, to deliver the grim news of Napoleon's plans to the English intelligence officers stationed there. Maxim would stay near Toulouse and see what else he could learn.

"Here," he said, thrusting the folded paper toward the other man.

Leclerc did not immediately take it. "A message for you, sir," he said instead, holding out a folded paper of his own.

Maxim took the note—unsigned, but written in the familiar hand of Zebadiah Scott.

You are wanted at home, Your Grace.

Maxim sat down heavily in the chair he had just vacated, probing his mind for some reaction to this oblique announcement of his grandfather's death. Not sorrow, when the man had once shown himself so indifferent to Maxim's own. Not grief for a man who had done everything he could to earn his place in hell.

Not relief, either, for the man's death merely foisted a new set of responsibilities onto Maxim's shoulders, responsibilities he had been told time and again he could not hope to fulfill.

No matter how hard he looked within himself, all he found was a familiar emptiness, the same hole he'd had in his chest for twenty-five years, more or less. But as his brief stint as a married man had so forcibly reminded him, heartlessness was more comfortable than the alternative.

Maxim turned the paper over in his hands, as if searching for something more. But the message was written in plain English, not encrypted—at least, not in the conventional sense. He grasped his new mission perfectly. He must return home at least long enough to claim the title of Duke of Hartwell. Scott had always been a stickler when it came to his men fulfilling their domestic duties.

Whether Maxim could correctly be called "one of Scott's men" was another question.

"Sir?" Leclerc ventured. "What is it?"

"It would seem," Maxim answered, rising, "that I have inherited a title and a pretty piece of property to go with it." His voice was thick with bitterness. "Since I must take myself to London to claim it, I suppose I'll just deliver these latest reports myself." He tucked what he'd written into his breast pocket, intending to destroy the papers later. The message would be safer in his head.

"When will you return?"

Maxim glanced around the meagerly furnished cottage. There would be little enough to pack. "I don't know. Here? Perhaps never." If the intelligence he had gathered proved right, in a matter of weeks, new battle lines would be drawn.

Leclerc nodded and turned to leave. But on the threshold, he hesitated. "Please, sir, won't you take me with you?" Though the young man's face was in shadow, Maxim could hear the fear in his voice. His fellow Frenchmen might deem his working for an Englishman as a betrayal—even if none of them ever knew the half of it. "We could say I was your valet—even in England, a French valet would not raise suspicions. You would merely be thought a gentleman at the height of fashion."

He was not wrong. Despite the war, the English passion for all things French had not subsided. The surge of refugees following the Terror had slowed in the years since, but Leclerc had good reason to want to get away.

And the Crown had good reason to want to keep an eye on him, for under the proper pressure, he could reveal secrets he didn't even realize he was keeping.

"Be ready to leave at moonrise," Maxim agreed.

"*Merci.*" Leclerc's shoulders slumped with the word, as if gratitude had made him weak. "Will we travel straight to London, sir?"

While mentally plotting out the journey, Maxim's thoughts skidded slightly off the direct path.

Toward Brighton, as it happened.

He'd made it his business to know where his wife was and what she was doing, so he knew Caro had taken up residence there. Just as she'd taken up residence in his thoughts, despite his determination to put ample time and distance between them.

Perhaps distance wasn't the answer. Perhaps seeing her, once more, would renew his resolve. Yes, his first thought should be the secure delivery of vital military intelligence. But Brighton hardly lay out of his way. A half a day's delay, at most.

He considered both his duty and his answer before he gave a sharp nod. "Almost."

Chapter 5

Fanny Drummond could not remember ever having been more annoyed. Or amused. Annoyed *because* she was amused. She did not want to find Lieutenant Hopkins even the slightest bit attractive.

She'd been watching General Scott's matchmaking schemes unfold for long enough to know what was what, though the men themselves seemed to be oblivious to them. She knew half the men in the Underground fancied themselves smitten with her, despite the stern demeanor she'd adopted and the widow's weeds she'd worn well past the point of necessity. She'd hoped the somber clothes and the somber expression would cause them to take her seriously. Instead, they'd turned her into a housekeeper—"the matron at a home for wayward boys," she'd only half joked.

This visit to Brighton—this *assignment*—was her one chance to prove she could be something more.

"Stand up straight." She spoke sharply to Lieutenant Hopkins—Fitz—the better to cover her own nervousness.

Even after he pushed away from the wall against which he'd been leaning and unfolded his arms, his posture was still loose limbed and rangy. "Better?" he asked, smiling.

"Footmen don't smile."

Not that she had a great deal of experience with footmen. She came of respectable stock, but not the sort of family with a bevy of menservants at its beck and call. But at least she knew they were meant to appear impassive—an expression that did not seem to be within Lieutenant Hopkins's repertoire.

Fanny, on the other hand, had devoted herself to preparing for her role here: she'd put off her widow's weeds in favor of softer, lighter fashions, so that her being out and about did not raise too many eyebrows; she had purchased and read two guidebooks on Brighton so she would be familiar with the town and all it offered; and she'd spent a few days after she had arrived learning what she could of Lady Chesleigh from the locals before presenting herself at the door with Mrs. Scott's letter of introduction.

This was her third visit to the house in Royal Crescent, the first being properly brief for new acquaintances, but the second prolonged by bad weather. And today, today they were to make a visit together to Donaldson's circulating library, and on the marchioness's suggestion. Fanny had connived to have the trip coincide with Lady Chesleigh's footman's half day, to provide an excuse for Lieutenant Hopkins to accompany them in the guise of Fanny's manservant...who was still smiling.

"I did suggest passing me off as your cousin," he reminded her.

Worse and worse. General Scott had said as much himself, but she had not wanted anything that smacked of intimacy between them. "Hush now," she retorted in a whisper, "before I demote you to boot boy."

He was young. Five years younger than she, at least. But those broad shoulders and intelligent gray eyes did not belong to a boy.

"*Distant* cousin?" he offered, with an expression of mock contrition. At her scowl, his smile deepened to a grin. "At least I didn't say *betrothed.*"

Her cheeks heated. She knew where he'd come up with such a notion: recently, another agent, Captain Addison, had had to pretend that the target of his investigation was his wife. Even more shocking, the lady in question had turned out to be Lieutenant Hopkins's sister. Fanny had overheard the other men in the Underground speculating in whispered but ribald tones about the degree of commitment to his part Addison's assignment must have entailed. And those speculations could not all have been incorrect, for the captain and Miss Hopkins were now wed.

Fortunately, Lady Chesleigh's appearance on the stairs prevented Fanny from having to make any reply.

"Good afternoon, Mrs. Drummond," she said, not sparing Lieutenant Hopkins a glance. "What a lovely day for an outing."

"It is indeed," Fanny agreed. Though it was past the first week of October, the sun was still sending out its summer warmth, here pleasantly cooled by the wind blowing across the water. The fresh breeze tangled Fanny's muslin skirts about her legs and teased at Lady Chesleigh's diaphanous veil as they set out, Lieutenant Hopkins following at a discreet distance.

"And how do you find German Place?" Lady Chesleigh asked.

"Oh, very well," Fanny said. She'd chosen the location with care: in a respectable part of town, but befitting a widow of less than extravagant means. "Though the parlor is small," she added, to discourage any thought Lady Chesleigh might have of calling on her. The rooms had been ready-furnished, and Fanny made do with the services of a cookmaid who did not live in.

The freedoms of the arrangement suited Fanny just fine. And despite her reservations about Lieutenant Hopkins's ability to act his part with conviction, he'd hit it off with some of the other servants belonging to the neighborhood and been able to provide Fanny with a good deal of useful information about Lady Chesleigh's household.

"The houses here were all built on the presumption that no one would spend much time inside them," Lady Chesleigh assured her.

Given the variety of other places one might congregate in Brighton—the theater, the assembly rooms, the churches, the shops, the beach itself—the presumption was not entirely unreasonable. But Fanny knew that Lady Chesleigh had a reputation for keeping to herself, in spite of frequent invitations. She considered this outing to the circulating library, so early in their acquaintance, a triumph.

They walked along at a leisurely pace. Though Royal Crescent stood on the far eastern edge of town, the distance between any two points in Brighton was not great. Fanny could almost wish they had farther to go. After so long in the Underground, she still marveled at every chance she got to stretch her legs and breathe in the fresh air.

"The seaside agrees with you," Lady Chesleigh remarked when Fanny paused to tip her face to the sun before stepping inside the comparatively dark bookshop.

Beneath the young marchioness's scrutiny, Fanny blushed, then scolded herself for the reaction. She must remember to act as if she'd been in company before. "You are too kind," she said.

Fitz was holding open the door to Donaldson's circulating library, both his posture and his expression as footman-like as she had ever seen them. As she turned her head, the better to avoid Lady Chesleigh's gaze, however, she caught his eye. Agreement with Lady Chesleigh's words—nay, more than that—*approval* glittered there. Not the shy glances he'd occasionally sent her in the Underground when he'd thought she wasn't looking. Something bolder. Something that sent awareness shooting along her nerves like a spark.

It was not a look a manservant should be giving his lady employer.

To reprimand him here and now would only call attention to his impudence, however. Lady Chesleigh, whose eye had been caught by a display of the latest titles just inside the door, might not even have noticed the look. Once Fanny slipped past him into the library, she dared to glance back and discovered his expression was once more suitably blank. Perhaps his look of desire had been a figment of her imagination.

Disappointment flickered through her at the thought, but she ruthlessly stamped it out. She was here *on assignment*. A dalliance with Fitz Hopkins would ruin...everything.

"What sorts of reading do you enjoy, Mrs. Drummond?" Lady Chesleigh was asking as she perused the new books.

Fanny hurried to her side. "With all my heart, ma'am, I wish I could tell you that I devote myself to history and philosophy and sermons, but the truth of the matter is, I mostly read novels."

"I quite often find more philosophical truths in a well-written novel than in those dusty tomes. And," she added with a wry laugh, "in the less well-written novels there is often more moralizing than a sermon."

"How clever you are," Fanny said. "I confess, I weigh books on a far more trivial scale. Does it bring a tear to my eye? Does it make my hair stand on end?"

Lady Chesleigh gave a mild smile. "It amounts to much the same thing."

"Now this," said Fanny, reaching for a book, "would just suit me—the latest by Robin Ratliff. *The Brigand's Captive*. Oooh." She wriggled as if a shiver of delight had just traveled up her spine.

"The Persephone Press does offer its readers ample entertainment." The smile slipped from Lady Chesleigh's lips as she turned from the display. "But I cannot abide Mr. Ratliff's work. Too predictable and implausible. If ever I have an opportunity of meeting him, I intend to remind him that the character with all the appearance of villainy sometimes *is* the villain."

Was that remark about villainy an oblique reference to her husband? If so, it was the closest she had come, in their brief acquaintance, of mentioning him, and Fanny wondered whether she had intended to reveal so much.

The extraordinary tale of Lady Caroline Brent's sudden marriage to the notorious marquess and his almost equally sudden abandonment of his bride had somehow led Fanny to expect a woman defeated by the experiences life had handed her—dull eyes, faded cheeks, curved shoulders.

And if not that, then she had imagined a posture of defiance—a woman who met the stares and whispers of passersby with chin raised and teeth bared, a woman more than willing to give them something to gossip about.

Lady Chesleigh was neither. Despite a stated preference for novels, Fanny had in fact read enough philosophy to call her stoic. She moved about town with her shoulders back, but her face covered. She lived frugally, particularly for a marchioness. She entertained rarely and did not dress in the latest fashions. If she had ever taken a lover in the six long years of her husband's absence, no one, not even the servants, breathed a word about it. She was difficult either to pity or to judge.

Despite the manifest differences in both situation and status, Fanny was intimately familiar with the strategies Lady Chesleigh employed. The composed demeanor. The cool reserve. Garments that served as both shields and weapons.

She recognized too the signs of something simmering just beneath that placid surface. Something it cost the marchioness a great deal to contain.

Lady Chesleigh moved deeper into the shop, while Fanny remained at the table near the door. She heard the proprietor speak deferentially to Lady Chesleigh. In another moment, the man's shadow fell across the books nearest to Fanny.

"Good morning, ma'am. May I welcome you to Brighton? I do not recall seeing you at Donaldson's before."

"Yes, thank you," Fanny said, letting the cover of the book at which she'd been looking fall closed before favoring the man with a smile. "I've only just arrived."

"Then perhaps you'd enjoy some books on the history of the area?" he suggested.

After a sideways glance of longing at the Robin Ratliff novels, Fanny followed him to another area of the library, where he left her to browse. After choosing two or three titles at random, she went to the desk where he had indicated she would sign her name and pay her subscription fee.

As she withdrew a guinea from her reticule, she marveled at the power of having a purseful of them at her own disposal. She had known, of course, that various cases required agents to be outfitted in a particular way, and even sometimes supplied with ready coin, but the amount of the bank draft Colonel Millrose had handed her, for transportation, clothes, "and other sundries," had made her goggle.

Or would have done, if she had not spent more than a year schooling her every expression into perfect composure.

Something of her present pleasure must have been visible, though, for Lady Chesleigh, who had joined her at the desk with three volumes of her own, remarked upon it. "There is really nothing to equal the power of selecting one's own books, is there?"

"No, indeed," Fanny agreed. But they were walking home, their combined selections in Fitz's capable hands, before she could bring herself to confess, "Reading is something of a guilty pleasure. My late husband did not like to see me with a book in my hands. Particularly not the sort of books that give women unrealistic expectations about the world, as he put it."

As if in response to her words, Fitz made a noise in his throat. She was surprised he had even heard her, as he followed several steps behind, all propriety again. Was he trying to caution her? Well, it *had* been a rather clumsy attempt at urging a confidence from Lady Chesleigh, for all it was also the truth.

Lady Chesleigh paused and turned toward her, an expression not just of sympathy but empathy in her dark eyes. "My father was much the same."

And your husband? Fanny found herself inordinately curious about the man, and more than a little tempted to warn the poor woman that he was about to return. But what plausible explanation could she give for possessing such knowledge?

Lady Chesleigh adjusted her parasol so she could loop her arm through Fanny's. As they resumed walking, Fanny felt a twinge of something like guilt. But this was her mission. To grow close to the marchioness, close enough that she could report on her husband's behavior. She must only hope she could appear convincingly surprised when Lord Chesleigh appeared.

"Tell me more about yourself, Mrs. Drummond."

Fanny narrowly stopped herself from stumbling. Not that she hadn't prepared for this moment, at least as rigorously as she'd prepared for all the others. She'd concocted half a dozen different answers and practiced them before her mirror in the privacy of her rooms. The truth was too pedestrian, unsuited to the acquaintance of a marchioness.

Nevertheless, it was the truth that now rose to her lips and slipped out, unbidden and unwelcome. "My father was a solicitor in London, my lady. I am the youngest of six brothers and sisters, all now scattered. I met Captain Drummond at a public assembly and agreed to marry him soon thereafter."

She half expected Lady Chesleigh to release her arm and bid her good day right then. A future duchess, even a lonely one, need not associate herself with someone who must rely on the most generous interpretation of facts to call herself either the wife or daughter of a gentleman.

But Lady Chesleigh only nodded encouragingly. "And were you happy in your choice?"

An odd query, really—surely she would not want to be asked the same in return? Or did she long for a friend in whom she could confide her feelings about her long-absent husband?

"He was handsome and clever, dashing in his red coat, and always merry among his friends," Fanny replied, not quite answering her question. "My mama urged caution, but I was past one and twenty and could not imagine what there was to wait for."

Despite the fact that she had been marrying a near stranger, Fanny had indeed expected many things from her marriage. She had imagined that life with an army officer would involve travel and chances to meet interesting people. At the very least, she had expected companionship. Children. Eventually, perhaps, love.

Not loneliness.

"I did not understand, then, how useful it might be to discover certain matters before marrying. A man's feelings about books, for example."

Those who had come to know her in recent years—including Fitz—would be shocked to learn that before her marriage, she had been generally regarded as warm spirited and eager to please.

Years of disappointment, dismissal, derision had turned her to ice.

The young marchioness patted her arm and favored her with a slightly wry, but genuinely compassionate smile. "I was twenty when I wed, and I too imagined I knew how the world worked."

Fanny managed to return Lady Chesleigh's smile, her own rather thin, though no less real. If she had not meant to be so forthcoming, neither had she expected to be met with understanding.

"I fear, my lady, that the world depends upon young women being kept ignorant of a great many things."

Lady Chesleigh paused and darted her gaze toward the water. Afternoon sun gilded the rippling waves, but Fanny did not think it was only brightness that had caused her eyes to narrow. "Please, call me Caro." Fanny stiffened in surprise at the invitation to familiarity, as the marchioness dipped her head in the direction of a charming little shop. "Will you join me for tea, Mrs. Drummond?"

"Fanny," she urged when she could trust herself to speak. "And tea would be most welcome."

Fitz stepped forward to open the door for them, the stack of books balanced easily in the crook of his other arm. Fanny sent him a sympathetic glance. He would have to stand outside and wait for them, and the day was warm. As Lady Chesleigh stepped into the tea shop, Fitz gave Fanny a wink, the movement of his eye so swift she could have persuaded herself she had imagined it, if he had not also mouthed the words, "Good work."

It did not feel like work—or at least, not the work she had imagined herself setting out to do. Nothing, in fact, was going according to Fanny's careful plan, which had certainly not anticipated the intimacy of Christian names and shared confidences about the poor foundations for their overly hasty marriages. What more might an hour over tea and cakes produce?

Laughter, as it turned out.

Lady Chesleigh—Caro—was an incisive observer with a sharp and subtle wit. And her laugh was surprisingly rich, inviting listeners to join in, in spite of themselves. Nothing in Fanny's research had prepared her for it, and she could not remember the last time she had laughed. Fortunately, the tea shop was otherwise empty of patrons, who might have been scandalized by the impropriety of it.

Fanny had seen men grow garrulous on brandy and tobacco; she had never imagined a cup of oolong with lemon biscuits could have a similar effect. When she at last stood to leave, she felt curiously light headed. Fitz's glance when they emerged—surprised and appreciative—made her lift her fingertips to her cheeks, which were warm and probably flushed. She was tempted to inspect her reflection in the shop's front window, but Caro saved her from her vanity by setting off down the street.

She was still giggling about the notorious ladies' bathing machine attendant, Martha Gunn, infamous for tossing reluctant bathers into the water, when they arrived at Royal Crescent. Fitz preceded them up the steps to open the door, but it opened a few inches before he could reach it. A wide-eyed maidservant peeped out, then swung the door wider.

"Oh, thank goodness you're back, milady."

"What is it, Tilly?" Caro hurried up the steps.

"A visitor, ma'am." The girl swallowed, as if speaking the name required additional fortitude. "His Grace, the Duke of Hartwell."

Caro drew in a sharp breath through her nose. Fanny could hear that sound of surprise and alarm even from several feet away. She darted a glance toward Fitz, who was standing ramrod straight, his gaze focused on some distant point, giving a very good impression of a servant who had no concern in the matters being discussed. But she knew he understood what the duke's arrival meant as well as she did.

"M-my husband's grandfather," Caro explained, looking over her shoulder at Fanny. "I have never met the man—why, I didn't think he even knew of my existence. What reason could he have for seeking me out now? And here? Something must have happened."

Fanny wished once more for the power to utter something like a warning. The only power she had at present, however, was to behave as a lady would under such circumstances. She must excuse herself and go.

Before she could make a move in that direction, however, Caro rocked back onto a lower step and reached out to lay a staying hand on Fanny's arm. "Won't you come inside for a moment? Your manservant can leave my books on the hall table."

Clearly, she wanted to avoid having to face her guest alone. Fanny nodded and let her slip her arm once more through the crook of Fanny's elbow and lead her up the remaining steps and into the house. Inside, tension curled through the air like fog rolling in off the water. The nervous maid bobbed a curtsy and nodded toward the staircase. "Mrs. Horn showed His Grace to the drawing room, milady."

Though Fanny could feel the reluctance in Caro's footsteps, they nonetheless climbed steadily to the first floor. Only on the threshold of the drawing room did she truly hesitate, reaching up a hand to smooth her hair and discovering she still wore her veiled bonnet. After drawing a steadying breath, she uncoiled her arm from Fanny's, removed her gloves and then her bonnet, and laid them on the seat of a delicate chair nearby. Against her auburn hair, her fingers were pale as she fluffed and straightened, until she was perfectly composed, until the woman who had laughed in the tea shop was nowhere to be seen.

Belatedly, Fanny realized she had acquired a great deal of information about the people and pastimes of Brighton today, but very little about Caro herself. When the door opened, Fanny did not know whether to expect her to shriek, weep, or perhaps even faint at the first sight of her guest, the Duke of Hartwell.

For of course the visitor was not her husband's grandfather.

It was her husband.

Even knowing what she did, Fanny had to stifle a gasp as she stepped into the room behind her friend. Mrs. Scott had mentioned something about the man having been injured as a child. But neither she nor anyone else of Fanny's acquaintance, excepting General Scott, had actually seen him, and for all his loquacity, the general had not been forthcoming about such details.

The present Duke of Hartwell was a giant of a man, tall and broad shouldered, with dark hair and eyes, his complexion sun warmed, as if he had recently come from a more southerly clime. In the bookshop Caro had said something about the appearance of villainy. Fanny wasn't sure what villains were meant to look like; weren't Hartwell's particular attributes—stature and strength—as often ascribed to heroes? Tall, dark, and handsome, and all that?

Except the duke was not handsome. His scowl, which judging from the lines of his face must form a nearly permanent part of his expression, only highlighted his crooked nose, sunken cheek, and a jagged scar running from temple to jaw. *Brooding, hulking*...those were the adjectives that leaped to mind when she saw him, and though she couldn't quite make herself look away, neither did she want to take one step closer.

Caro, however, marched up to him. "Oh. I thought *you* might be the one who was dead," she said in a voice so cool and matter of fact even Fanny envied it. The duke himself stood stock still, rather like a mastiff warily watching the approach of a kitten with a puffed-up tail.

Caro's metaphorical tail remained sleek, however, betraying not even a twitch of annoyance. "My condolences on the passing of your grandfather" were her next words, accompanied by a slight curtsy, a deferential dip of her head, though the set of her chin remained firm. Then she raised her eyes to his face again. "Now that you've delivered the news, you may be on your way."

Chapter 6

When Caro had stepped into the room, Maxim had fully expected her to erupt in anger. Anger was understandable, justifiable. Familiar. He'd lived with anger all his life.

Her calm put him at a disadvantage. But he could work with cold dismissal.

He knew how to use it to make things worse.

"On my way? Why would you assume I don't intend to stay, my dear?"

Something like a tremor passed through Caro, but she stiffened her spine against it. "Past experience, I suppose."

"Where else would I go?" he prodded, determined to break through her façade.

"To hell, for all I care."

Inwardly, he smiled. Oh, yes. She was angry all right. She hated him, just as he'd hoped.

He waited for a sense of triumph to surge through him at this confirmation, but it never came.

When he'd left all those years ago, he'd done so in spectacularly callous fashion. He'd intended to keep her from persuading herself that she cared for him, to keep her from imagining that he could ever care for her.

Now he understood that if such had truly been his goal, he should have hoped not for anger and hatred, but indifference.

A gasp behind Caro dragged his attention to the still-open door and the pale-haired woman standing there. "Introduce me to your friend," he said.

Caro turned and reached out a hand to draw the other woman further into the room. "Mrs. Drummond." In the stranger's expression he saw the familiar glimmers of disgust and fear at his appearance, along with amazement that his wife could speak of his inevitable damnation with undisguised anticipation. "May I present His Grace, the Duke of Hartwell." Mrs. Drummond dipped into a shaky curtsy. "Hartwell, this is Mrs. Drummond."

He bowed, hating the sound of his title even more on Caro's lips. "Ma'am."

"I should—" Mrs. Drummond began, then paused, as if weighing whether to give in to the impulse to flee or stay and offer support, no matter how feeble, to her friend.

Caro relieved her of the burden of a decision. "My dear Mrs. Drummond," she said, turning her back on him, "you have been so kind as to give me your afternoon when you must be wishing to enjoy those books you chose at Donaldson's."

"It's been my pleasure, Lady Che—" She broke off, uncertain, and darted a glance toward him. "I'll show myself out."

Caro stepped to the door beside her. "You will call early tomorrow? For our usual stroll?"

The other woman blinked, as if surprised by the request, but quickly recovered. "Of course."

"Thank you, my friend."

He expected Caro to fly at him the moment the door closed behind Mrs. Drummond. Instead, she stood with her back to him, her shoulders rigid, the posture of one battling a desire to walk away. But when she at last spoke, her voice was still infuriatingly calm. "Did you enjoy Paris?" she asked, as if he'd been gone a month at most.

He pretended the answer required reflection. "Not particularly."

In the autumn and winter of 1802, Paris had been overrun by merrymaking Englishmen pretending the war was over. He hadn't tarried there long.

"What a pity." She sounded like someone speaking to a stranger. Which, of course, she was.

He had never been—would never be—anything else to her.

Finally, she turned toward him, her expression blank. "And why are you here, again?"

He felt something like pity then. He could not change the past, but he might have spared her this. "You need a cup of tea," he declared. "Ring for some fresh water."

Her slightly unfocused gaze settled on the tray an astonished Mrs. Horn had insisted on bringing him when he'd arrived. He wondered whether he was about to have a teapot lobbed at his head. "I had tea with Mrs. Drummond," she said.

"Sit down, at least. You've had a shock."

A laugh, not quite hysterical, burbled from her.

Another man would have gone to her, taken her by the elbow, gently led her to a chair. He turned, inexorably, to stone. "Surely you heard rumors about my grandfather's health? You should have anticipated that I would have no choice but to return to England for a time. Certain matters related to my inheritance must be handled face-to-face."

She lifted her gaze to him. She was still the only woman—almost the only person—who could look at him without flinching. "I heard nothing of the sort. In any case, what I wish to know is why you are *here*, in Brighton. If it were only a matter of informing me of your grandfather's death, a letter would have sufficed. Rest assured, I would've asked Mrs. Horn to see that appropriate measures were taken. Crape would already have been hung and—"

"No." She jerked at the force of the word. "I don't mourn the man, and I forbid you to."

A shimmer of gold in her eyes flared at the command in his voice, and he belatedly caught yet another error in his judgment. No doubt he had just guaranteed that she would wear all black from this point forward, forever—and damn him, but she would look no less beautiful.

"Then I could have ordered myself new calling cards, at least." The sharpness of her retort, its sarcastic, bitter tone, offered less comfort than he had anticipated. "In any case, you had no need to come in person."

What did it mean that he had wanted, gone out of his way even, to see her? Over the years, he'd grown quite adept at dismissing her from his thoughts—a skill made necessary by the frequency with which she intruded there. From Toulouse, the journey to London would not ordinarily have taken him through Brighton. But then he'd let himself imagine her furious reaction to his sudden reappearance. The spark of fire in her eyes and in her hair.

He should have contented himself with that mental image, rather than insisting on admiring it firsthand.

Before he could frame a response, she spoke again, and this time, he heard something close to fear in her voice. "But since you're here, now what?"

"Now?" he answered coolly. "Now you are the Duchess of Hartwell. Your acquaintance and entertainments will be even more highly sought. You may look down your nose at all but the queen herself, if you wish." He let his gaze travel over her.

There was something distressingly familiar about the pale green muslin of her gown.

For six years, and however unwillingly, he had carried a picture of his wife in his mind, the way she had looked that morning in his study, when she had come to him, book in hand, something dangerously like affection in her eyes, and he had…well, *panicked*, he supposed, and told her he was bound for Paris.

She had been wearing a dress of pale green muslin. He'd hated that dress, all her dresses, on sight. Oh, she'd looked pretty enough in them— she looked pretty in anything and probably, if his senses other than sight could be trusted, would look even prettier in nothing at all. But it had been autumn, and she had been wearing a spring dress—spring of a year or two past, if he didn't miss his guess.

Those out-of-season, out-of-fashion dresses had been one more reminder of Caro's damnable family, her father especially, who had run up debts and then expected his daughter to scrimp and sacrifice and had not even shown the decency to balk at marrying her to a monster.

He'd ordered her to buy a new wardrobe, complete. Something befitting a marchioness. Had she done it?

Or was she still wearing the old things to spite him?

He had expected her to be angry, yes. He had not expected to feel anger himself.

"I will tell Sellers to increase your pin money," he added.

At that, she sent a glance toward the far end of the long room where her escritoire sat, the movement so quick he could almost convince himself he had imagined it.

In an obvious effort to retain her calm, she sat down beside the tea table and carefully arranged her skirts around her. "And you, sir?" she asked, as if this were merely an ordinary social call. "Will you stay in England or return to…Paris?" That slight hesitation conveyed not doubt, but knowledge, as if she understood full well that he had not been in the French capital all these years. Had he forgotten how clever she was?

"That remains to be seen."

His business in London was urgent, and he had intended to travel on before nightfall. Then again, the notion that he might stay longer in her company clearly made her unhappy. "Are you so eager to be rid of me, madam wife?" He sat down across from her in one of the elegant upholstered chairs, too small for his frame, and stretched out his booted legs. Whatever it took to increase her discomfort, to remind her how terrible he was. "But of course. How thoughtless of me. Your lover is expected this evening, perhaps."

Color fanned across her cheeks. "On the servants' half day? How predictable."

Damn him for wishing her to deny it outright. "You will be alone, then? All the better."

Her eyes flared. Oh, he'd intended to alarm her—and was gratified to see he'd succeeded. But even so, a frisson of... *something*, something that wasn't fear, passed between them. No, she was not indifferent to him.

Neither was he indifferent to her.

"I daresay a few days at the seaside would prove most enjoyable," he went on.

"The Old Ship offers acceptable accommodations," she replied. He could almost admire her show of calm. "Shall I ring for Mrs. Horn and have her send someone to make arrangements?"

"That won't be necessary."

Her breasts rose and fell on a sharp, silent breath. "Surely you don't expect an invitation to stay in my house?"

"*Your* house?" He made his voice light, easy, even as hers began to betray her agitation. "I'm afraid there's a flaw in your logic, my dear. Is not this house leased by *my* solicitor? Using *my* money?" Her control slipped from her with his every word, and he gathered it eagerly to himself. "Therefore, it is, under any reasonable interpretation of the law, mine."

Her cheeks were pink and her respirations uneven. "There's a flaw in *your* logic, too," she replied, her voice quieter than he had expected. "If I were dear to you, you would not have abandoned me six years ago."

Abandoned.

Her voice, earlier so cool and bright, had grown brittle enough to crack beneath the weight of that single word.

No, not indifferent at all.

"You left me without cause, without explanation, without—"

"No." With an idle flick of his hand, he waved away her accusations, wondering when he had last troubled to defend himself. "I left you *with* a house in London, a staff of servants, ready access to funds to meet all your material needs, and the title of marchioness—itself no insignificant weapon for self-defense." She arched a skeptical brow. "The only thing I removed from your life was my person, my disagreeable person, and if you were so unwise as to pine for me in my absence, well..." He brushed an imaginary speck of lint off his sleeve. "I cannot help you."

"One need not *pine* to wonder what has become of someone. Surely, in six years' time, you might at least have written...."

"What could I have told you that you would have wished to hear?"

She glanced down at her hands, folded tightly in her lap. "What if you had died...?"

A laugh ghosted from him at her oblique answer to his question. "Then you would have been a wealthy widow."

Far from appearing reassured, she flinched. Laying her hands on the arms of the chair, she pushed to standing, perhaps to disguise the involuntary movement. "I should go and speak to Mrs. Horn about dinner," she said, suiting her actions to her words, "though I suspect she's already scrambling to prepare your favorite dishes."

"I hope she will not trouble herself overmuch. I am a man of simple appetites."

Her hand, which had been reaching for the door, fell to her side, and she shot a quelling look over her shoulder.

"As for where you will sleep..." The coolness had returned to her voice, but still, he detected the slightest tremor. Was she wondering whether he intended to slake his simple appetites in her bed?

"Mrs. Horn already directed my man to put my things in an unoccupied suite of rooms at the back of the house," he told her. "She said that there, I would run no danger of troubling the mistress."

Something—amusement? relief?—flickered through her eyes, though it did not travel deep enough to change her expression. When she thought of those nights together, so long ago, did she remember them with pleasure or pain?

He turned away from her, toward the large bow window at the front of the house, overlooking the water. The sun was setting, painting the channel and the pebbled strand and the glass itself with its reflected glory.

The next time he saw its colors, he would be on his way to London.

When he turned back, she was gone.

Chapter 7

When sunrise began to streak the sky, Caro untangled herself from the bed where she had passed a sleepless night. She had dined on a tray in her room rather than face him over the table, and retired soon after—a mistake, she had soon discovered. Lying in the dark led to thinking in the dark, and hadn't she learned to avoid that after all these years?

She had not locked the door to her chamber; she knew full well it would not stop her husband if he wanted to come to her. His intent to master the stubborn lock on Lord Earnshaw's library door had led them to this pass.

She had lain stiff as a board, listening and waiting—for what, she did not know.

But she'd heard no more than a few indecipherable murmurs through the wall that divided the two bedchambers, the opening and closing of doors other than her own, and once, something that might have been a snore. When exhaustion at last forced her rigid muscles to slacken, she had looked up at the ceiling and tried to picture the stars in the sky beyond, so that she might count them.

All she could picture in her mind's eye was him.

She had not forgotten his scars. In fact, it was possible her memory had exaggerated them, made them more than they really were. But his appearance had never bothered her, never frightened her. *He* had never frightened her—at least, not at first.

Now, she better understood the sort of pain he was prepared to cause.

After six years, his outward appearance was largely unchanged. A little older, a little more haggard, a little more sun browned—one might say much the same of her, she supposed, though she had always taken scrupulous care with her complexion.

The inward changes, however... She was not the same person she had been, a naïve girl whose reading had given her romantic aspirations, who imagined she had escaped her father's cruelty. Whether her husband had changed—was capable of change—was something that could only be discovered with time. But time with him, thank God, was fleeting. In a few hours, he would be gone.

The Duke of Hartwell. The rumors of his rupture with his grandfather must have had some truth in them, after all. She had suspected as much, when the man had never so much as acknowledged her existence. And now, she was a duchess, a woman with an important role to fill in society— though mostly dependent on whether her husband chose to fill his. She could not predict how her life would change from this point forward, with one exception.

Her family's letters, when they came, would demand even more.

When the first glimmers of sunrise began to dispel the night's gloom, she rose and dressed without ringing for her maid. Through the bow window in her bedchamber, identical to the window in the drawing room below, she looked out on the expanse of silvery gray water, a shade or two darker than the sky. Wind and sea dueled, neither showing any signs of tiring. It would be cold on the strand. Uncomfortable. Even if Fanny Drummond had understood her invitation, she would not expect to meet her at this hour, under these conditions. But Caro could not wait another moment.

On the landing, someone had left a tray on the hall table between the two doors. Ordinarily, she took breakfast only after she returned from her walk. But perhaps Mrs. Horn had anticipated that Caro would need some fortification this morning. Or perhaps the repast had been left for...their guest. Hearing no bustle of departure from the other room, Caro filled a cup with as much as she could of the steaming coffee, added sugar, and took great delight in swallowing half of the black brew before she reached the ground floor.

Despite the early hour, Geoffrey, the footman, stood at the ready in the entry hall. "You needn't step out this morning," she assured him, handing off her mostly empty cup. She thought she caught a glimmer of relief in his face as he took it from her, opened the door, and bowed her through it.

The sharp morning air stole her breath, but it carried with it a welcome greeting.

"I'm here," called Mrs. Drummond, rounding the western end of Royal Crescent. "So sorry to be late." Her manservant trudged along behind her, looking sleepy, his wig askew enough to reveal ginger hair beneath.

"Not late," Caro reassured her as they met at the foot of the stairs. "I'm setting out half an hour earlier than usual, at least. I…" Fanny's eyes were already searching her face through the veil. Not much point in denying it. "I didn't sleep a wink." Though the morning light wasn't especially bright, she found herself squinting against it as a headache pierced her temples.

"You poor dear. He didn't—" Fanny's cheeks flamed. "Oh, I beg your pardon. It wasn't my intention to ask an improper question. I was merely worried—"

"He didn't," Caro reassured her, looping her arm through her friend's and feeling some of the night's tension ease from her shoulders. "And by the time we return, he will be gone again."

"Gone? I…see."

From her expression, she plainly *didn't* see, and she certainly might be forgiven her lack of understanding. Caro herself felt befuddled. They walked along in silence for some time, the scuff of their walking boots nearly lost to the noise of wind and water. She glanced over her shoulder to spy the drowsy footman leaning against a paling, pretending to watch their progress from a distance. "He has important business in London," she explained, her voice low. "He merely stopped in Brighton to"—*Unsettle me? Upset me? Undo whatever meager peace the passage of six years has brought?*—"deliver the news of his grandfather's passing."

"Of course." Fanny managed, somehow, to make it sound as if the Duke of Hartwell's behavior was eminently reasonable. "I ought to have offered my condolences yesterday, but I was—"

"Surprised? Not more than I was, I assure you. But I never met the man, and Hartwell…" She recalled his harsh words at her suggestion the household observe the usual practices of mourning. "I don't believe Hartwell and his grandfather were close."

Fanny made a murmur but said nothing more.

"I suppose word of my husband's return is already being bandied about?" Caro asked when they had walked another dozen yards, the pounding in her head only growing worse, rather than being cleared by the sea air.

Fanny's arm stiffened. "I'm no gossip. But…yes. I fear it is."

Of course, he would be the subject of rumors. When hadn't he been? And the people of Brighton, though generally respectful, had never truly managed to hide their curiosity about Caro's unusual situation. At least it was not high season, the town crowded with visitors ready to carry the news to every corner of the kingdom.

"Does he intend to stay in England, I wonder?" Fanny's question sounded idle, as if she did not expect an answer, so Caro did not attempt one. Her headache had grown severe enough to unsettle her stomach.

"Oh!" She lifted her free hand, undecided whether to press it to her temple, or her belly.

"Caro, dear." Fanny slid her arm free, only to grasp her by the shoulders, the better to study her face. "Are you all right?"

"Megrim," she managed to grind out.

"We should turn back this very minute. You need to lie down."

Caro glanced toward Royal Crescent, but she could no longer judge how far they had come. Even as she tried to focus, the distance stretched and shrank, the smooth surface of the Marine Parade undulating like the waves of the sea. "I fear I'm going to be sick."

Thank God, Fanny was a sensible woman. Swiftly, she lifted Caro's veil and tucked it out of the way. A grateful Caro sucked in an unmuffled breath. "You look dreadful," Fanny declared, alternating between searching in her reticule and signaling to her servant. "I usually have one or two... ah, yes. Here. A peppermint drop. It might help soothe your stomach."

She pressed the wrapped sweet into Caro's hand. Caro fumbled a little with the paper, but eventually succeeded in popping the confection in her mouth. The rush of peppermint drove back the nausea and momentarily sharpened her senses. "Thank you," she managed to whisper.

"I can't abide smelling salts," Fanny explained sheepishly. She was like a peppermint drop herself, cool and sweet all at once, stronger somehow than Caro had expected. She looped her arm around Caro's waist, gathering her tight to her side and clearly prepared to bear her weight. "Do you think you can walk now?"

"I'm sure I can. I just need..." She tried to focus on Royal Crescent in the distance. A man was walking toward them. Fanny's servant. Then the solitary figure split and became two men—and the row of houses was nothing more than a speck at the end of a long tunnel. How had they come so far? "I just need a...moment to...rest." And then she was slipping through Fanny's grasp as the ground rushed upward and the sky mercifully dimmed.

But the thunder! Oh, it made her teeth rattle; the storm that followed would be terrible indeed. She tried to tug at Fanny's hems and warn her to seek shelter, but she couldn't reach her, couldn't reach anything...she needed all her strength just to hold herself together...

No, not thunder...footsteps. Running footsteps. And voices. A man. Men. Shouting—at her? She couldn't for the life of her make out the words....

She turned her head, intending to ask the fellow to repeat himself, and was promptly and spectacularly sick.

Then everything went black.

* * * *

Leclerc spent half an hour polishing these boots. He'll have my head.

The shallow, ridiculous thought caught Maxim off guard, and he drove it away with a shake. His mind's attempt, perhaps, to protect him from the grim reality of the situation. He couldn't make sense of what he was seeing: Caro lying on the ground, curled in upon herself, moaning. From the drawing room window, he'd watched her leave the house not a quarter of an hour ago. She'd looked perfectly fit. Perfect.

"Fetch a physician," he ordered the woman's—Mrs. Drummond's—servant. "Go!"

He could've sworn he'd said as much once already, but the young man had only goggled at him. He'd lost his wig in the dash toward Caro, and his rust-red hair glowed, even in the gray morning light. When understanding now swept across the other man's features, Maxim realized his first shouted order had not been delivered in English. "Yes, sir," he said at last and hurried away.

"What happened?" Maxim ground out as he bent to lift Caro into his arms.

"A megrim, she said." Mrs. Drummond was pale, but not, thank God, hysterical. "I didn't know she was prone to headaches."

Neither did I.

He hardly knew his wife at all. Did not recognize the shape of her body gathered against his chest, could muster only the vaguest recollection of her rosewater scent.

But he had not forgotten that unaccountable, undeniable need to protect her.

Especially from himself.

"Can you manage?" Mrs. Drummond reached out a hand but stopped short of daring to catch his arm when he glared at her.

Turning, he began to trudge across the roadway, disguising his limp. Caro, who had moaned when he picked her up, was now distressingly silent. They hadn't got far from Royal Crescent, but Mrs. Drummond's man was still there before them, with a short, silver-haired man in tow. Mrs. Horn herself opened the front door and gasped at the sight of her mistress's gray-tinged complexion and the beads of sweat that had formed on her brow and upper lip.

"Straight to bed with her," the doctor said.

Maxim let Mrs. Horn and Mrs. Drummond precede him up the stairs, out of practicality rather than mere politeness. By the time he reached the door to Caro's bedchamber, the housekeeper had smoothed and turned back the linens and Mrs. Drummond was at the washstand, pouring water from the pitcher into the basin and dampening a cloth.

Before he deposited his wife on the bed, Mrs. Horn untied Caro's bonnet and removed it. A coil of red-brown hair tumbled loose, more vivid even than usual against her sickly pallor. As he laid her on the plush bed, she exhaled deeply but her body did not uncoil. While Mrs. Drummond sponged Caro's pale face, Mrs. Horn removed her shoes, unbuttoned her pelisse, and finally slipped off her tattered kid gloves, revealing palms scraped raw by the roadway. She must have thrown out her hands instinctively as she'd fallen; Mrs. Drummond dabbed carefully around a similar wound on Caro's cheek, the one that had been pressed against his breast.

"I am Trefrey," the physician said, removing his coat and laying it aside with his hat. "I assume I have the honor of addressing the Duke of Hartwell?"

My, but word had traveled fast.

"Honor?" Maxim gritted past his clenched jaw. "Just do your job, man."

"Of course, Your Grace. If the lady will—" He gestured toward the door with a sweep of one arm, as if to usher Mrs. Drummond and her delicate sensibilities from the room.

"Certainly not" was her tart reply, her eyes barely leaving Caro's face. Mrs. Horn gave a curt nod of silent agreement with her refusal.

Trefrey sighed. "Very well. Who can tell me what happened?"

"She rose early," Maxim began. At various points throughout the night, he'd caught himself straining for any sound of movement from her room.

"As she always does," interjected the housekeeper. "She takes a morning constitutional."

"And today," added Mrs. Drummond, "she invited me to join her. When she stepped out, I thought she looked wan, and she told me she hadn't slept well. She blamed it on a megrim."

Trefrey took in the information as he examined her, lifting her limp wrist from the bed to check her pulse, lowering his ear to her chest to listen to her breathing. "A migraine is a possibility. Several of my patients suffer most acutely when the weather is about to turn." With his broad thumb, he

drew up one eyelid, then the other. Caro showed no signs of consciousness.
"She vomited, the boy said."

"Yes."

"Had she eaten anything?"

"She never takes a bite of breakfast before she goes out," Mrs. Horn
fretted, "no matter how often I caution her—"

"You." Maxim rounded the end of the bed and faced Mrs. Drummond,
driving her slowly back toward the wall as he approached. "You gave her
something. I saw you."

"A p-p-peppermint drop," Mrs. Drummond choked out, her pale blue
eyes wide with undisguised panic. "T-t-to soothe her stomach. P-p-perfectly
harmless."

"Now, now, Your Grace," the physician soothed, as if a mad duke was an
ordinary fixture in the sickrooms he visited. "I've never yet seen someone
laid low by a sweet. Have you any more, ma'am?"

Maxim stepped back just far enough to allow her to retrieve her reticule.
She dumped its contents on Caro's dressing table: a key, a handkerchief, a
few coins, and three or four paper-wrapped shapes. The physician picked
up one, untwisted the paper, sniffed the contents, and popped the sugary
droplet into his mouth. "Not the culprit," he opined once the sweet had
melted away.

"But you still think it was something—something she took in. Not
merely a headache."

"Difficult to say. Has anyone else been taken ill?"

Mrs. Horn started to shake her head, then gasped. "Geoffrey. The
footman. Started complaining of the gripes just this morning and had to
be relieved from his duties."

"There, you see." Trefrey nodded sagely. "It will be something they
both ate. Something from the larder."

The housekeeper looked both stricken by and scornful at the suggestion.
"I keep a clean kitchen, sir," she insisted.

"Will my wife recover?" Maxim paused slightly between each word to
keep from shouting. He wanted to strangle someone, and as Mrs. Drummond
had managed to slither out of his reach, the physician would do.

"Oh, yes. In a day or two, she'll be right as rain. A nice, strong purgative
will help things along." He fished in the little leather satchel he had brought
and withdrew a small, corked bottle. "A spoonful should do the trick," he
said, holding it out. "And one for the footman too."

Maxim reached for it, but Mrs. Horn snatched the bottle away first. "That's no task for a man, Your Grace. Besides, I thought you meant to be on your way at first light. It's well past that."

Her subtle scolding was far less than he deserved. "I—" He glanced from the housekeeper to the physician. "This morning's events have, of course, altered my plans." He couldn't leave her like this, even if he should.

Mrs. Drummond had resumed sponging Caro's brow, but she gave a skeptical sniff. Did she imagine *he* was somehow responsible for his wife's sudden bout of illness?

"Mrs. Horn," he said, turning back toward the housekeeper, "is there a manservant in the household who could be trusted to deliver some important papers to London?"

The housekeeper shook her head. "I'm afraid the only manservant here is Geoffrey. And your valet, of course."

"Leclerc would not be well suited to the task." He spoke no more than a few words of English and read none at all. He had never been to London. It was far too easy to imagine him lost, robbed, or worse.

While they spoke, Trefrey closed his satchel, donned his greatcoat, and picked up his hat. "I shall call again this evening to see how the patient fares," he said to Maxim. "But if you have concerns in the meantime, Mrs. Horn knows where to find me."

Maxim nodded once; Trefrey bowed and was gone. For a moment, the only sound in the room was the slosh of water in the washbasin as Mrs. Drummond refreshed the cloth she had been using.

"If it's as important as that, you may have the use of my manservant, Your Grace." She did not look at him as she spoke, and the offer sounded reluctant. "We've just come from London, so you can be sure he knows his way around town, and you've seen firsthand that he's both quick and trustworthy."

Had he seen any such thing? If the young man hadn't been loitering, half-asleep, he would have been closer when Caro fell. And while he *had* managed to fetch a physician promptly, a sea bathing town must be lousy with men like Trefrey, so it had hardly been a Herculean task.

Maxim eyed Mrs. Drummond's bent head uncertainly. His suspicions had not been entirely eliminated by the physician's performance with the peppermint drop. Still, the loan of her manservant would be a help....

"Mrs. Horn," he said, "would you step into the corridor for just a moment?"

Nodding, the housekeeper slipped the bottle of physic into her pocket and left the room. Her eyes grew wide when he followed her and closed the door. "What can you tell me about Mrs. Drummond?" he asked, his voice low.

"Very little, Your Grace. She's only been in Brighton less than a fortnight. Said to be an army officer's widow—introduced to Her Grace by a mutual friend."

"And who is that?"

"A Mrs. Scott, who was here in Brighton all of September…"

Unease trickled down Maxim's spine, though he tried to stem its progress with logic. *Scott* was a common enough surname. No reason to assume—

"…with her husband, General Scott," the housekeeper finished.

A string of curses—an unholy mixture of Breton, French, and English—rose to his lips, but he swallowed them back. With any other man, he might still have convinced himself it was a coincidence. But Scott left too little to chance.

The general would have known where matters stood with the late duke's health. He must have anticipated Maxim would visit Caro on his return to England. Mrs. Drummond's presence in Brighton, however, suggested that Scott had wanted to keep an eye on him. But why? And why would he send a woman to do the job? Unless Mrs. Drummond was merely a cover for…

"As for that manservant of hers," Mrs. Horn continued, her tone sharpening, "you'd be doing the housekeepers of Brighton a favor to send him out of the way for a bit. He's already a great favorite among the serving girls hereabouts, if you catch my meaning."

"I understand perfectly." He knew just how a man in Scott's service might go about gathering useful information and observing household comings and goings undetected. Mrs. Drummond and her "servant" had obviously been placed here ahead of Maxim's arrival. Had something happened to make the general suspicious of his loyalty?

And was his wife a witting or unwitting part of Scott's scheme?

"I need to change my boots," he said, turning toward his own chamber. He needed a moment to think. He needed some way to test, some way to determine whether he'd lost the general's trust. If he had, then the message he'd brought all this way would fall on deaf ears, and that could spell disaster.

The message he'd brought all this way…

"Tell Mrs. Drummond I thank her for her kind offer," he said, abruptly changing direction in favor of the drawing room and its writing desk. "I'll have things ready for her man in half an hour." More than enough time to devise and encrypt another message.

Its reception would tell him all he needed to know about where he stood with General Scott.

Chapter 8

"Come in," Maxim said when a tap sounded on the drawing room door. He'd just sealed the letter to be delivered and now carefully unfolded himself from the delicate chair, more suited to an elf than a man of his size.

Just as Mrs. Drummond's manservant opened the door, Maxim spied his cipher wheel—two interlocking metal discs that could be set to create a basic encryption, the substitution of one letter for another in a regular pattern—still lying on the desktop. Swiftly he slid open the shallow drawer and dropped it inside. No one in Scott's camp would have any trouble deciphering a simple Caesar cipher, but best not to be so obvious about his methods that he inadvertently revealed what he knew of theirs.

When he turned from the desk, the other man gave no sign of having seen anything. "What's your name?" Maxim asked.

"Hopkins, sir. Fitz Hopkins."

He was tall and well built, ideal for playing the part of a footman, if one were willing to ignore the shock of red hair and freckles, which made him look younger than he really was. On the beach, a quick glance had placed him at eighteen at most, but now Maxim judged him in his midtwenties. Caro's age. Perhaps an officer, perhaps not. Likely not long in Scott's service, either way. And yet there were signs—not visible scars, but something in his visage—that said he had faced danger.

He was brave enough to size Maxim up, at any rate, which few men of his acquaintance were. He showed none of a manservant's deference.

"Mrs. Drummond told you what's wanted?"

"Aye, sir. Papers delivered to London."

"Important papers, Hopkins," Maxim stressed. "You must make haste."

Something dangerously close to a grin lit the younger man's features. "Not a problem, sir."

Maxim snatched up two letters from the otherwise empty desktop. The first was addressed to Sellers, his solicitor. "This," he lied, handing it to Hopkins, "is an urgent matter. You must hand it to this man and no other, and wait for a reply. You are likely to be asked to carry something to me in return." Sellers no doubt had a mountain of his grandfather's papers for Maxim to sort through, the dullest stuff imaginable. "This," he said, laying the second letter on the man's open palm, the encrypted note addressed to Scott at his Audley Street home, "you may leave with whoever opens the door. No reply."

Hopkins looked at the direction on both letters, nodded, and tucked them into his breast pocket. "Understood, sir." He bowed, and when he lifted his head, Maxim could read nothing in the man's expression. He'd been trained well.

"On your way," Maxim ordered, and with a nod, Hopkins was gone. Maxim listened until the front door closed, then returned to the desk to retrieve his cipher wheel. The smooth slide of the drawer was impeded this time by the corner of a letter, topmost in a thick packet of letters bound with a length of blue embroidery silk tied in a bow. He picked up the disc and tucked it in his pocket, all the while studying the writing on the letter uppermost: a man's hand, almost certainly. Caro's not-so-mythical lover?

With a grumble, he picked up the bundle and took it across the long room with him to the chair in which he'd sat the day before. He never felt guilt at prying into others' secrets. After all, he was a spy. And yet two or three silent moments ticked by before he could persuade himself to run his thumb over a corner of the stack of letters, fanning them like a deck of cards. Every one addressed to Caro. Not all written by the same gentleman's hand.

He did not know what to feel. Jealousy? Regret? Relief?

Grasping one end of the blue silk thread between thumb and forefinger, he tugged the knot loose and picked up and opened the topmost letter, the paper of which was wrinkled, as if the sheet had been crumpled, then smoothed. An indication of frustration at its contents? Or distress? Darting his eyes down the page, he saw that it was signed by her father, and the sensation in his chest that might have been relief was burned away in a furnace blast of fury. The bastard wanted money, he realized as he read more carefully, and no insignificant sum at that. It wasn't a begging, pleading, importuning letter, either. It was a demand. Or rather, a threat.

He turned to the next letter, and the next. Every one of them from some member of Caro's worthless family. Every one a request. Mostly for funds, large amounts and small, but occasionally for some other form of assistance, to wield a marchioness's influence, to wager her reputation on their behalf.

How many times over the past six years had he reassured himself that he'd left her better off than he'd found her, with a generous allowance and a title and a position in society no one would dare try to flout or exploit?

When in fact he'd wounded her and abandoned her to a circling pack of bloodthirsty scavengers.

With the deliberate motions he'd mastered more than half a lifetime ago, he refolded the letters, restacked them as they had been originally, retied the bundle, and returned it to its place in the drawer. It no longer required conscious thought to restore things in such a way that no one would ever suspect they had been disturbed.

By the time he left the drawing room, only his thoughts were still ruffled, disorderly, out of sorts.

In the rear bedchamber, he toed off his ruined boots. The *thump, thump* against the floor brought Leclerc from the dressing room.

"Oh, sir. There you are!" He spoke in rapid French and his eyes were wide with surprise, even before he saw the condition of Maxim's boots. "I have had your things packed these two hours at least. I understood you wanted to—my God, what has happened here?"

"The duchess was taken ill. We do not travel today. Bring me hot water and fresh clothes."

"But of course, sir. I won't be a moment."

True to his word, Leclerc hurried about his duties, murmuring expressions of pity and surprise all the while, apologizing that he had heard nothing of the mistress's unfortunate situation, as her ignorant servants spoke only English.

"What of your important business in London, sir? If you wish it, I will gladly go on your behalf and—"

"That won't be necessary. I've already sent a letter with Mrs. Drummond's manservant. The lad knows the city well."

"Ah. How fortunate, sir." Relief gusted from him in the form of a self-deprecating laugh. "Who knows where I might have ended up?"

In a quarter of an hour, Maxim was washed and dressed and on his way back to Caro's chamber when he passed a little table, equidistant between the two doors. He had not noticed it there before, but now the silver coffeepot beckoned to him. Brushing a fingertip over the metal, he found it cool to the touch. A pity. Perhaps Mrs. Horn could be prevailed upon to send up a fresh pot, though it was now past midmorning.

But when he opened Caro's door, any thought of refreshment fled from his mind. The housekeeper was not within. Mrs. Drummond sat on the edge of the bed, no longer sponging his wife's brow, but simply holding her hand. The linens, Caro's nightgown, a vase of flowers—all were fresh and crisp, but the stench of sickness still hung on the air. Even the aromatic concoction of herbs and spices bubbling away in a little posset pot could not drive it away.

"I've sent your man on his way," he said with the closest to a nod of thanks that he could muster. "Is she improved?"

Mrs. Drummond started and turned to face him but did not rise. "We managed to rouse her enough to safely administer the purgative. Of course, it has made her weaker." Beneath a down-filled coverlet, Caro shivered. "She's insensible again."

"Leave us."

He gave the order without heat, but nevertheless Mrs. Drummond stiffened in defiance. Her eyes were the cool, pale blue of ice chips, but the fear he had glimpsed in them earlier this morning, and yesterday afternoon, had melted into loathing. "Haven't you done enough already, Your Grace?"

He could almost admire her sangfroid, though he knew it was part of a performance. Acting was a necessary skill in this line of work, and Scott would not have sent an untutored innocent into the beast's lair.

When he took two measured steps toward the bed, however, she slid uncertainly from her perch on the edge of the mattress. Perhaps the glimmerings of fear in her expression had been real. Another step, and she rounded the foot of the bed and moved toward the door.

"Tell Mrs. Horn I will sit with the duchess for a time and that we are not to be disturbed," he said, keeping his voice terrifyingly soft. "My wife needs her rest."

He heard the door latch click, once to open, once to close. He presumed Mrs. Drummond had heard, perhaps even acknowledged, his order. But he could not take his eyes from Caro's form, dwarfed by the mountain of bedding that surrounded her, nearly as pale as the bleached linen on which she lay shivering.

She was lying on her side, facing away from him, so he moved to the other side of the bed and looked down at her. The scrape on her cheek was vivid, glistening with some salve intended to keep it from becoming a scar. Gently, he lifted first her right hand, and then the left. The scrapes on the heels of her hands were less red, the skin there tougher. He skated a fingertip around the injury, pausing over her wedding ring, surprised to see she still wore it.

With a silent oath, he toed off his second pair of boots for the day, then shrugged out of his coat and tossed it over a tufted bench at the foot of the bed. Setting his good knee to the mattress, he crawled his way toward her; she showed no signs of waking.

Only when he stretched his length beside her, surrounding her with his warmth, did she respond. A murmur of sound, nothing more, against his chest.

"Mmm."

Foolish hope surged in his breast. *The start of a word.* The start of a word he'd dreamed of hearing for six years.

When I'm in your bed, you may call me Maxim.

The muffled hum faded from her lips and disappeared into silence.

Bah. He had grown soft—soft in the head. Imagining she wanted him still—had ever wanted him.

But he held her to him all the same, tightly enough that his body absorbed her tremors and she relaxed in his arms, falling at last into a more restful slumber. Against her scalp, he whispered warm, soft words in the language of his childhood...all the cold, hard things he would do to punish her father, whoever had made her sick, everyone who had ever hurt her.

And at the top of the list? Underscored twice with thick, black ink?

His own wretched name.

Chapter 9

Fitz had visited General Scott's office in the Horse Guards only once before. After he'd sufficiently recovered from the injuries he had sustained at the hands of his French kidnappers, Scott had brought him here to order him to take leave in the country. No, not *order*, for Fitz had been at liberty to refuse, and had. *Suggest,* then. *Encourage. The Underground is no place to recover one's nerves,* Scott had insisted.

Too late, Fitz had realized the old man might have been right.

The office itself had not changed in the intervening months: dark blue curtains had been looped back haphazardly from the tall window to let in light; the rug was just shy of threadbare; Scott's desktop was still littered with an impossible jumble of paperwork. The only difference was that the usual haze of tobacco smoke had cleared, though Scott still clutched his unlit pipe between his teeth as he studied the letter Fitz had given him.

"What does it say, sir?" Fitz asked when Scott's lips curled into a wry smile around the pipestem.

"That I may go to hell. Oh, not in so many words," he added with a reassuring chuckle as he laid the empty pipe in an equally empty ashtray and tossed the letter to join the mountain of papers. "This shabbily encrypted note purports to contain information about the movement of French troops, information that would of course be invaluable—if I didn't suspect it had been made out of whole cloth."

"But why would Hartwell do such a thing?"

"To check whether he's being watched."

"By me?" Fitz couldn't quite keep the nervousness from his voice. He'd learned the hard way he was far from invincible, and the duke did not look the sort to shy away from violence.

"By *me*—though the British Army aren't the only ones who want what Hartwell has. This was the more important document, he told you?" Scott asked, picking up the other letter. At Fitz's nod, the general opened it without disturbing the seal and scanned its contents. "Merely a letter to his solicitor, pertaining to estate business. Nothing too urgent. Yes,"—he nodded as he refolded the note—"I'd say that he doesn't quite trust you, either. Must've wanted to test you a bit, see how you'd carry out your commission. Very well." He handed the resealed letter back to Fitz, who turned it over in his fingers. It looked exactly as it had when Hartwell had first given it to him; no one would guess it had been read. "Take that to Mr.—ah—Sellers and ferry whatever he gives you back to Hartwell, quick as you can. Give him no reason to doubt that you followed his instructions precisely. We'll hope that reassures him." Something faraway glimmered in Scott's eyes, though they hid behind smudged spectacles. "Perhaps sorting through some dusty old paperwork will prove beneficial for Hartwell's soul."

Doubting the duke was even possessed of such a thing, Fitz tucked the letter into his breast pocket. "And what of the duchess's sudden illness this morning? Do you believe she—or, or Mrs. Drummond—is in danger from Hartwell? Shouldn't she come back to London, just to be safe?"

For all Fitz's determination to be subtle, even matter of fact, when mentioning Fanny, his stammer earned him a speculative glance from Scott. "Has Mrs. Drummond expressed concern, Lieutenant Hopkins? Reluctance to continue her mission?"

"No, sir."

Scott unthreaded his spectacles from behind his ears and tossed them onto the desktop, where a slide of letters and other documents promptly buried them. Fitz wondered how many pairs he had lost that way. "Naturally, you would not want to see any lady come to harm. But"—a smile once more played about Scott's lips—"I am persuaded that this lady would not appreciate any attempt to gainsay her wishes—no matter how well intentioned. She strikes me as someone who wants the freedom to make her own decisions."

Fitz nodded once, a little sharply. He didn't begrudge her her freedom. In fact, he'd been quietly admiring her strength and her fortitude for some time. Which was not to say there was anything particular in his interest in Fanny Drummond. It was just that…well, all those weeks stuck in the Underground—a man had to have something to occupy his mind.

"Do I have your permission to tell her that Hartwell suspects me—and therefore, her?"

"By all means, she should know. But don't expect her to reach the same conclusion you seem to have reached about whether she ought to continue in Brighton. You each have your uses there. The duchess needs a friend, a confidant. And Hartwell needs...well,"—he folded his arms over his chest and tipped back in his chair—"I confess my interest in the case is not limited strictly to his skills in espionage."

Fitz made no attempt to hide either his surprise or his confusion. Scott chuckled. "Go on," he urged, waving Fitz toward the door with the fingers of one hand. "With any luck, you can be back in Brighton before nightfall."

Sunset was streaking the sky over the channel when he arrived, but all was dark by the time he opened the door to Fanny's sitting room and slipped inside. She must already have retired, though the hour was not that late. He tried to tamp down the surge of disappointment that passed through him. He had no urgent news, after all.

And then a single word—"Well?"—came from the shadows.

He followed that sound to the corner of the room and then waited as she lit a candle. Its flame illuminated only a quarter of the small room, but it was more than enough light to reveal the worry in her face.

"I've just dropped off a whole crate of papers and ledgers and such at Royal Crescent," he said, stepping closer. "A present from the duke's solicitor. Mrs. Horn says the footman who was taken ill is much improved, just a bit of a headache now, and the duchess is resting peacefully."

"I'm glad to hear it." The flickering light might have disguised the skepticism in her expression, but he could hear it plainly in her voice. "His Grace tossed me out on my ear." On her lips, the honorific became an insult. "Shortly after you left."

"Mrs. Horn says he sat with her all day himself," he tried to reassure her. "She seemed quite touched by his show of devotion."

"Devotion?" Fanny scoffed, unfolding the leg that had been curled beneath her and standing. "A few hours hardly make up for years of neglect. For all we know, he poisoned her."

"Do you really believe he's capable of that?" Fitz asked, astonished.

"There's very little I wouldn't believe of one of Scott's men."

"Is that what you think of us—of me?"

For answer, she carried the candlestick to the nearby mantel and touched the candle's flame to the wick of another. By that doubled light, he could make out the details of the small sitting room. The rose-patterned wallpaper. The aubergine velvet chaise longue on which she had been reclining. A small table beside it, and on its polished surface, a book lying open, facedown. A history of Brighton—he knew that much from having carried the thing home from the circulating library. He wondered whether she'd put it aside reluctantly, only as the light faded, or given up early on.

"My husband was devoted too. Devoted to his work. To keeping up appearances. To making sure I knew my place." Her voice dropped to little more than a whisper. "Do you know why I've spent more than a year in the Underground?"

"Colonel Millrose told some of the men it was because you knew something you shouldn't, that your Captain Drummond let slip…"

Even as he spoke the words, he recognized their hollow sound. Of course there must be married officers who shared more than was wise with their wives, in part because they couldn't bring themselves to keep secrets from the women they loved.

Fitz had never met Drummond, but from what Fanny had just said, her husband hadn't been the sort.

His gaze fell once more on the book, and he recalled what Fanny had told the Duchess of Hartwell outside the circulating library just the day before. How her husband had denied her even the simple pleasure of reading novels.

Confirming his sudden understanding of the situation, Fanny shook her head. "No. It wasn't a slip. It was a trap. You see, on what turned out to be his final assignment, he was partnered with the Magpie," she explained, using the code name given to Major Langley Stanhope for his ability to mimic voices. "Robert and I had half of a house in Marylebone. Magpie was always popping in and out with an update on the mission, but equally ready to talk with me about things my husband believed a woman incapable of understanding. Weighty matters. News of the day. Politics.

"Robert disapproved of our…*friendship*, I suppose you might have called it. It was certainly never anything more, despite what my husband imagined. But his jealousy got the better of him. One day, he—he told me something about their assignment. Something I had no business knowing. I think he assumed I would say Major Stanhope had already revealed as much, and his suspicions about us would be confirmed. Only Magpie would never have done something so foolish. So dangerous." Her gaze was focused on the floor, but her thoughts were considerably further away. "Robert must have realized right away the mistake he'd made, though he tried to pass it off as nothing. And it might have been…until he died. Afterward, when Colonel Millrose questioned me, I proved Robert right," she said, snapping her attention back to Fitz with a stilted, humorless smile. "I was too naïve to keep quiet. I made it clear I knew more than I ought. So, down into the Underground I went."

"My God." She had been married for years to a man who held her at arm's length, who seemed to have imagined this curious and clever woman incapable of serious thought. And when he died, that man's compatriots had—without irony—all but imprisoned her for knowing too much. "They only wanted to keep you safe," Fitz murmured consolingly, stepping closer still, hands outstretched as if to grasp hers.

"Safe? Safe from what?" She rounded on him, and he dropped his arms to his sides. "The knowledge of what men are willing to do to acquire secrets? What they must sometimes endure to keep them?" Her pale eyes scoured his face, as if searching for the shadow of bruises there, the memory of what the French agents had done to him while he'd been their prisoner. He could not quite read her expression.

"Hartwell suspects," he told her, hoping to convey the seriousness of their present situation. "Who we are. Why we're here."

"Let him suspect all he wants," she retorted flatly. "I won't stand by and see Caro—the duchess—sacrificed to this ridiculous game."

The venom she laid on that word, *game*.... Was she trying to make him defensive? If he argued with her, it would only confirm in her mind that he was just like all the rest.

But she must have at least a hint of doubt, or else she would not require confirmation. Perhaps she had not quite made up her mind about him?

"Fanny," he ventured. Her eyes flared, but she did not protest the familiarity. "I don't intend to stand in your way. But I—I also care for you. A great deal. Enough to want to make sure you aren't hurt."

A flush of color brightened her cheeks, as if she were not quite indifferent to his concern. "I have to do this, Fitz. I have to prove that I'm more than a glorified housekeeper. More than an ornament."

Her cool beauty had the effect of making her seem untouchable, something altogether too delicate for a man's rough hands. But in this moment, beneath the warm glow of the candles, he saw only the beautiful fierceness of her determination, and he ached to reach out to her.

"Prove to whom?" he asked. "Not to me."

"To myself."

He could only nod his understanding, though he knew too well what she felt. Hadn't he joined the army to prove himself a better man than the one with whom he shared his name? "Then you must go on being a friend to the duchess, no matter what the duke says or does. Together, we'll figure out whose side Hartwell is on."

"Thank you."

The silence that settled between them was charged, like the air before a storm. "It's late," he said after a moment. "I should go. Don't want the gossips thinking we're more to each other than manservant and mistress."

"No," she agreed.

But was it his imagination, or had her breath had quickened at the notion of *more*? It was all he could do to keep himself from staring hungrily at the rise and fall of her bosom, disguised though it was by a light woolen shawl. God, but he could not remember ever wanting to kiss a woman as much as he wanted to kiss this one, right now. But how dangerous that would be, how disruptive to their mission, how spectacularly presumptuous of him, given all she had just revealed.

"I'll say good night, Fanny."

In spite of his determination to do the right thing, his voice rose on a questioning note, as if his leaving might be in doubt.

She nodded, then rose up on her tiptoes and pressed her lips to his, her mouth puckered at first, in the manner of one who intends to offer nothing more than a swift peck of gratitude or to bid an acquaintance farewell.

Then her lips softened and clung to his. She tasted of peppermint, cool and sweet. He wanted to wrap his arms around her and devour her on the spot. But too soon, she rocked back onto her heels, dabbing at the corners of her mouth with the knuckle of her first finger. Her eyes darted first to the floor, then his shoulder, and finally his face, as if apprehensive of his reaction. "I shouldn't have done that." Her own eyes were uncharacteristically dark, but more with desire than with regret, he thought.

"Probably not," he agreed, then grinned. "But maybe you'd better do it again to be certain."

"Fitz!" She dipped her head, but not before he caught a glimpse of an answering smile. "Good night." She stepped back to let him pass, then stopped him with a hand against his chest. "Don't be late tomorrow," she warned, recovering some of her usual severity, though there was still heat in her cool eyes. And in the warmth of her palm over his heart...

Suddenly his quarters in the attic seemed very far away—and not nearly private enough for the dreams he expected would plague him. He glanced toward the door that led to her bedchamber, where he'd carried her trunk on the day of their arrival. He could think of one sure way to make certain he was here when she wanted him in the morning.

Her fingers curled against his lapel, half pushing him away, half drawing him closer.

In the back of his head, he heard General Scott's words about Fanny wanting the freedom to make her own decisions. But he had a choice to make, too. A choice and a chance to make her see that one of Scott's men was capable of treating her as she deserved to be treated.

"Till tomorrow, Fanny."

He left her with a wink and a bow and returned to his musty room and his narrow cot, filled with sensations he had not felt in a very long time.

Anticipation, chief among them.

And hope.

Chapter 10

Caro squinted against the light pouring into her bedchamber, testing what her eyes could bear. Her head still ached, and her mouth tasted as if she'd tried to eat her down-filled pillow. Overall, she felt rather like someone who had consumed several glasses of wine too many at dinner. She knew the feeling because she'd tried it as a means of forgetting…once. It had failed on several levels, chief among them the fact that she hadn't forgotten anything.

But now, she really couldn't remember. Judging by the light, it was midday, or even later. And she was still abed, still wearing her nightdress? That was more than merely oversleeping. But hadn't she walked that morning, as she always did? She remembered strolling arm in arm with Fanny Drummond…. No, that had been the day before, the visit to the circulating library. They'd taken tea together, too. And when she had returned home…

A shudder—almost a spasm—passed through her, the sensation of falling and struggling to catch herself. Her limbs and her nightdress whispered across the bed linens as she tried to regain control, to master the throb in her head and the wave of nausea that accompanied it, to push herself more upright and take stock of her surroundings.

In a chair that had been moved from near the window to the head of the bed sprawled Hartwell, fast asleep. His head was tipped back against the chair's back, his lips parted slightly. Something—the light, the pose, the reflected color of rose brocade—softened him. At this angle, the worst of his scars were not visible, and even his nose appeared merely patrician. Not difficult to picture how he would have looked before the accident, without the accident. Almost handsome…

"I won't ask if you like what you see." He spoke without opening his eyes, without turning his head, without giving any sign of wakefulness at all. But his deep voice was alert and mocking.

"I was never bothered by your scars. Never frightened of them."

"Perhaps you should have been."

"Why? Your scars aren't what make you a beast," she declared, her heart stuttering at her boldness.

He opened his eyes then, and turned to face her, destroying the illusion. "I would ask how you're feeling," he said in that familiar wry tone, as he sat upright. He wore no coat. The open book that had been resting against his chest began to slide down his waistcoat, and he caught it with one hand. "But your sharp tongue and quick wit suggest you're on your way to a complete recovery."

"Recovery?" she echoed in a confused murmur, gathering the linens against her chest, a pathetic shield against his dark, penetrating gaze. "I—I'm not myself, it's true. My head hurts, and I can't decide whether the sensation in my belly is queasiness or hunger."

He closed his book with a snap and tapped it twice against his withered thigh before letting it rest there. "The latter, I would guess. You haven't eaten anything since dinner, two nights past—and I rather suspect you didn't eat much then."

"*Two* nights past?" She glanced toward the bow window and the water beyond. Gray waves lapped lazily at the pebbled beach as flashes of memory came back to her. She *had* walked in the morning with Fanny, though she'd been tired after a sleepless night. Such a headache—her present one was nothing more than a shadow of it. And the taste of peppermint...

"I've been ill—"

"Yes. At times, violently."

Heat rushed into her cheeks, and the burn led her to discover the previously unknown injury there. She lifted her fingertips to prod its edges, then studied her scraped palms. "I...fainted. But how did I—?" She glanced around her room.

"I carried you back to your bed," he said. She squeezed shut her eyes, not sure whether she was trying to call up the memory of being wrapped in his arms, or push it away. "Mrs. Drummond's manservant found some quack named Trefrey who said it must have been caused by something you ate and prescribed a purgative. Your footman, Geoffrey, was taken ill too, though not as severely."

"Oh." Weakly, she slid back down among the pillows. She remembered none of it. "And so you...sat with me. All night?"

"And all morning, and most of yesterday too. Yes." He made it sound as if it were the most ordinary thing in the world.

Oh, she did not doubt there were husbands who kept vigil at their wives' sickbeds. But *her* husband? When he had spent six years demonstrating how very little he cared? *Why?* she wanted to demand.

"You said you had important business," she reminded him instead.

"London has waited this long. It can wait a little longer. But speaking of urgent matters…" He pushed to stand, stretched the stiffness from his back. "If Mrs. Horn isn't camped outside your bedchamber door, I'll be shocked, and I've heard Mrs. Drummond's voice below at least twice, calling to check on you. These new-built houses aren't much for privacy, are they?" he remarked with a glance toward the window. Here, the elevation spared them the prying eyes of passersby, but the dining room was something of a fishbowl.

It was, she supposed, a not-so-roundabout way of faulting her choice, of criticizing her for taking this place when he had deserted her in a perfectly good house in town.

"I wanted something that had only ever been mine," she said, her voice weaker than she would've liked.

To her shock, he nodded. "I never had much desire to visit one of these seaside towns. But after sitting here all these hours, watching the water, I begin to understand the appeal."

There was a sort of longing in his words. In her mind, he'd been like the sea: powerful, remorseless. If he wanted to remake his world, he could do so—had done so—with little more than a snap of his fingers.

But perhaps truly erasing the past was not quite as easy as it seemed. Even for him.

"I should go," he said, tossing the book onto the seat of the chair and striding toward the door.

Go? she wanted to call after him. *How far? Your bedchamber, London, the other side of the globe? And for how long? A few hours' rest? A lifetime?*

She said nothing, though, her sudden bewilderment only amplified by her weakness. Of course she wanted him gone, wanted her peace—meager though it might sometimes be—restored to her. And yet, she watched his broad shoulders disappear through the doorway with the same strange wistfulness with which he had regarded the waters of the English Channel.

Before she could begin to sort through the tangle of her emotions, Mrs. Horn came bustling in. "Ah, there you are! Isn't it grand to see Your Grace sitting up—or very near it, at least? How are you feeling?"

"I—I'm not certain," Caro answered honestly.

"And it's no wonder, poorly as you've been. I've sent down to the kitchen for some beef tea and hot water. You'll be all the better for a wash and fresh nightgown...." Here, she disappeared into the dressing room, and her voice grew muffled, so that Caro could only make out occasional words, something about "strength" and "stale air" and Geoffrey, the poor footman.

"Did the duke really sit up with me all night?" she asked when Mrs. Horn reappeared with an armful of fresh linen.

"Oh, aye. Right fierce about it too. Nearly drove Mrs. Drummond to distraction—oh, and here I am forgetting that she left a note for you." She reached into the slit pocket of her dark gray worsted and pulled out a folded slip of hot-pressed paper, from Caro's own writing desk, it appeared. "I couldn't like it—nursing's not a job for a man—but he insisted. Wouldn't let me do more than bring him a tray and close the drapes," she said, tsking at the discovery that they had since been opened, and drawing them nearly shut again. Caro blinked at the sudden dimness, relieved by it and yet still craning to glimpse the sliver of water just visible in the gap she had left. "To look at him, you wouldn't know he had it in him to be so gentle—beggin' your pardon, Your Grace."

Caro shook her head, brushing off the apology and appearing to agree with the housekeeper's assessment, though that would be a lie. She *had* seen his gentle side, once.

To distract herself from unwelcome memories, she flicked open Fanny's note. Before she could read a word, however, two housemaids came in, one with a tray and the other lugging a canister of the promised hot water, and Caro had to submit herself to being bathed and dressed and very nearly fed. It required almost all her strength to persuade Mrs. Horn she was capable of wielding her own spoon.

Muttering a protest under her breath all the while, the housekeeper busied herself with picking up around the room: she smoothed one of the duke's discarded coats over her arm, gathered up damp towels from the washstand and an empty glass from the bedside table. Proof, if Caro had needed it, that her husband had indeed spent hours by her side.

The last item Mrs. Horn collected was the book he had tossed onto the chair. She turned the spine toward her, made a scoffing noise in her throat, and shook her head in open disbelief.

"What is it?" Caro ventured, dabbing at the beef tea dribbling down her chin.

"The last part of some tall tale about a highwayman, by that fellow... what's his name? Oh, yes. Robin Ratliff. When His Grace asked for it, particular-like, you could have knocked me over with a feather. I offered to send round to Donaldson's for something better, but he said he wanted that book, and no other. Felt certain you would have it somewhere, and sure enough, Tilly found it in a crate in the attic. And when I gave it to him, he chuckled real strange-like and said, 'Well, at least she didn't use it to kindle a fire.'" Again she shook her head, tucking the book into the crook of the arm that held the coat.

"It was a gift," Caro explained. "A thoughtful one, at the time. But I've since lost my taste for gothic romances."

"I shouldn't wonder," the housekeeper declared. "A lot of stuff and nonsense, if you ask me. The sort of thing that has housemaids sneaking candles into their beds, reading when they should be asleep." Her shoulders rose and fell with a despairing sigh.

Caro focused all her attention on finishing what she could of the beef tea and was shuffling her hips down in the bed again, exhausted by the effort, when the crinkle of paper reminded her of Fanny's note. Rescuing it from the linens, she smoothed away its wrinkles but still had to squint to make out the hurriedly written lines, hampered both by the ache in her temples and the lack of light in the room.

Dear Caro,

I can't convince myself that you'll ever see this, but if it should somehow come into your hands, please take pity on me and send word that you are safe. I can be at your side in half a moment.

F.

Despite the difficulties, she read it through twice. *Safe?* Not *well?* And whom did Fanny suspect of keeping her post from her? Caro's headache, subdued by the broth, now threatened to roar back to life.

It must've been frightening for Fanny to witness Caro suddenly take ill, but this felt like more than ordinary concern. Caro recalled what Mrs. Horn had said about Mrs. Drummond's reluctance to leave, despite the duke's insistence. Her friend's fear rubbed uneasily against her husband's unprecedented show of care and concern. The whole episode had been caused by something she ate, according to the physician, but she could not remember taking a bite. Nor could she remember ever having been so sick in her life. Surely Fanny didn't imagine Caro was in real danger, or that the duke was capable of—

"How's our patient, Mrs. Horn?" Still clad only in shirtsleeves, Hartwell nearly filled the doorway, one shoulder leaning against the frame. Though he'd spoken to the housekeeper, his gaze was focused squarely on Caro—or rather, the note she held.

Caro hid it in her hand, ignoring the prickle of pain when the paper's sharp corners prodded the abrasions on her palm. "Better, thank you. But tired."

"Then by all means, rest, my dear," he said. "Ah, and there's my coat." Pushing himself upright, he turned toward the housekeeper and stretched out a hand. "Leclerc will scold me for my carelessness."

Mrs. Horn hustled toward him, juggling the various objects she had collected to get to the garment. "Oughtn't I have it sponged and pressed?"

"No need," he insisted, shrugging into it, careless of the wrinkles. "I'm only stepping out for a breath of fresh air—unless I'm wanted here?" Quicker than seemed possible, his dark eyes were once more focused on Caro.

She swallowed. "I'm fine. You needn't worry about me anymore."

His answering expression held that same wistful note she'd seen earlier, but he quickly masked it with what she once might have called a scowl. Only now did she see the shadow of something more in it. With a dip of his head, and without another word to either of them, he turned and left.

Mrs. Horn rearranged her armload once again in order to free her hands to carry away the tray that was still lying over Caro's lap. "You rest now, Your Grace."

"I will," she promised. She really didn't think she could do otherwise. "But please,"—she dropped her voice a notch lower and sent a glance toward the empty doorway—"will you go to Mrs. Drummond yourself, reassure her that I am well, and ask her to call on me tomorrow morning?"

The housekeeper looked mildly surprised by the request, but not displeased. "Of course, ma'am. She'll be relieved to hear it. But do you really think you'll be ready for company tomorrow?"

"This was merely a bout of indigestion," she insisted, as if saying it out loud would make it true. "I refuse to let it keep me bedridden. And Mrs. Drummond isn't company. She is a friend."

"Yes, ma'am." Despite her burden, Mrs. Horn managed a shallow curtsy and backed her way from the room. Caro closed her eyes as the door shut behind her. Turning on her side, she slid Fanny's note beneath her pillow.

Fatigue and weakness made her limbs heavy, but sleep did not immediately come. She kept replaying Fanny's words in her head.

Send word that you are safe....

Was she? Or was she foolish enough to open her heart to her husband again?

* * * *

The next morning, she felt almost herself, enough better that the previous day's worries could be dismissed as fretfulness. Under Mrs. Horn's watchful eye, she managed tea and toast and coddled eggs, and submitted to having her hair combed and loosely arranged. When she called for a morning gown, however, the housekeeper's brow sank into a maternal frown.

"Another day in bed would suit you better," she insisted.

"I couldn't possibly. Besides, Mrs. Drummond is to call soon—"

"Let me show her up here."

Caro shook her head. "I'm not an invalid—though I might yet become one, if you don't let me move about a bit, stretch my limbs. Is Geoffrey back at his post?"

"Aye, Your Grace," Mrs. Horn confessed, looking sheepish.

"Then surely I can survive a quarter of an hour in the drawing room, being fussed over by my friend."

Reluctantly, Mrs. Horn agreed and brought a loose-fitting gown of fawn-colored poplin and a rose-pink cashmere shawl, "so you don't take a chill." The dress was hardly more confining than a nightgown, but in it, Caro felt a step closer to normality.

Strong enough, at least, to ask, "And where is my husband, this morning?" They'd reached the top of the stairs, and she found that her knees wanted to wobble.

"Sea bathing, Your Grace."

Automatically, Caro made a noise of surprise, though really, she did not know the duke's habits well enough to express any such thing.

"Leastways, I think that's what his servant was trying to say," Mrs. Horn went on. "I can't understand a word of that babble he speaks, but he does a fair pantomime. Ah, and speak of the devil." A meticulously but not expensively dressed young man with narrow features and dark hair and eyes was ascending the steps in front of them. "I can't make him understand that he ought to use the servants' stairs."

"A gentleman's valet is a law unto himself," Caro told her in a low, laughing whisper. Then, she addressed the young man in French. "You must be Mr. Leclerc."

"Oh, yes, ma'am," he replied in the same language, making a willowy bow. The rest of his speech came so rapidly she hadn't a prayer of understanding half of it—her governess's French really had been abysmal—but she caught a word here and there. "Lovely" and "pleasure" and "health"—an effusive string of flattery, as best she could tell.

"See?" Mrs. Horn opined dismissively, not troubling to lower her voice. "Babble."

Nevertheless, Caro graciously inclined her head and smiled, and Leclerc pressed himself against the wall so that she and Mrs. Horn might pass. She wished him a good morning, and he did the same before hurrying the rest of the way up the stairs and disappearing into the back bedchamber.

Mrs. Horn continued to natter about Frenchmen and the likelihood that His Grace would catch his death of a cold, but the descent required all of Caro's focus. Though her head no longer throbbed, neither was it perfectly clear and steady.

After what seemed an eternity, they reached the first-floor landing and passed through the door to the drawing room. Fanny, waiting just inside, leaped to her feet and came forward, hands outstretched. "I've been so worried," she said, and if her face had not made the fact plain, the sob in her voice would have.

Mrs. Horn surrendered Caro to Fanny and backed out with a curtsy, closing the doors behind her. "You needn't have been," Caro tried to reassure her friend, in spite of a wobbly exhale as she sank into a chair.

"With all due respect, you weren't there. Not really. I've never seen someone fade away so quickly. Your skin was gray, my dear, absolutely gray, and you went from talking rationally to insensate as quickly as if you'd fainted."

"I'm sorry to have made such a spectacle of myself over a bit of dyspepsia."

"Dyspepsia?" One of Fanny's pale, delicate brows arched.

"Dr. Trefrey said…"

Fanny pressed her lips together as if trying to hold back her doubts.

"What else could it have been?" Caro tried to sound dismissive.

Pale blue eyes searched her face. Fanny opened her mouth as if to speak and then shook her head. "Let's not dwell on it, shall we? You're better now."

Suddenly Caro wasn't willing to let go of the subject. "Why did you say you feared for my safety?"

"Pardon?"

"In your note—you did not ask me to send word that I was *well*, but rather that I was *safe*. As if you had reason to think I might not be."

"Oh, I—" Fanny, who had been seated opposite her, rose and stepped to the window, as if to study the view. "I suspect I was distraught. Don't, please, read too much into a hastily scribbled letter."

"Did…" The question caught in her throat, and dislodging it required her to press her fingertips into her breastbone. "Did my husband…threaten you?"

Fanny spun around. "Whatever would make you ask such a thing?"

"Mrs. Horn said that when he insisted upon staying with me, you were displeased. I thought he might have said...something." She caught her lower lip in her teeth, hardly knowing what she wanted Fanny to answer. If he really were the monster the world believed him to be, threatening a lady would only be further proof.

"He..." Fanny knotted her fingers in front of her. "He all but accused me of poisoning you." The awful words hung on the air, punctuated by a nervous laugh. "With a peppermint drop."

It was indeed a terrible allegation.

It was not, however, the only terrible allegation that had been made.

"Meanwhile, you..." Caro struggled to make sense of the fragments of conversation. "You must also have feared that someone—that he—that my husband—"

"No. That is, I—" Fanny stuttered, rocking onto her toes and back again. "I suppose it planted the idea in my mind, the idea that something nefarious might have happened, and well, the duke does have a certain... reputation."

She spoke only the truth: dreadful rumors surrounded the man. Still Caro sucked in a sharp breath through her nose. She'd insisted time and again that she wasn't afraid of him.

Perhaps you should have been.

"I overstepped." Fanny's cheeks flushed almost red. "Can you forgive me?"

Before Caro could answer, one of the drawing room doors opened, revealing the Duke of Hartwell. His color was high too, and for a moment she wondered whether he had overheard their conversation. But he didn't look angry—at least, not any angrier than usual. Damp had darkened his overlong hair even further and made it curl against his collar almost boyishly. His chest rose and fell with deeply drawn breaths, as if he'd hurried up the stairs.

"I apologize for interrupting," he said with a bow. "I was told only that you'd come down, Caro. Not that you had company."

Fanny curtsied. "I should go."

"Not on my account," he said, holding up a hand. "I'm just on my way to change."

"Your man, Leclerc, said you'd gone sea bathing."

His brows shot up. "Bit brisk for that, I'd say. I was rowing. I asked Leclerc to find me a boat. Thought I might work off a bit of—" *Restlessness? Spleen?* Whatever it was he'd hoped to exorcise, he did not finish the sentence. "Yes. Well. I'll leave you ladies to it." He bowed once more, then fixed his gaze on Caro. "I'm glad you're feeling better. But don't overtax yourself, my dear."

She recognized something in the tone of those last words, the softness and warmth with which he had once whispered to her in French. Her scalp prickled—in apprehension, she told herself. Oh, his newfound concern for her was charming, all right.

But when had the man ever shown any inclination to charm?

As soon as he was gone, Fanny stepped toward her, this time with her hands at her sides. "I'll go too. But please believe my concern was kindly meant."

A fresh wave of weariness washed over Caro. She was tired, so tired, of being alone. But who could she, should she trust—her friend? her husband?

Both were little more than strangers.

Fanny was almost to the door before Caro mustered a shaky "wait."

She half turned, looking at Caro over her shoulder, but saying nothing.

"I don't believe he would hurt me," Caro said at last.

A curious mix of emotions washed over Fanny's face. Sympathy. Exasperation. "He already has."

Caro closed her eyes, let the words tumble around her aching skull. Nothing made any sense. "Will you send Mrs. Horn to me? I need to lie down."

"Yes, of course."

"And Fanny—"

"Yes?"

"Come back again tomorrow. Please?"

Pleasure and relief gleamed like tears in the other woman's pale eyes. With a nod, she was gone.

Chapter 11

Maxim tapped quietly against Caro's bedchamber door. Almost too quietly to be heard. When he got no response, he laid a hand on the knob. If it was locked, he would turn and go. The worn leather case full of lock picks never left his pocket. But he could not stoop to—

The knob turned easily in his hand.

Caro lay on the bed fully clothed, facing the door this time, her eyes closed, her breathing soft and even. He should let her rest. He'd only wanted—well, *needed*, if he were honest—to see that she was well.

That need was a knife to the gut, a sharp and sudden pain, its damage all out of proportion to the size of the wound.

And he would know, having been stabbed more than once.

He'd learned to survive in a hard school. Self-preservation was second nature. And yet his selfishness when it came to Caro astonished him. *He* had brought her to this pass—oh, he'd done nothing to cause this strange, sudden illness, to be sure, though the sight of her pale and lifeless on the strand had nearly driven him mad. But for all the rest—her isolation, her family's disrespect—the burden of guilt was his. He'd told her he'd set out to punish her father by marrying her.

Instead, he had punished her.

Then again, would it not have been a greater punishment to her if he'd stayed? He was no fit husband for a woman like her. She deserved better than a man whose scars had left him little more than a monster, inside and out.

But with only the minor inconveniences of a flight of stairs or a closed door between them, he couldn't keep away from her; not six years ago, not now. Her beauty, her liveliness, her quick tongue—even the memory of them—drew him like an enchantment.

If time and distance had not severed his attraction to her, what could?

Perhaps something more official. Something permanent. An annulment? He'd dismissed the notion once, but he was a damned duke now—no longer a powerless little boy. This time, he would leave her with half his fortune at her disposal and the promise that he would never intrude or interfere again. She would be free to seek happiness with a man who was worthy of her. *Yes.* Yes, that was it. He would go to London and explore the possibility.

As soon as she was fully recovered.

Just a few more days…

She blinked up at him twice and gave a soft gasp. "I didn't hear you come in."

"Forgive me. I didn't mean to wake you." But he made no move to go.

She pushed herself up on one elbow. "How long have I been asleep? Did you want something?"

Dear God. Had anyone ever asked a more dangerous question? He stepped farther into the room and closed the door behind him. "I was going to offer to read to you." He gestured with the book in his hand. "If you wish it."

Her eyes narrowed and her chin drew back, surprised at first, then skeptical. "Oh. More Robin Ratliff, I suppose." Her tone made it clear that she suspected an intent to torment her.

So, Mrs. Horn had told her about that, had she? The knife in his gut twisted, driving a little deeper. "No. God, no." He'd wanted to know whether Caro had kept the books he'd bought for her, kept them with her…and perhaps also to torment himself with that nonsensical fantasy of villains who could somehow become heroes. "It's—" He glanced down at the book. "Mrs. Horn said you brought it back from the bookshop the other day. Poetry, I believe."

Her expression wary, she considered his answer. "Thompson, yes. *The Four Seasons.*"

He took a step closer. "May I?"

Shifting onto her back, she levered herself more upright against the mountain of pillows and gave the slightest of nods.

Relief shuddered from him. Before she could think better of her choice, he circled the end of the bed and took up the chair. But what was he doing? This was the opposite of leaving her in peace.

Wasn't it?

"Where shall I begin?"

She was watching the low gray clouds outside the window, blanketing a stormy sea. "At the end. Autumn." As she listened, her eyes never left the rough water, the hard set of her jaw never relented, seemingly impervious to the poem's gentle rhythms.

After a quarter of an hour, he snapped the book shut. "You despise this—despise me."

She had turned toward the sound of the book closing but did not meet his eyes. "I hardly know you."

Maxim nodded curtly, stung by her words, though he had no right to be. "And for that, I suppose you must account yourself lucky."

"Why?" she snapped back. "Why must I do any such thing? Why are you doing this? A few days ago, you walked back into my life, daring me to vent my fury at you, and now you—you're sitting at my bedside, reading poetry, all but daring me to—to—" She broke off on a strangled cry of frustration and dropped her head into her hands.

"Daring you to what?"

She sent him a sidelong glance. "You must know you have a marvelous voice. The sort of voice that can make a woman's pulse race, even if you're only rattling off—oh, I don't know." She paused to search for something outlandish. "Mathematical equations."

In spite of himself, he chuckled, astonished but pleased by her praise. "Pythagoras's theorem, the square of the hypotenuse, that sort of thing?"

"I daresay simple addition would do the trick. But don't"—she sat upright again and lifted a peremptory finger—"try it." Her voice dropped a notch lower, serious again as she repeated her earlier question: "Why are you doing this?"

"I don't know," he said honestly. To avoid his future? To revisit his past? But neither of those was an answer, really. Not an answer to satisfy her. Not even to satisfy himself.

"You are my husband. I am your wife. But this—" She gestured between them. "This is not a marriage."

She was right, of course. That was precisely why he'd intended to offer her an annulment. But when it came time to speak the words, he realized he couldn't give her up without a fight. Whether it was easier or better or safer to keep himself apart from her, as he'd always told himself, was no longer clear to him. Lonelier, certainly.

And if he had another chance, any chance, to ease a lifetime of loneliness, shouldn't he seize it?

His heart thudded in his chest, harder than it had when he'd rowed out against the inrushing tide. He'd been strong before, brave before. But this was strength and bravery of a different order. What if she refused him? What if she was happier alone?

Despite his *marvelous* voice, he could manage only a whisper. "Could it be?"

"I don't know you," she repeated, looking back toward the window, as if she could not answer him without more information. "Neither do you know me."

"No," he agreed. "But will you give me leave to learn? To try?"

"I'm not sure I should."

His heart leaped—a movement so violent he did not at first recognize it as joy, as hope.

She hadn't said no.

Gently, he laid the book beside her on the bed and rose. "Join me for dinner tonight." An offer, not an order. "Or better yet, I will ask Mrs. Horn to send up two trays and join you here."

She dropped her gaze to the book and watched her fingertip trace the embossing on its cover. An eternity passed, eons in which glaciers moved and continents drifted, before she at last said, "All right."

* * * *

Caro hadn't the slightest idea what Hartwell expected to accomplish by dining in her room—unless it was to make more work for the servants.

One of the housemaids had dragged the chair from the bedside to the window to join its mate, and poor Geoffrey had been recruited to place the table from the corridor between them. Once the dropped leaf had been lifted and the leg swung around to support it, the narrow rectangular tabletop doubled to become a square, though still hardly spacious for dining.

Meanwhile, Mrs. Horn had fussed over the menu, uncertain what might suit both Caro's still-delicate stomach and a gentleman's heartier appetite, until Caro had quite literally put her foot down. "You will *not* prepare two meals. The duke can get by on an invalid's diet for one evening, or else not eat at all," she had declared.

"Very well, Your Grace," Mrs. Horn had conceded, "I will agree to a simple menu." Defiance twinkled in her eye. "If you will agree to change your gown."

The last thing Caro wanted was to make it seem as if she had been preening for her husband. She did not want to reveal any more of herself to him than absolutely necessary. Not her décolletage. Not her soul.

"Very well, Mrs. Horn. The primrose silk, if you please." Papa had gotten a bargain on it, though she had protested that she looked wretched in yellow. Given her present pallor, she would look worse still.

She had not accounted for the softening glow of candlelight. Or the warmth that flooded her cheeks when he entered the room. Leclerc must have taken a page from Mrs. Horn's book of bargaining, for the duke looked fully the part for once. His hair had been trimmed and the knot in his cravat was nothing short of elegant. And when he seated himself across from her at the intimate little table, their knees brushing, she was so distracted by the look in his eyes, she almost forgot his scars.

Why are you doing this? she wanted to ask again.

Six years ago, she had been willing to give him anything, everything. Then he'd revealed a capacity for cruelty beyond even her father's. The show of strength it had taken to hold her head up when he had abandoned her, to start anew in a place where she knew no one...it had left her too weak to shake off her family's grasping, greedy hands.

But she must find the strength to stand firm now, not to let him draw her in, only to trample her once more.

"Shall we begin?" she said, setting her chin and picking up her spoon as she dared him to look down at the bowl of clear broth sitting before him.

He glanced at his place, and his expression settled into those familiar, wry lines: a lopsided smile, made more so by his injuries. But when he raised his eyes to her again, they were twinkling. "Ah, a consommé." He took a spoonful, looking at her all the while. "How lovely."

"Does it make you think of France?" she taunted.

"Well, where I've been most recently, the fare is heartier. Peasant dishes, you know."

"Oh?"

"Yes, in the south. Near the Pyrenees." And he launched into a description of scenery so breathtaking, it might have come from a guidebook—or a Robin Ratliff novel. She wanted to close her eyes and lose herself in its evocative beauty.

Why in God's name had she told him she liked the sound of his voice?

He had never revealed so much to her before, and yet there was something strangely impersonal in his tales about the people and the food and the charming little cottage in which he had lived with only Leclerc to tend to him.

"Is it not a dangerous place for an Englishman at present," she asked when he paused, "the South of France?"

His eyes shuttered, though the half smile never slid from his face. "Ah, but you see, when in France, I am a Frenchman."

Once she had finished her soup, he rose, retrieved the dinner plates from the window ledge, and laid one at each place. With a flourish, he lifted the covers to reveal boiled chicken, boiled potatoes, and for dessert, boiled custard. She choked back her laugh into a cough.

"And when in England…?" she prompted, as soon as he was seated again.

He took a sip of wine and then lifted his shoulders, the gesture so characteristically French she had to stifle another laugh. "In England, I am a duke."

A duke who expressed no dismay at his bland, meager dinner. She would give him credit for that, at least.

Leaning back against his chair, he glanced toward the window, though the darkness beyond offered no view save their own reflections in the glass. "I did not know you enjoyed the seaside."

She poked at the chicken with her fork. "As it turns out, I don't." He made a sound of surprise, but she gave him no other opportunity to react. "What is the farthest from your birthplace you have ever traveled?"

For a moment, she thought he would refuse to answer. "Dominica," he said at last, a slight frown notched between his brow, as if the reply had required concentration. "Though Egypt must run a close second."

She tried to imagine it—the voyages, the climates, the wonderful strangeness of places she would never see.

"Brighton," she said, tipping the point of her knife toward her chest to indicate the limits of her own travels. "Perhaps I should have gone farther afield? I might've packed my trunks and gone all the way to…" Now she twirled her wrist, inscribing a circle in the air with the knife. "Oh, Northumberland, say. Deposited myself on your grandfather's doorstep, and—"

"No." His eyes flashed as he leaned toward her. "You didn't—tell me you didn't really consider doing such a thing?"

She met him over the table, mere inches separating them. "And if I had, what of it? Would it have been an unreasonable reaction to the situation in which I found myself six years ago? You might recall I had no desire to return to my father."

"Caro, I—"

At this distance, it became quite clear that the look in his eyes was not anger but fear.

"Don't say you're sorry," she told him, hardening herself. She too had been afraid. "Sorry is for children."

He pushed away from the table and stood. "Very well. I did what I had to do."

"As did I." She also stood, abruptly enough to make the dishes rattle. "You wished to know me better, sir, and now you do. Do you like what you see?"

With blazing eyes, he looked her up and down, his breath now coming in rasps. Muttering an oath—in French, she was sure of it; perhaps she would ask Leclerc its meaning—he turned and strode from the room.

Her hand trembling, she plucked up her wineglass and drained the contents, heedless of either her head or her stomach. Tears burned hot behind her eyes. *Damn you,* she wanted to shout after him—a plain, old English curse.

But the tears did not come and the words did not pass her lips, and she was left wondering whether that was a sign of weakness, or of strength.

Chapter 12

Maxim rose earlier yet the next morning, while darkness still clung to the sky, eager to work his muscles, breathe in the sharp air, and drive out the nightmares that had plagued him during the few hours he'd slept. He slipped on his clothes in silence—Leclerc's snores thundering from the alcove that served for a dressing room would have drowned out any noise he happened to make, in any case—and stumped as lightly as he could along the corridor, determined not to hesitate as he passed Caro's door.

He thought he had imagined the worst possible scenarios involving his wife: for some time after he'd returned to France, for instance, he had worried that he might have left her with child, that he sat hundreds of miles away, unknowing, as she suffered in childbed and died.

But never, not once, had he considered that she might have gone to Chesleigh Court. To his grandfather.

A shudder wracked him even before he stepped out into the cold morning air. Pushing aside the question of how his grandfather would have reacted to her arrival, what the man would have done—to her, not for her—Maxim flipped up the collar of his greatcoat and set out for the empty strand below. The boat Leclerc had managed to procure him was a bit larger and heavier than Maxim would have liked, but when he had considered the language barrier and tried to picture Leclerc miming what was wanted, he had decided it would be unfair to complain.

The tide was high and the sea glassy calm as he scraped the boat across the shingle and pushed it into the channel, wading through the shallows and leaping in just before the water was high enough to spill over the tops of his boots. Grabbing the oars, he began to pull, driving himself farther and farther from shore. He was tempted to row until he reached France or his heart gave out, whichever came first.

With each stroke, he relived last night's disastrous dinner, Caro's distrust and anger, every bit of which he deserved—and more. Things might've been different between them, once upon a time. If he had not been so hardheaded. Hard hearted.

His grandfather had made almost all of Maxim's life a misery, but blame for the last six years fell squarely on Maxim's own shoulders. Well, his and Napoleon's.

When the entire town of Brighton was little more than a speck in the distance, he turned the boat, though his arms and shoulders had not yet begun to burn. The tide was heading out now, the water increasingly choppy, and more than half his work was still to come. His back to the shore, he began to row.

And that was when he noticed the water bubbling through a crack in the bottom of the boat.

He dropped down on one knee to investigate. A small crack. Not much water. Troubling nonetheless. Shrugging out of his coat, the better to free his movements, he began to row faster. More than half the return distance to travel, still, and the crack began to widen. He could feel the drag as the bottom of the boat began to fill with water.

The tin pail he had spotted yesterday was now nowhere to be found. He had nothing more than his hat or his hands with which to bail—and neither would do him a damn bit of good. His lungs began to ache as he willed the boat to move faster, and icy water soaked through the soles of his boots.

When the boat began to ride low enough that waves splashed over the sides, he tugged off his boots and tossed them overboard. Soon enough he would have to swim, and they would only weigh him down.

A hundred yards from shore, the crack became a gash, as the water grew ravenous and began to tear the little boat asunder, the better to devour it. Dropping the oars, he gathered his resolve, stood, and dove.

He remembered nothing of the accident that had split his face and nearly his skull, mangled his leg, and almost cost him his life. But surely this pain must be comparable? His lungs, his heart, his muscles all screamed in protest at the cold and the effort required to fight against the outgoing tide, to gain even an inch toward shore.

Give up! His grandfather's ghost was in the waves and wind, howling at him to surrender, dragging him under. His feet touched bottom.

Do you like what you see? Caro's voice, this time. The challenge in Caro's flashing eyes.

Yes, he wanted to call out, *yes!* His feet touched bottom, but his head was still above water.

He dragged himself along the sea floor—scraping and scrabbling with toes, knees, hands—as every few moments a wave washed over him, stealing his breath, knocking him down. A few yards more, a few feet more...

Finally, he collapsed onto the pebbled beach and everything went dark.

* * * *

After breakfast in her chambers, Caro went down to the drawing room in ample time to be there before Fanny arrived and ready to distract her friend from noticing the shadows beneath her eyes.

She wasn't sorry she'd said those things to her husband—sorry was for children, just as she'd told him. But the finality of it still sent a pang through her heart. Somehow, hope had managed to lie dormant there after all that had happened, after all this time.

Well, it surely had been rooted out for good now.

She sat down at her writing desk. Her father's letter was still awaiting a response, and if she began it now, she would have a ready and honest excuse to explain her foul mood when her friend arrived. Should she plead with Papa, or tell him to do his worst? If she had two thousand pounds, she wouldn't give it to him. At least, she didn't think she would. Since she didn't have anything approaching that sum, the question of what she would do with it was moot.

As she reached for the drawer, her eyes fell on a large wooden crate on the floor beside the desk.

She had just knelt to investigate when Fanny entered at the far end of the room. "Oh," Fanny said, "those must be the important papers my footman was sent to retrieve."

Caro had forgotten all about her husband's urgent business in London. She eyed the crate skeptically. "What sort of papers, I wonder?" They didn't look terribly important, tucked into a corner and ignored.

Fanny shrugged and came toward her, holding out a hand to help her rise. "Who can say? But how are you feeling?"

"Oh, much improved," Caro said, glancing over her shoulder at the crate. "And yesterday—"

"There's absolutely nothing to discuss. Or forgive," she added preemptively, looping her arm through Fanny's as they turned and walked toward the sofa. "Hartwell has always invited sordid speculation and vicious rumors. Who can say what he might be capable of? Certainly, when I married him, I hardly knew what to believe...."

Once more the crate drew her eye, as yesterday's words came rushing back to her.

I don't know you.

Might that unassuming box contain something that would at last truly help her understand her husband?

She thought back to the fear she had glimpsed in his eyes when she had mentioned the prospect of her going to his grandfather. What sort of man had the late duke been? And what had happened to create the gulf between him and his grandson and heir?

"How difficult would it be to open such a crate?" she asked.

A frown creased Fanny's brow. "You would need something sturdy to pry with. If you were going to do such a thing. Which, speaking as your friend, I consider ill advised."

"Like a paper knife?" Caro freed her arm to grasp Fanny's hand instead. "Will you help me?"

"What will your husband say?"

"He's gone out boating again. He'll never know."

With a trembling nod—either fear or anticipation, Caro could not decide which—Fanny agreed. After fishing in the drawer of the escritoire for the paper knife, she presented the blunt-tipped implement to her friend, handle first, and then hesitated. "I suppose I'd better be the one, just in case. That way, you cannot be blamed." Following Fanny's advice, she pried loose the tacks that held the lid in place, and then, drawing a steadying breath, she opened the crate.

The contents—stacks of documents and baize-covered ledgers—were still neatly arranged, despite what must have been a jostling journey. She felt almost disappointed at their mundanity. Brushing aside the packing straw, she reached for the first ledger and opened the cover.

Columns and rows of faded numbers greeted her eyes. The dates at the top of each page were many decades in the past. Though Caro was reasonably good with figures and had had the careful management of her pin money and her small household's accounts, what lay before her was far beyond her scope of understanding.

She turned toward Fanny, seated on the floor beside her. "What does this mean?"

Fanny peered over her shoulder. "Oh. I have some familiarity with this sort of record keeping. Gains, you see, here,"—she ran a fingertip down one column—"and losses there. I suspect the Duke of Hartwell's holdings are quite complex. I can look through them if you like—is there something in particular you want to know?"

Caro lifted the stack of ledgers and deposited them in Fanny's lap. "I'm not sure." Money troubles could, she supposed, be at the root of her husband's conflict with his grandfather. "Something to explain why the late duke and the present one were at odds."

"Were they?" Fanny's mild question was the sort one asked to be polite, rather than urging gossip. When Caro offered no reply, she bent her head to her task.

Caro, meanwhile, began to riffle through what remained. Scores of legal documents, with bold seals and impossibly perfect copperplate. Matters pertaining to landholdings, the breeding of horses, a ship that had foundered off the coast of Canada and a subsequent claim on the insurance for lost cargo. All perfectly ordinary, she gathered, if one were wildly wealthy and powerful.

Laying those papers aside, she came to a letter book, in which the late duke's secretary had meticulously recorded correspondence: every letter the duke had sent or received, every letter the secretary had sent or received on his behalf. Nothing revelatory, beyond the fact that the duke had been a prolific correspondent. She scanned through the list of names and dates, occasionally a memorandum as to the topic, all of it stretching back decades. Any one of the letters might have been the key to her quest, and she would never know. How ridiculous of her to have imagined she would find her answer in this rough-hewn crate.

And then a name leaped out at her. Chesleigh. A letter received from her husband, dated the day after he had left her—*just for a few weeks,* she had tried to tell herself, as she'd watched his carriage disappear. Three hundred fourteen weeks, as it had turned out. Beside her husband's name, the secretary had written *marriage.* Her eyes raced down the remainder of that page and onto the next, and the next, but she found no indication a reply had been sent. She wondered whether the late duke had even seen the letter.

"What," she wondered aloud, half to Fanny, half to herself, "could people with everything anyone could want at their fingertips find to fight about?"

"Not money," Fanny replied, her nose still buried in a ledger. "I can't find any indication of difficulties. No unpaid debts. No valuable pieces of property sold off. No sign of an unscrupulous steward trying to hide his tracks. No wayward daughter auctioned to the highest bidder." She followed the last with a rueful laugh. "Perhaps I *have* read too many novels."

"No such thing," Caro insisted, patting her friend's knee. "Besides, I don't think there was a daughter. At least, Hartwell has never mentioned any family except his grandfather. No aunts, uncles, cousins. His father died when he was a boy, I gather."

Fanny nodded, her lips pressed together, thoughtful. "What of his mother?"

"I don't know." She furrowed her brow, trying to sort through the rumors she remembered, to sift the plausible from the outlandish. "I believe she was French."

At least, that had been the more ordinary explanation given for her husband's dark hair and eyes; at the time, she had discounted the stories that claimed he was descended from the devil himself.

Fanny closed the ledger she'd been studying and tapped her first finger softly against the cover. "French, you say? I suppose that might have caused some hard feelings...if, for instance, his son—his only son, it seems—married against his wishes. And of course there are more than a few men with a particularly strong animosity toward the nation across the channel," she added, tipping her head toward the bow window.

When in France, I am a Frenchman.

Last night, she'd almost laughed at those words. But could they hold the key?

"Perhaps we need to go back further," she said, digging once more through the contents of the crate. "If the real conflict was between the late duke and his son, that could have involved something that took place forty, fifty, sixty years ago." She still wasn't sure what she was looking for.

But she knew when she had found it.

At the very bottom of the box, almost lost beneath a tuft of packing straw, lay a thin bundle of letters, tied with black ribbon so old, it crumbled away when she tried to untie it.

Pleading letters, angry letters. She wanted to close her eyes against them, at first, their contents familiar and wretched. Without conscious thought, she glanced up to her writing desk and her family's letters secreted there.

Dragging in a breath, praying for strength, she began to read more carefully, the faded ink that told first of the late Lord Chesleigh's Grand Tour, his fascination with the culture and customs of Breton; then of one young woman in particular, her unsurpassed beauty and goodness; and finally, of his marriage and the birth of a child. All those details were interspersed with pleas: for acknowledgment, for assistance. And then, one final letter, written in a more delicate hand and composed entirely in French: from Lady Chesleigh, reporting the death of her husband from an apoplexy and the hourly expected death of her young son, who in desperation had been sent for the physician for his father, was caught in a storm, and was trampled beneath his horse's iron-rimmed hooves.

The tears that last night had refused to fall now streamed freely down her cheeks. Her fingers fumbled as she sought and found the letter book and raced through its pages, searching in it for some record of these letters' receipt and whether any response had been made. She found nothing.

"Fanny," she sobbed. "Help me. There must be something. Something from the summer of 1783. Or after. His mother..." Met with confusion, she thrust the last letter into Fanny's hands.

"I—I can't read this." Fanny's cheeks flushed with embarrassment. "It's...not written in English."

"It's from the duke's daughter-in-law. There was...an accident," she explained, quickly translating.

"Oh, dear God," Fanny said, when she had finished. "And the others?"

"All from his son, begging for her recognition, for a reconciliation."

Fanny's face settled into grim, knowing lines. "Which never came." Her fingers danced over the piles of account books that now surrounded her. "Here. Here are the years."

Together, they bent over the ledger, scouring its pages for any signpost that would lead to an answer of what had become of the poor young widow.

The first came in the form of a large sum paid to a physician named Allen. The second, the regular payment of tuition to Eton, beginning in the autumn of 1784. "That must, I think, be for the present duke?" Fanny said, her voice uncertain.

"Surely the old duke would've wanted his grandson educated in a manner befitting his future role," Caro agreed.

"This is odd," Fanny said a few pages later, underscoring a number with her thumbnail. "For the purchase of some property in...in Quebec? You don't suppose—"

"Oh, dear God. He...he must have intended to send her away. Maxim's mother." She spoke his given name without hesitation, without thought.

"Did she go?"

She might, of course, have been an avaricious woman, eager to flee her present troubles. But Caro couldn't reconcile such a description with the woman who had penned that letter. "I'm not sure. Perhaps she had no choice. He might've threatened her life. She must have been persuaded it was for the best."

"Yes, I suppose. But why not send her back to France?"

"Too close?" Caro suggested. "Perhaps he wanted to make it difficult for her family to intervene. I wonder if—I wonder if he knew." *He,* meaning Maxim. A desperately injured boy, his whole life ripped away from him in little more than an instant. Sobs threatened to choke her. "Oh, God. Th-the ship—" Heedless of the disorder she created, she tore through a previously discarded stack of legal documents. "This ship. It went down. He—he was reimbursed for the loss of c-c-cargo. It was bound for—"

"Canada," Fanny breathed.

It was all the rankest speculation, hardly worthy of the pages of the most torrid tome in Donaldson's library. Yet her heart sank in her chest beneath the weighty truth of it.

In her hands, she held the final fragments of the curse that had turned her husband into a monster.

Distantly, she heard the knocker on the front door fall, and then a shout and the hurry of footsteps. Her eyes flew to the clock on the mantel; more time had passed than she'd realized. "He's home," she said, and began stuffing papers back into the crate. "Hurry."

The door swung open well before she was ready, and for a moment, her mind frantically engaged in concocting some excuse for prying into his private business, she did not register more than his presence.

"Your Grace," Fanny exclaimed, leaping to her feet. "What has happened?"

"Just let," he rasped out, "me catch...my breath."

Finally Caro saw him, waving Fanny off as he staggered into the room, without hat or coat, shoes or stockings, fine silt clinging to his tattered clothes and his salt-stiffened hair, blood staining his knees and speckling his shirt.

"What happened to you?" Caro screeched, rushing toward him.

He let her wrap an arm around his waist and lead him to a small sofa. Through his damp clothes, she could feel his hard, sinewy body, cold as ice. "I t-took...a s-swim...after all. B-b-boat...sank," he managed to stammer through blue-tinged lips.

"Fanny, fetch Dr. Trefrey," she demanded, urging him to lie back, though the delicate piece of furniture was far too small for him to recline fully.

"Like hell," he ground out as he tipped his head back onto the arm of the sofa, one leg propped partly on the cushions, the other foot still resting on the floor.

"Then fetch Mrs. Horn. Towels, blankets, hot water—go!" She draped him with the only cover the room afforded, her light woolen shawl, as Fanny ran from the room.

"B-b-be f-f-fine, now," he mumbled, his eyes fluttering closed. "S-s-survived worse."

Those words were perhaps the only ones that could have dragged her eyes from his face. She glanced over her shoulder toward the crate in the corner, its lid propped against the wall, its contents strewn about the floor. Proof that he had, indeed, survived far worse than she had previously understood.

Somehow, his bleary gaze must have followed hers. When she turned back, he was looking up at her, and the blazing fury she saw in his eyes seemed to have been strong enough to drive the Atlantic's chill from his blood, at least temporarily.

"Caro," he said, still breathing heavily, "what the devil have you done?"

Chapter 13

Almost immediately, Maxim regretted raising his voice. For one thing, it hurt like hell, his throat already raw from swallowing and then purging what had felt like half the water in the channel. For another, Caro's stark expression—carved into her face by guilt and worry and things he couldn't even name—was enough to flay open whatever parts of him the shingled beach had left intact.

"What in God's name did you hope to find?" he demanded of her, the question quieter, but no less urgent.

"An explanation."

"For what?"

Her gaze cut back to the box of papers. "Your hard feelings toward your grandfather."

All at once, the flash of indignation that had temporarily warmed him fled and his body recalled its battered and chilled state. A bone-deep shudder passed through him, rattling his teeth, rattling the little sofa on which he sat. He had imagined her trying to discover how much money she could wheedle for her family, or the name of some far-flung ducal property to which she could repair, alone. Not searching for—and finding—the clues that would strip away whatever thin layer of protection he had managed to build between his present life and the torments of his youth.

He dug his fingers—or tried; his hands didn't seem to want to work properly—into the thin pink shawl Caro had draped over him, as if he could hold himself together with it. "And di-di-d-d-did you f-f-f-find—?"

The door of the drawing room swung open without warning, revealing what must be every servant belonging to the place. Mrs. Horn sounded an incoherent alarm as she strode into the room and deposited a tray on the table. "You need something to warm yourself, Your Grace. A cup of tea, first," she ordered as she poured, "and then a nice hot bath." A sharp nod at the maids and manservant gawking from the doorway sent them scampering to the stairwell with their steaming cannisters of water.

Maxim couldn't seem to make his arms obey enough to reach for the cup and saucer she held out to him. Caro stepped forward, took the tea from Mrs. Horn, and perched herself on the edge of the cushion beside him, heedless of the dirt or the damp. "Here," she said, holding the cup to his lips.

He wanted to despise the pity shadowing her eyes. That crate could only contain a fragment of the truth; she didn't know the half of why he hated his grandfather. Anyway, he didn't want—didn't *deserve* her pity.

Did he?

When she tipped the cup, he took a scalding gulp of tea, craving a sharper, more focusing pain than the ache of muscles or the sting of various scrapes. Ordinarily, he never drank the brew without wishing it were either red wine or black coffee. But he could not help but welcome its hot sweetness as it seared its way down his throat and into his belly.

Perhaps his grandfather had not been entirely right about him. Perhaps there was some part of him that was really an Englishman.

Caro tilted the cup away. "Be careful. You'll burn yourself."

Did it matter? To her? To anyone?

The warmth spread inside him, but he still shook uncontrollably, his teeth rattling against the delicate china when she tipped up the cup again. With a gargantuan force of will, he released his hold on the shawl and brought up one of his own hands to encircle hers, hoping if not to steady the cup then at least to time its tremors with his own.

Mrs. Horn, who had stepped momentarily from the room, returned with a pair of blankets and wrapped them around his shoulders. "Gracious, sir," she fretted as she gave him a closer inspection. "Look at your hands. I'll find what's left of Dr. Trefrey's salve for them."

Belatedly, he realized that Caro's knuckles were smeared with his blood. But he couldn't let her go—wouldn't let her go. And she made no effort to free herself, simply urged him to go on drinking.

After refilling the cup for a second time, Mrs. Horn excused herself again and soon returned with Leclerc, whose expression was nearly as shocked as Caro's had been. "A hot bath is what's wanted now, Your Grace," the housekeeper said.

Maxim didn't disagree; the tea had warmed him enough that he was becoming more aware of the rest of his injuries, as well as the grit that had managed to work its way *everywhere* beneath his remaining clothes. Despite his willingness, however, it took the combined efforts of the other three to get him to his feet and then up the stairs to his bedchamber.

A fire already blazed in the hearth, and before it sat a copper tub, steam rising from it in swirling, inviting clouds. Once even Leclerc had gone, he stripped off his tattered garments and sank into the tub, wincing as the water hit his abrasions.

Gradually, the heat penetrated his cold, stiff muscles. Cupping his hands, he sluiced water over his chest and his arms, rinsing away the grit and salt from his battered body, then slid low enough to do the same for his hair.

When he opened his eyes after shaking the water from them, Leclerc was there, holding out a cordial glass.

"Qu'est-ce que c'est?" Maxim rasped.

"Something for your pain," the young man replied in French. "Laudanum." He shaped the word oddly, not as a Frenchman would, but probably as he'd heard it on the lips of Mrs. Horn or that quack, Trefrey.

"Bah." Maxim waved the glass away. He'd been given enough as a boy that he'd come to crave the stuff and had had to learn to do without. Never again.

Leclerc gave a reluctant nod and set the glass aside. "Something else, sir?"

"Rien." The word of refusal scraped his tortured throat. Tipping his head back against the edge of the tub, he listened as the young man padded from the room.

The moment his eyes drifted closed, he saw the cracked bottom of the boat again, felt the icy claws of the sea—of his grandfather—dragging him to his death. He sat up with a start, sloshing water over the side of the tub, sensing he wasn't alone.

"Still here?" he said, in French. "Then fetch me my dressing gown."

From behind him came the quiet answer, in English. "It's not Monsieur Leclerc." Caro's voice.

"You needn't worry about me," he insisted hoarsely, when he'd recovered from the surprise. "I'm fine." When she didn't take the hint and go, he added, "If you wish it, I'll tell Leclerc to pack my things, and we'll leave in the morning." It was the last thing he wanted, but after last night, what use was it to trouble her longer?

He heard her draw and release a slow, shivery breath. Relief?

"Out of sight, out of mind, I suppose?" The mocking note in her voice was unmistakable—and closer. Rather than retreating, she'd stepped further into the room. "Only I don't find it works that way, do you? You can have no idea how much time and energy I've spent trying not to think of you over the last six years."

Oh, the stories he could tell of how hard—and how fruitlessly—he'd worked to forget her... A wry answering laugh gusted from his weary chest. "Can I not?"

That reply seemed to catch her off guard. "At least," she retorted after a moment, "you know why you left."

Did he? In all those years, he'd never managed to concoct an explanation that would make sense to her. His reasons for leaving didn't really make sense, even to him.

"I wracked my brain, trying to understand how I'd displeased you," she told him, "what I'd done to drive you away."

"You didn't—"

"I even," she spoke across him, her words punctuated by a laugh that was almost a sob, "managed at one point to convince myself that you had been sent on some secret mission for king and country."

A shudder passed through him, stirring the now-tepid bath. "The simplest explanation is usually the correct one, my dear. Perhaps I *am* the heartless monster I was rumored to be."

"No," she said. But her protest sounded unconvincing—and unconvinced.

"The water's grown cold." He laid his forearms along the tub's sides. "I'm getting out."

It was her cue to leave. A threat. She didn't want to see what was, for now, hidden by copper and murky bathwater, any more than he wanted to show her.

But she didn't flee. "I'm your wife," she said, albeit a trifle hesitantly.

So he stood.

Rivulets ran down his chest and over his torso, tracing his injuries as he unfolded himself from the tub; droplets splashed into the water from his fingertips when he dropped his arms to his sides. No sense in covering himself. He couldn't imagine Caro had found anything in the crate that truly explained the extent of his suffering. But his body would be explanation enough.

With his back to her, she would see little more than the thin scars on his shoulders, the ghostly memories of a few boyhood birchings and one or two more recent wounds. Oh, and the knotted and twisted sinews of his thigh, where they'd fought to hold the pieces of his broken leg together. The front was far worse. But she wanted to know, didn't she? Wanted to see?

Still standing in the tub, he turned to face her.

She was carrying a stack of towels, and the fading scrape on her cheek had been underscored by a smudge of something. Dust, ink. He blamed the contents of the crate. Her hair was slipping from its pins, and her dress looked like a castoff. He could've mistaken her for a housemaid, and the discovery irritated him beyond measure. She was a *duchess*, for God's sake. He'd made her a duchess—thinking, somehow, that he was doing the right thing, for once.

Her eyes, which were locked on his face, blinked but did not wander.

"Go on," he urged, softening his rough voice as much as he was able. "Look."

He'd spent most of a lifetime shielding others—even, occasionally, himself—from the extent of his gruesome scars. He'd never kept a valet; he'd taken care to dress and bathe only after he'd sent the servants, even Leclerc, from the room. Still, when her gaze began to drift lower, he was caught off guard by the vulnerability that washed over him, stronger even than the icy waves that had tried to make him their prisoner forever.

This room's windows were comparatively small, nothing like the wall of glass in the rooms facing the channel. And the light passing through them was gray, filtered through clouds and a spit of rain. But it was still midday, and thus bright enough to reveal…everything.

He watched her eyes scan slowly downward, taking in the breadth of his chest, the size of his arms. His *maman* had delighted in telling him that he was built like the men of her family, tall and broad shouldered, even as a boy; the fact that he looked more like a sturdy French peasant than his own father had only further displeased his grandfather. Nevertheless, after the accident, he had worked hard to strengthen his upper body, to make up for the weakness of the lower. And because he was angry, always angry, he'd done most of that honing with his fists. Now Caro could see the truth of him, scraped by this morning's misadventure, scattered with scars and bruises that never seemed to fade, sun browned where a true gentleman shouldn't be.

Light as a feather, her gaze drifted lower, over a pair of broken ribs. And woven between them, a long, jagged, puckered seam—the remnant of a more recent knife wound, hastily stitched up, which he'd really thought might be the end of him.

Lower still. He knew just when she reached his groin: one daring look, then away, a maidenly flush of color across her cheekbones, then a swift glance back. His cock wasn't hard—that frigid dawn swim had sent his bollocks into a retreat from which even the warm bath hadn't yet coaxed them—but it was still large. And ugly. Just like the rest of him.

Finally, her gaze came to rest on his leg, and the ghastly cleft in his thigh where the horse's hoof had torn through it and part of the muscle had withered away. Everything mangled, nothing whole. The reason his grandfather had sneered and told him he would never walk again. The proof that he'd defied the old bastard through sheer force of will.

Her eyes dropped to the curved edge of the tub, and then the floor. To her credit, she didn't run. Or faint. She stood in silence, the only sign of her distress the way her arms curled tighter around the linens.

"Seen enough?" In the quiet, the question sounded harsher than he'd intended.

Her chin came up, and her gaze settled once more on his face. "What I see is a survivor." She stepped closer. "But what concerns me more are the scars I can't see."

Although the fire had warmed the room to the point of stuffiness, a shudder passed through him, making the water around his knees ripple. "What did you find in that trunk?"

"Dry yourself," she ordered, holding out the linens. "You'll waste all the benefit of that hot bath, standing there like that. And besides, you're dripping on my floor."

Strangely enough, the sheer normalcy of her words made his heart lift. He had long since passed the point of coddling, hadn't ever wanted her pity. Grabbing a towel from the top of the stack, he dried his arms and chest, then dropped it onto the floor to soak up both the little puddles he'd already made and the larger one he caused by stepping out of the tub.

Caro might have deposited the rest of the linens nearby and left the room, but she didn't. Neither did she stare or scrutinize, though she was close enough now to see with perfect clarity what before might have been blessedly indistinct. She behaved as if seeing her husband in the altogether was an ordinary, everyday occurrence.

As it might have been if they'd spent the last six years together.

He didn't know if he believed it, didn't know if he could bear it—her utter calm, both in the face of the visible scars and in her awareness of the existence of invisible ones. He certainly didn't deserve her compassion, wasn't even sure if *compassion* was the word for what she seemed prepared now to extend to him.

As he reached for the dressing gown Leclerc had laid over a nearby chair, she spoke two quiet words. "Don't go."

Swiftly, he turned toward her, the silk sliding from his grasp enough to knock over the cordial glass, which shattered and spattered its contents over the floor. "A dose of laudanum," he explained, surprised by the almost regretful tone he heard in his own voice. "Leclerc brought it."

She lifted her frown from the mess to his face. "Are you in a great deal of pain?"

He was not sure how to answer that question. He was sore—his muscles, his throat, his various scrapes and bruises. But *pain* was relative. He'd certainly hurt worse.

"Just tired," he answered with a shake of his head as he slipped his arms into the sleeves of the dressing gown.

"Then lie down," she insisted. "Rest."

"You said…"

Her hand came around his elbow, her touch light and cool through the silk. With gentle pressure she urged him toward his bed. "You said you would tell Leclerc to pack your things so you could be gone in the morning. If I wished it." He looked down at her, but she was busying herself with turning back the coverlet. "But I wish you to stay." She'd said just that on their wedding night. Why hadn't he listened then? "There are things for us to discuss, I think, after you have had some time to recover from this misadventure."

He didn't dread the notion of such a conversation as much as he thought he should. Instead, he let her settle him into the bed like a child. "Stay with me," he murmured, his eyelids drifting shut of their own volition as he sank into the pillows.

"I suppose that's only fair," she conceded, and he heard the sound of her dragging a chair across the floor. "If I had the voice for it, I would offer to read to you."

Was she…teasing him? *Flirting* with him? "No. Just sit. Just…you."

"Very well. I'll stay until you fall asleep."

Already, slumber beckoned, its waves considerably warmer and gentler than the ones he'd battled earlier that day. This time, he didn't try to resist.

The gentle brush of Caro's fingertips across his brow was surely nothing but a dream.…

Chapter 14

Fanny arrived at German Place before she realized she'd left her pelisse, gloves, and bonnet at Royal Crescent. In her bewildered state, she'd hardly felt the chill. Now, however, her numb fingers fumbled to insert the key into the keyhole so she could enter her rooms. Before she could manage it, the door opened from within, and Fitz stood before her, frowning.

"Th-the Duke of Hartwell's boat c-capsized," she stammered. "He nearly drowned."

"I know it," he said. "I'm the one who helped him home." When he stepped back so she could enter, she saw that his coat was streaked with silt and damp in patches. "While you were visiting with the duchess, I happened to see Hartwell drag himself out of the water and onto the beach. It took some doing to rouse him, but I managed—no way I could've carried him without help, otherwise."

"Y-you saved his life," she managed, her jaw still clenched to prevent her teeth from chattering.

"This time," he acknowledged cryptically. "But I thought it was imperative to alert General Scott to what had happened as soon as possible." He nodded toward the small table where she took her meals, at present pressed into service as a writing desk, with sheets of letter paper, quill trimmings, and an uncorked bottle of ink spread across its top. "I've just sent word by a messenger. I'm sorry—I thought I'd be done in time to return to Royal Crescent and escort you back here. Where on earth are your gloves?" Evidently forgetting that he was still meant to be her footman, he reached for her bare hand and began to chafe it between his palms.

"Things were…chaotic," she replied, once she was able to make herself to focus on something other than the heat of his touch, which spread through her whole body with remarkable quickness. "Servants scurrying everywhere. Hartwell refused a physician. W-will he be all right, do you think?"

Fitz nodded reassuringly. "Sore, of course. Tired. But an ox like that is far more difficult to kill than you might imagine." He took up her other hand and began to rub it. "What were you and the duchess talking about for so long before that?"

She withdrew her fingers from Fitz's grasp, though they were still cold, and braced for his disapproval. "We opened the crate."

His arms fell to his sides. "The crate I brought back from London? Hartwell's private papers?" She nodded. "Why?"

"The duchess was...curious. And I suppose I was too. A little."

Fitz set his mouth in a hard line. "Don't you suppose that if General Scott wanted the contents of that crate inspected, it would've been done already?" Her heart began to pound. "Good God. What were you thinking?" *What the devil have you done?*

His words echoed the duke's accusatory question. She couldn't meet Fitz's suddenly steely eyes. "The duchess hoped to discover what might have been the cause of her husband's falling-out with his grandfather."

He paused to consider her answer. "And did she?"

She curled her hands into fists and thrust them behind her back. She would not let herself pine for his touch. "I think so, yes."

He nodded curtly, once. "Well, what's done is done. Did you happen to notice anything else, while you were at it? Anything useful to the mission?"

"I'm not certain." What ought she to have been looking for? "Hartwell is as rich as Croesus now. I should think he would be very difficult to bribe." Her mind raced. "You don't—you don't suppose he'll kill her for prying, do you?"

An incredulous laugh huffed from his chest, and he ran his hand through his bright hair, making it stand on end. He hadn't worn his footman's wig since the morning Caro had collapsed on the beach. He really looked nothing like a servant.

"For all those months you've spent in the Underground, you still don't know much about men, do you?" he asked with an exaggerated sigh. "All the standing around I've been doing since we arrived has given me an opportunity to observe some things where the duke and duchess are concerned. Hartwell doesn't want to kill his wife. He wants to kiss her."

"What?" Fanny shook her head, unwilling or unable to give such a ridiculous notion any space in her mind. "He sounded furious with her...."

"Oh, yes," he agreed. "Ironically, I've never met a secret agent who takes kindly to others' snooping."

"And yet, you think he—? But he abandoned her, all those years ago," she reminded him. "Besides, I've done some observing of my own. I saw his face when he first set eyes on her in Brighton. He clearly intended to frighten her with that surprise arrival, to hurt her all over again. And I—" She bit her lip, almost afraid to speak her fear aloud. "I don't believe for a moment that she had dyspepsia. *Someone* gave her something—"

"You said before that you thought he poisoned her." He still sounded skeptical.

Fanny lifted her chin the slightest possible degree. "You can't deny, he's a dangerous man."

"Hartwell *is* dangerous," he conceded. "Dangerous enough that if he wanted his wife dead, she would be." Fanny gasped, but he seemed not to hear her. He began to pace, crossing the room in half a dozen long strides before stopping at the table. "And also dangerous enough that..." He grabbed one of the ladder-back chairs but neither offered it to her, nor sat down himself. His fingers drummed absently against the top rail. "When I was in London, Scott hinted that there were others who would want the information Hartwell has."

"Something in that crate?"

"Possibly. But it's more likely to be something he knows." He paused his drumming to raise one long finger and tap it against his temple. "And if someone doesn't want him to pass that information along, they would do whatever was necessary to keep him quiet."

"Are you suggesting...?"

"That it's possible the duchess ate or drank something meant for her husband? Or that this morning's boating accident might not have been so accidental?" He nodded grimly. "Yes, I suppose I am."

"Fitz!" Fanny reached for the door. "If they're in danger, we've got to warn them."

"Not yet." She turned back to face him. "For one thing, he knows who we are and why we were sent here. He's already suspicious. I'm not sure he'd believe us without proof. For another, we stand a far better chance of finding out who's after him if that person still believes no one suspects."

All perfectly logical points.

But Fanny was not in a mood for logic where her friend's safety was concerned.

"General Scott sent me here to make sure Caro was safe."

"And he sent *me* along to make sure *you* were. Listen," he went on, before she could protest his protectiveness, "partners take care of one another. That's how it's supposed to work."

Partners?

She took an uncertain step toward him, away from the door, and he nodded encouragingly. "I know you won't like to hear this, but sometimes waiting is part of the mission too."

She sighed. "How long?"

"In an hour, say, I'll go back to Royal Crescent to check on things. I'll leave word for Her Grace that the sight of the duke in distress overwhelmed your delicate sensibilities, and you came back here to recover. I promise you, nothing bad will happen in an hour. Our would-be assassin, if he even exists, will need time to puzzle over his failures and plot his next attack. And in the meantime, perhaps the duke and duchess will have a chance to...work out some of their differences." Mischief twinkled in his eyes.

"Oh, yes," she said, fighting to keep her own eyes from rolling. "Right. I nearly forgot. Though personally I should've thought all the coughing up seawater and shouting might interfere with the kissing."

"Doubt me if you will." He grinned. "But Hartwell's just fought for his life and won. His heart is racing, and in spite of that dip in the channel, his blood is hot. And after a good fight, well..." He lifted his hands as if to indicate that the conclusion must be obvious. "A man likes to f—"

Though he broke off before finishing the forbidden word, she knew full well what he had been about to say. One did not spend months in the company of soldiers, men hardened by war, without occasionally hearing things that would've burned most ladies' ears.

Heat bloomed in her chest, rushing up into her head.

And downward too. Below her belly. Between her thighs.

"I'm sorry, Fanny," he said, letting the wooden chair rattle back into its place as he stepped toward her. "I forgot who I was talking to, I guess. I shouldn't have—"

She held up a hand to stay him—his progress across the room, his apology. Her head spun. It took every bit of her remaining wherewithal to make her way across the room to the velvet chaise and sink down onto its foot.

"Is that true?"

Fitz took a cautious step toward her, and when she didn't object, came closer still. "It's just talk," he said, reaching out for her hands again. She surrendered them to him; her fingers were still cold. "Men talk a great deal too much."

"Yes." He was being kind, trying to comfort her, imagining she'd been bothered by a naughty word. "At least, I hope that's it. Because otherwise, you see, I might be forced to conclude that I simply never in my life inspired that kind of passion. I can recall any number of arguments with my husband, and not one of them ever led to kissing," she confessed, hating the shakiness in her voice. "To say nothing of f—"

In one swift, smooth motion, he pulled her onto her feet and into his arms, covering her mouth with his. She hadn't an opportunity to raise her defenses, to stiffen her spine or pucker her lips. Just a gasp of surprise at the softness of his kiss, the hardness of his body, the strength of his arms wrapped around her.

"Hot," he murmured against her mouth. "Sweet."

"Peppermint drops," she tried to explain between kisses.

His chuckle vibrated through her. "No. Just you."

The temptation to go on kissing him was strong enough that she made herself pull away. Reluctantly, he let her step out of the circle of his embrace. "You...ah..." She turned toward the window. No view of the water here, just the houses across the way, filtered through a sheer silk drapery with a shabby hem. "You needn't put on a show of affection to humor me."

"A show?" In two steps, he was behind her, not touching her, yet she'd never been so aware of another's presence. "Hasn't this footman charade pretty well established that I'm no actor? I thought for sure you must have known for weeks how much I wanted to kiss you."

Fanny thought back to the night before last, how he'd made a joke and walked away from her. "Y-you have?" she asked doubtfully. "But why?"

A soft laugh ghosted over her scalp. "Because I'm a contrary fellow, Fan. In the Underground, you always looked so cool and aloof. Never a hair out of place." His fingertip skated along the nape of her neck, where a few stubborn curls had sprung free during the windy walk without a bonnet. "I found myself imagining how you'd look with your hair tumbling down and a flush on your cheeks." Lower and lower his finger slipped, tracing the gathered edge of her simple sprigged muslin. "Without those dull, high-necked gowns."

But her widow's weeds had been safe, familiar. She'd grown comfortable in the role of icy matron. As prim, proper Mrs. Drummond, she'd persuaded Colonel Millrose to teach her about bookkeeping and business matters and to let her run the tobacco shop that disguised the real operations of the Underground. And that role, in turn, must have persuaded General Scott she was ready for more responsibility yet.

She, who had once been valued solely for her beauty, who had been told time and again not to bother her pretty head about politics or the war, was in Brighton on a mission at the behest of the foremost intelligence officer in the British Army.

"What makes you so certain that dour, black-gowned woman isn't the real me?"

"This."

A tremor of desire traveled up her spine when he dropped his lips to that delicate crescent of skin at the top of her back. She had no hope of containing it, disguising it. She wasn't passionless, after all.

But in giving in to passion, what might she be forced to give up?

"We shouldn't…" She sighed as his arm came around her waist, drawing their bodies together. "*I* shouldn't…" She sagged against him. Fitz's touch called her back to a time before her marriage, when there had been soft, pretty things. And amusements. And flirtations.

"Why?"

She was running out of excuses. "How old are you, Lieutenant Hopkins?"

"Four and twenty, ma'am," he teased, as his lips found the sensitive place where her neck joined her shoulder. Her husband's kisses had certainly never left her feeling this way, all achy and trembling.

"And it doesn't bother you that I'm, um…" How could she be expected to do sums when he was kissing her like that? "Almost seven years older?"

He nipped her earlobe. "I'm too busy being scandalized by your blatant seduction of your footman. Why are you fighting this, Fanny?" he breathed against her cheek.

"Perhaps because I was told—" she turned in his arms, laid her palms flat against the wall of his chest, and made herself meet his gray eyes, darker and stormier than she had yet seen them—"that a good fight would make you want to—"

He swept her into a kiss, off her feet, and onto the velvet chaise, all in one fluid motion. Bending over her, he propped himself up with his forearm resting against the chaise's rolled top and one knee pressing into the cushion between her spread thighs. His free hand roamed down her throat, over her collarbone, along the neckline of her gown, which earlier in the day she would have described as modest but seemed now to have dipped to daring lows.

He broke off the kiss to draw a ragged breath and tipped his forehead against hers. "Still think you don't inspire passion, Fanny?" he teased. "Tell me what you want. What you need."

"I..." She snagged her lower lip between her teeth, surprised to find it pleasantly swollen. "I assumed you would...just..." She lifted her lips in a tentative thrust.

His lips brushed against her temple. "Why, you greedy minx. But what's the hurry? We've got an hour, remember?"

An hour? "I don't...know...."

"Now, don't be shy." She could feel his smile against his brow.

Tears sprang into her eyes and burned her throat. "I'm not," she insisted, surprised by her own fretfulness. "I don't...I don't know what you mean. What more is there?"

She sobbed when he lifted his body away from hers, levering himself more upright. She could feel him looking down at her, but she resisted raising her eyes to his with every fiber of her being. "Please," she whispered to his cravat.

"Do you mean to say that Drummond only—that he never—he never... *pleased* you? In bed?"

"I've never found the act unpleasant," she reassured him. "After the first few times, of course."

A muscle ticked along Fitz's jaw. A moment past, she had thought the hesitation in his speech was due to embarrassment, or perhaps an attempt to be delicate. Now she saw he was angry.

"It wouldn't be my place to declare myself a marvelous lover," he said. "But I think I can say with some certainty that your husband was a lousy one." Dipping his head, he softly kissed her burning cheek. "With your permission, Fanny, might I try for something better than 'not unpleasant'?"

Finally, she met his pewter gaze. "Yes."

The set of his expression was almost grimly determined as he hoisted himself off her entirely, shed his coat, and tossed it in the direction of the wooden chair. She jerked automatically toward the sound of it hitting the floor instead. "Never mind it, Fanny," he told her, as he bent to remove her half boots. After unlacing each boot and tugging it off, he set the pair aside with far more care than he'd shown his coat. Finally, he lowered himself to the floor beside her, arranging some of the pillows that had been pushed off the chaise under his knees. "Are you comfortable?"

"I think so?"

"If there's anything you don't like—or anything you find you *do*—you have only to tell me," he said, as if such honesty were the simplest thing in the world.

And perhaps it was. She nodded her understanding.

He raised one hand to cup her face, sweeping the pad of his thumb over her eyebrow and down her cheek, before leaning in to kiss her, more gently than before. Just a soft, warm press of lips, his own slightly parted. Then another. And another. Until her mouth wanted to cling to his and she found herself straining to follow when, between kisses, he pulled ever so slightly away.

When their lips met the next time, he did not draw back but held her to him, the touch of both his hand and his mouth firming as he touched the tip of his tongue to the seam of her lips. Startled at first, she didn't know how to respond. "Open for me," he murmured, and when she did, the kiss became something wilder, hungrier, as their tongues met, then danced, then clashed. Her hands, which had been lying at her sides, rose up over his chest and shoulders, her fingers spearing into his coppery hair as he plundered her mouth. Kisses, she was discovering, had the curious ability to make one want more kisses and more than kisses all at once.

His mouth moved to the turn of her jaw, her throat, the little hollow beneath her ear, kissing her, tasting her. Then lower—her collarbone, the neckline of her dress, the gentle swell of her bosom. His free hand, which had been resting near her waist, swept higher, to brush against the underside of her breast.

In the whole of her life, no one—not even Fanny—had ever paid as much attention to her desires as Fitz was paying now. He divined her every sigh or gasp, the unsubtle movement of her hips against the velvet. "Do you like that, my sweet?" he asked. He swept the pad of his thumb across her nipple, bringing it to an aching peak. "May I kiss you here too?"

When a shaky groan proved an insufficiently clear answer, she managed to hiss out, "Yes." And he took that peak between his lips, the delicate layers of muslin suddenly no barrier at all. When her dress was nearly sheer in that place, and her breath was coming in ragged pants, he moved his mouth to the other nipple and began the sweet torment anew.

Nor were his hands still. One curled possessively against the back of her skull, while the other left her breast to trail further down her body, stopping at her calf to trace the pattern on her clocked stockings before sliding higher again. His fingers skated along her knee and upward, past her garters, her skirts gathering around his wrist as he went.

When his fingertips reached the soft skin of her thighs, not quite her private curls, he lifted his head from her breast and sought her gaze, his own dark with another question. "Do you need to be touched?"

Somehow, she managed a nod.

This, she told herself, was the beginning of a return to the familiar—though she could not ever remember a time when that place between her legs had ached so. Did he know even that?

He did. Knew too how to turn the ache into a throb as he toyed with her curls and traced the seam along the top of her thigh. On a sigh, she let her legs fall open, praying he also knew how to ease the sensation he'd so skillfully built.

"That's right," he praised her. "Let me see you." Following his heated gaze downward, she discovered that her skirts had risen almost to her waist, revealing...*everything.* She thought perhaps she ought to be mortified, lying there, totally exposed, in the light of midday. But when he looked at her with such undisguised admiration, watching his fingertip slide deeper into her feminine folds and murmuring, "So pretty and wet," embarrassment was the last emotion she could muster.

"Kiss me," she pleaded.

His fingertip flicked across a spot so marvelously sensitive, her breath stuttered in her chest. "Here?" he asked, favoring her with a lazy, wicked grin. Shock rushed through her, another wave of heat. She'd never imagined such a thing.

Perhaps it was time to let her imagination run wild.

"Yes," she breathed. "There."

Lowering his head, he rewarded her with the most wonderfully wicked kiss imaginable.

His tongue and his fingers worked in concert, teasing her, ratcheting her pleasure higher and higher. She gripped his hair and lifted her hips, chasing...something. Racing toward...something. It fluttered there, in the distance, all around her, inside her—until it burst, like fireworks over Vauxhall Gardens, explosion after explosion of color and light, bright sparks that washed over her and rippled through her, making her gasp with joy.

In the aftermath, she let one arm drop over the side of the chaise and leaned her cheek against the tufted velvet. She did not know that tears had leaked from the corners of her eyes until his thumb had whisked them away. She looked up to see her desire reflected in his gaze, glistening on his lips and chin. "Not unpleasant, dare I hope?" he teased.

Her fingers curled around the corner of one of the cushions that had fallen to the floor. If she'd had the strength, she would have whacked him with it.

He must have read her thoughts. Laughing, he fished in his breast pocket for a handkerchief to wipe his hand and face, then tucked it away and withdrew his pocket watch to check the time. "Just under an hour, too." He winked. "But now I suppose I must see to my other duties," he said, pushing up from his knees to stand.

She brushed her skirts down to her knees and scooted her hips higher on the chaise. "Your other—y-you mean, you're going to go? Without...?" Her eyes fell to his evident arousal, tenting the fall of his breeches.

Another laugh rumbled from his chest, this one more wry, as he snatched up his coat from the floor, shook it out, and thrust his arms into the sleeves. "Three things," he said, returning to her side and leaning over to press a kiss against her brow, then lingering to whisper into her hair. "First, that greedy fellow has been known to get hard at the mere thought of you and must learn patience. Because, second, I intend to make you come a dozen times at least before he gets involved in the proceedings. And third, I promised you I would go to Royal Crescent in an hour to check on your friend—and Fanny?" He tucked a finger beneath her chin and lifted her gaze to meet his, serious and seductive all at once. "I keep my promises."

Chapter 15

Sometime past dawn, Caro rose, gave a most unladylike stretch, and circled her neck to ease the knot formed by drowsing all night in a chair.

Maxim slept on. In repose, his features had lost some of their habitual harshness. She wondered if there could ever come a time when he could surrender that mask in his waking hours too.

Maxim.

When had she resumed thinking of him by that name? When he'd left, she had vowed never to allow the intimacy of it, and all it represented, to intrude on her thoughts. But the events of the past day—the discovery of those horrible letters, his near drowning, the sight of his scarred body—had made him real to her in a way he hadn't been six years ago. Not a beast, but a man.

Maxim.

Resisting the urge to brush the dark hair from his brow again, she stepped silently to the door, returned to her own chamber, and rang the bell. Nan, the elder of the two housemaids, came to help her wash and dress and arrange her hair.

"Have Mrs. Horn bring up a breakfast tray. To Hartwell's chamber."

"Yes, Your Grace."

When she returned to his room, he was sitting up in bed, the dressing gown gaping open to reveal the mat of dark hair on his chest. Before she could make sense of the sudden desire to lay her hand, perhaps even her cheek, against it, he cleared his throat and gathered the two sides of the robe together again. "Good morning, Caro. I've just sent Leclerc to fetch me some coffee."

"You needn't have bothered," she said, stepping closer. "Mrs. Horn will be here shortly with a breakfast tray."

"I'm not an invalid," he protested, the familiar scowl beginning to cloud his features.

She met that look with a scolding one of her own, just enough to drive back some of his ferocity. "It's for both of us."

For a moment, he didn't seem to know what to say to that. His dark eyes looked her up and down. "You're dressed for walking."

"Yes." She'd reached the side of the bed and now rested her hip against the mattress. Over the course of the night, she'd imagined the conversation they must have today. But she couldn't bear the thought of facing him across the drawing room, or any other room in this house, this place to which she'd fled to be free of painful memories. "I thought, after breakfast, you might join me. If you feel up to it."

His voice was still hoarse but his color had returned to normal, and she knew he'd slept well. Yet behind his gaze glimmered something that might have been trepidation. As if he wasn't sure how to answer her.

Moments later, Mrs. Horn backed into the room carrying a loaded tray. "Here you be, Your Grace," she said, laying it across his lap. "And how are you feeling after yesterday's ordeal?"

"I feel fine," he rasped, speaking as much to Caro as to the housekeeper.

"Well, you've had a right dedicated nursemaid," Mrs. Horn replied with a saucy glance between the two of them. A frown of surprise notched the space between his brows when he realized that Caro had stayed by his side all night. "An' I hope now, we can enjoy a spell of good health in this house. Speaking of, that manservant of Mrs. Drummond's called yesterday afternoon with a message for you, Your Grace." She turned toward Caro. "But I didn't like to disturb you."

"Yes, what it is?"

"He said Mrs. Drummond was nearly done in by the shock of what happened to His Grace and had to be hurried home. Once she'd recovered, she wished to send her apologies and ask what assistance she could offer."

"The poor dear," Caro said, though not before she saw Maxim roll his eyes. "I'll go and send her a note of reassurance." She snatched a piece of toast from the tray, the contents of which her husband was already in the process of devouring. "When you are ready," she said to him, "come down."

Around a mouthful of eggs, he promised, "I won't be long."

She had just handed the message for Mrs. Drummond to Geoffrey when she heard Maxim's footsteps on the stairs. Having seen the damage to his leg, she marveled all the more at his ability to move with such apparent ease, the effort it must have required to walk at all.

When he reached the landing, she looked up to spy him sporting a drab duster, the sort of thing a gentleman might wear in the springtime, rather than the cool days of autumn. Her surprise must have shown in her face, for he answered her with a wry shrug. "I lost a few items in yesterday's duel with Proteus."

"Your greatcoat, I can understand. But no gloves? No hat?"

"Leclerc informed me this morning that my second-best hat has somehow been crushed and he has misplaced all my gloves," he explained as he joined her in the entry hall. "If I didn't know better, I'd think he was afraid to let me out of the house."

"The poor man doesn't know yet how contrary you are, especially when it comes to leaving when you're asked to stay," she teased. Or tried to.

The amusement that had been twinkling in his eyes faded. "I think he feels some misplaced sense of guilt. It was he who procured me the boat, after all. But neither of us saw that it was damaged."

Geoffrey stepped to the door as Maxim gestured toward it, and she moved to precede him. "Won't you be cold?"

Sunlight streamed into the entry hall and with it, a soft breeze—not warm, exactly, but nothing like the day before. Maxim's lips quirked. "I'll manage."

With quick fingers, she reached up to untie her veiled bonnet, then tugged off her gloves and tossed them onto a nearby table.

His piercing gaze swept over her face and hair. "Won't the good people of Brighton be scandalized?"

Caro lifted her chin. "I'll manage."

The sun off the water was nearly blinding when they first stepped outside. "A duel with Proteus," she repeated, watching as the light wind churned up playful waves, silver in some places and white in others. The breeze caressed her cheeks and teased loose a few strands of hair. "That's a poetic thought."

"No need to sound so surprised, ma'am," he retorted. "I'm not entirely an uncultured brute." As if to prove it, he extended an arm to her.

She threaded her bare hand around the crook of his elbow. Yesterday's research had yielded only hints about his upbringing and education. "Anyway, I'm glad you won the duel."

"Are you?" They walked along the Marine Parade in front of Royal Crescent, opposite the direction Caro ordinarily took. "I wondered if you wouldn't prefer to be a wealthy widow."

She waited to respond until the last of the houses were behind them. "I suppose that would be a less ambiguous status than the one I have endured these last years," she admitted and felt him stiffen at her honest words. "Then again, I look terrible in black."

He didn't laugh. "You would mourn me?" His voice was little more than a whisper.

Here, at the edge of town, the roadway dwindled into a rough path, bordered on either side by waving seagrasses. She paused to look out over the water, eyes narrowed against the sun, thinking not of yesterday, but all the days before. "In some ways, I already have."

He laid a hand over hers where it rested against his arm. "If it helps, so have I."

Unexpected grief squeezed her heart. Had he been lost to her all along?

"Why didn't you tell me the sort of man your grandfather was, what he did to you—to her?" Gathering her courage, she glanced up at him, only to find that he too was staring out to sea.

"To my mother, you mean?" He lifted one shoulder. "Because I swore after her death I would never speak to the man again—and I did my damnedest not to speak *of* him, either. I thought then that he had done the worst a man could do. I was wrong of course—but boys of twelve or thirteen often fancy they know everything."

"I will not ask, now...."

"No, no. You deserve to know—deserved to know six years ago, before binding yourself in marriage to...to whatever it is I have become."

"Maxim..." she breathed.

That earned her a brusque laugh. "He hated even my name, did you know? Because Maximilien was my other grandfather's name, my *grandpère's* name. My *maman* chose it to honor him, you see, but my grandfather did not think it suitable for a future duke."

"The name of emperors? Of kings?"

"Not English ones. He hated her for being French, and worse, Breton. Hated my father for the unforgivable sin of loving her, marrying her. He cut them off—no acknowledgment, no allowance. They would have been in desperate straits, if not for my late grandmother, the last Duchess of Hartwell, whose marriage settlements had provided a modest income for her only child after her death. I grew up in a cottage, with no more help for my mother than a maid of all work—that's why I was the one chosen to go out into the storm to fetch the doctor when my father was taken ill."

"Do you—do you remember the accident?"

"No. Nor the month or so afterward. My *maman* nursed me back from the brink of death more than once, and I have often thought—"

"Don't say it. Please."

He drew a ragged breath. "My grandfather said it, often, when he showed up later that summer. He mocked me for my looks, my invalidism, my accent. I had grown up speaking only French or Breton at home, you see, because my *maman* spoke almost no English." She could hear his affection for his mother in his voice, the faint echoes of her speech in his. "But he was a powerful man, and she had nothing. He took me away, locked me away—he hadn't the courage, I gather, simply to kill me. Or her. Afterward he sent her far away, to Quebec—or tried. She dr—"

"I know." She cut across him, trying once more to spare him from having to speak the words. She hadn't wanted to be right in her conjectures about the ship that had foundered and the—good God, the insurance money the late duke had gained by his daughter-in-law's death. "But he sent you to school?"

"Once I'd taught myself to walk again, taught myself to fight back against the heartless couple he'd hired to pretend to be my caretakers, yes. I think he could no longer deny that I might survive and so, as his heir, I must be brought up accordingly. I was packed off to Eton, where I learned… oh, many things. Chief among them that my classmates ventured fewer cruelties against me, the ugly crippled boy, when I was cruel to them first."

Briefly, she closed her eyes—against the sun, against his words, against the mental image of the tortures he had endured, the evidence of which she had seen on his naked body. Now she knew for certain just how deeply those wounds had also been carved on his heart. "And when you finished school?"

He hesitated only a moment, but his answer was glib, hiding more than it revealed. "I traveled the world. As young English gentlemen do. And when I came home, I married you."

Why? she wanted to ask. He might have abandoned her to her father's anger that night in Lord Earnshaw's library and thought nothing more on the matter. But he hadn't, and it had been that fact, more than any other, that she had clung to for reassurance over the years. Whatever he was, however he had been mistreated, there was still a spark of goodness in him.

"I know you wrote to tell your grandfather of our marriage. But why?"

This time, he didn't answer at all. "The contents of that crate revealed all this, did they? Old account books, mortgage papers, and the like?"

"There are letters too," she told him, gnawing at her lower lip. "From your father to his. One from your mother, about the accident. They made parts of the story perfectly clear." His expression darkened. "And your grandfather's secretary kept a detailed letter book, to log every bit of correspondence he received, including your letter. But I confess I did have to speculate a bit, puzzle out some connections. I couldn't make heads nor tails of the ledgers, but Mrs. Drummond helped—"

"Ah, yes. Mrs. Drummond." Her stomach knotted as he pulled his arm free from hers and took a few steps away. She could see nothing of his face now. Just his broad shoulders, taut beneath his coat, and his dark brown hair, tangled and tousled by the wind. "If you'd asked, I would have told you that you were welcome to waste your morning poring over decades of my grandfather's musty old account books. But when I think of that woman—"

"Remember, you are speaking of a lady," she cautioned. She wished she understood the source of the animosity that had sprung up between them.

He whirled on her. His scar leaped into prominence as his jaw clenched. "Mrs. Drummond is a—"

"A friend," she snapped, forestalling whatever epithet he had been about to offer. "She's shown me nothing but kindness and understanding since—"

"Since the day General Scott ordered her into your life?" Maxim supplied with something very close to a sneer.

Her breath left her in a rush, and she was sorely tempted to sink onto a nearby tuft of grasses. "I beg your pardon?"

"Mrs. Horn told me she was introduced to you by Mrs. Scott," he explained. "And I'll wager the value of everything in that wretched crate that Mrs. Scott was acting at her husband's behest. Mrs. Drummond, and her supposed manservant, work for the leader of British intelligence."

That sweet old man she'd beaten at whist? Fanny? *Impossible.* Maxim was lying to her—hadn't he just confessed how he'd learned to defend himself by attacking first?

Still, Fanny *had* introduced herself with a letter from the general's wife. "H-how do you—?"

"How do I know?" He turned back toward the water, his voice now alarmingly quiet, almost lost to the sounds of the wind and waves. "Because, my dear, so do I."

She did sink down then, the stiff grasses crunching beneath her, offering little in the way of cushion. He must have heard, because he glanced over his shoulder and then turned back and knelt beside her, his movements swift, though stiffer than they had been years ago in Lord Earnshaw's library. "I shouldn't have told you the truth so abruptly."

"But it is the truth?"

"Yes."

Her head spun as flashes of memory came and went, much like the documents in the crate: not a complete picture, but enough. "That—that's why the general was at our wedding. That's why you know how to pick locks." She could barely push the words past her suddenly parched lips.

"I was sixteen years old when I met then Colonel Scott, and already an accomplished thief. One does what one must to survive," he added with a slight shrug of something like embarrassment. "Scott put those skills to better uses, taught me new ones. For the first time in my life, the fact that I was half-French was a reason to be valued, not despised."

"Why didn't you tell me?"

"I ought to have done," he readily admitted. "That wasn't fair to you. But it has been the business of my life to collect information, not to share it about. Besides,"—a dry laugh gusted from him—"if you remember, when we met, the war was over."

A spy. She was married to a *spy.* "That's why you've traveled to so many places. Why you went to…to France. *He* sent you."

His shoulders rose and fell on a surprisingly shaky breath. "I can't lay the blame for that last trip at Scott's feet—though the work I ultimately did for him had a hand in keeping me away, it's true. I left four days after our wedding because I—" As if the next words were sharp in his throat, he swallowed twice before speaking them. "I found myself drawn to you, Caro, in a way I had not expected. Next thing I knew, I would be fancying that I *needed* you." The humorless sound with which he punctuated that sentence made it clear how alarming he found such a prospect.

But it also hinted that he had not triumphed over his fancy as fully as he might have wished. "And when you came to me that morning," he went on, "with that silly book in your hands, I was afraid…afraid you might try to persuade yourself you needed me too. I couldn't let that happen. Not for your sake. Nor for mine."

Of all the devastating discoveries of the day, this one might have been the worst: the realization that if Maxim's soul hadn't been so scarred by tragedy and torture, they might have built something from those moments, might have had a life together. Instead, all these years later, what did they have? An unexpected attraction, as he'd said, and very little else.

Could this moment be a chance to start again?

His forearm lay propped across his upraised knee, and she reached for his hand, turning it toward her until she could see the red abrasions scoring his palm. Then she laid her hand palm upward in his—her own, similar wound was considerably less stark now, pink and only a little tender. "I suppose after all this time you've realized you didn't—don't—really need me."

His fingers curled gently around hers, encircling her hand entirely in his. "My God, Caro," he whispered. "I'm here. What else must I say?"

She tugged against his grasp, not to free herself, but to encourage him to rise. Together, hand in hand, they walked on.

"Do you know why I came to Brighton?" she asked after a long silence. They were standing shoulder to shoulder now, looking outward. "Because the sea is powerful. And, to anyone with a lick of sense, more than a little terrifying. Like you."

"You said you weren't frightened of me."

"I wasn't. I'm not." She looked down the cliff's face and watched as the water tumbled the fine pebbles, sorting through them like a child, deciding which to toss away and which to keep. "But when you left...*then* I was frightened. Frightened and very, very angry. I was desperate to free myself from those feelings, to make it seem as if the distance between us was of my own choosing. So, I fled London and came here. I picked Royal Crescent because the houses overlook the water. I thought I could make myself stronger if I forced myself to face it—something I can't control, something I don't fully understand. Every day I walked along the water's edge, careful never to let it touch me. And every day, I very deliberately turned my back on it. Over and over again. I waited for the day when I could at last look with disdain on the people drawn to the sea's charms, all the while feeling nothing for it myself. Nothing at all."

He nodded his understanding. "I told myself I should have hoped to find you indifferent when you saw me again."

"But I wasn't," she confessed on a whisper. "I'm not."

He led her to a narrow set of steps—mere notches in the cliff's face, really—and down to the strand. Shrugging out of his duster, he made a place for her to sit. Then he tugged off his boots and his stockings. His calves, the only bit of him hidden from her view the day before, were muscular and sprinkled with dark hair.

"What are you doing?" she demanded, a question that became more urgent when he bent and began to unlace her ankle boots.

"You said you'd never set foot in the water in all the time you've been here. Shall we try putting a toe in? Together?"

Gripping her lightly by the hands, he led her out. With every step, she wanted to protest. The shingle was uncomfortable on the tender soles of her feet; the water, which rushed to surround her, was freezing. The first time it touched her, she squealed.

But he was the one who'd nearly drowned the day before, and he was already ankle deep. If the water frightened him, he had a very different way of dealing with his fear.

The water swirled and foamed over the tops of her feet, which quickly progressed from cold to numb. But she didn't retreat. She took a step, and another, until her hems were wet. Now that she'd come this far, she would readily have ventured deeper than was wise. Just as she'd always feared.

She raised her eyes to his face, and something in her expression made him catch his breath.

"You should hate me."

"I *have* hated you, sometimes," she admitted. "Perhaps even often. But hatred is not the opposite of—"

"No." The single word was firm, unwavering. She did not know whether it indicated agreement with what she had been about to say, or a refusal to hear the word spoken aloud.

Distracted, lost in one another's gaze, they were both caught off guard by a larger wave that broke around them and soaked them to the knees. He laughed; she joined him, then quickly sobered.

"Does…does all of this"—the spying, yes, but most of all his battered, distrustful heart—"mean you're bound to leave me again, someday?" she asked.

Urging her back toward dry land, he helped her to sit down before kneeling himself, dried and chafed her icy feet with the hems of his duster, and finally put her shoes on again. "I don't know if there's a way for me to make things right." He did not lift his eyes to her. "But all that's happened in the last few days has made me more determined than ever to free myself from my past. I'm bound to you, Caro, if you'll have me."

She stood unaided. "I still don't know if I can trust you."

With another sharp nod, he began stuffing his feet into his boots and his arms into his now hopelessly wrinkled coat. "Neither does General Scott," he said at last. "My assignment was to make the French believe I'm on their side. Something must have happened to persuade Scott they're right."

Maxim was suspected of turning traitor? Might he have? *When in France, I am a Frenchman,* he'd told her. She tried to shake off the suspicion, but six years was a very long time to pretend.

Together, though not touching, they began to walk along the beach, to a place where they could more easily ascend to the Marine Parade that ran along the top of the cliff. "Mrs. Drummond thinks you tried to poison me."

He paused and turned toward her. "Do you?" Fanny's accusation seemed not to surprise him. He was too used to people assuming the worst, she supposed. But she could see in his eyes that he did not want her to be one of them.

With a dismissive flick of her wrist, she tossed the ridiculous question aside. But afterward, her hand hovered between them, near his face. "May I?"

After the briefest hesitation, he nodded.

With an upward stroke of her fingertips, she traced his scar, from the edge of his jaw, where no whiskers grew, along his sunken cheekbone, around his eye, through his eyebrow and over his temple, the silvery line growing ever thinner, until it disappeared into his dark hair. That wound had healed, however imperfectly.

But what of those that were still raw? What if they never healed at all?

His eyelids squeezed shut. Did her touch give him pleasure or pain? "When you look at me that way," he whispered, turning his face into her hand and pressing a kiss against her palm, "it makes me wish I could be the man you seem to see."

"Maxim." She could not make up her mind whether to comfort or to scold. "Your scars are a sign to the world that the past has shaped who you are. But you don't have to be done changing, becoming the man you could be."

When his eyes flew open, she saw a blaze of disbelief, but also a flicker of hope.

"Your hand is cold," he said suddenly, reaching up to cover it, cupping her palm against his cheek.

"You should feel the rest of me."

A new emotion flared in the depths of his dark gaze. But he said nothing, just wrapped an arm around her shoulders to hurry her toward home, toward something much more than she had expected when they set out that morning.

She was laughing—excitement and nervousness tangled in her belly— when they reached the steps of the house. The sound caught in her throat as the door opened. "You have guests, Your Grace," Geoffrey said, his expression inscrutable.

"Who?" Maxim demanded.

But Caro, who had preceded him up the stairs, already knew the answer.

"You're letting in a draft, Caroline," scolded her father, gesturing imperiously for her to cross the threshold. "Marriage hasn't cured you of the habit of running about without being properly dressed, I see."

Oh, but she was cold, ever so much colder than she had been when standing ankle deep in the north Atlantic. Her heart thudded dully, struggling to move her suddenly congealed blood.

"Well," he said as he turned toward the dining room, where the rest of her family appeared to be enjoying a hearty repast, "I suppose you can afford both the bill for the coal and the cost of making yourself a spectacle."

"If she cannot," said her husband as he stepped up behind her, his voice as deep and rich as she had ever heard it, all hint of raspiness gone, "I can."

Chapter 16

Laughton started but recovered quickly, bowing and then waving an arm, as if inviting guests into his own home. "Ah. Chesleigh. I had no expectation of finding you here." Though the sounds of silver against china had fallen silent behind him, Maxim could see full well that the family was at present devouring the breakfast he'd once so pointedly denied them.

"It's Hartwell, now," Maxim said.

The effect of his voice on Caro's father was radically different from its effect on Caro herself. Color drained from the man's face, reminiscent of the night at Earnshaw's. He seemed to understand immediately that it had been one thing to flout the will of the disgraced heir presumptive, particularly when he had taken himself off to parts unknown.

Quite another to defy a duke to his face—his scarred and scowling face.

"I see," Laughton said when he had recovered himself and bowed a second time. "Do I offer my condolences, or my congratulations?"

"Neither," he replied. "We have no need of anything from you."

As that pleading stack of letters had made plain, however, the Brent family had need of many things…and expected Caro to provide them, even over her husband's prohibition. As if on cue, the family members arrayed themselves behind their pathetic patriarch: the aunt who fancied herself ill, the desperate and deluded wife and mother, the spoiled sister, and last of all, the debauched brother, wiping grease from his chin with the back of his hand, looking as if he'd just stumbled in from a hard night or three at the tables.

Of course, Maxim wasn't meant to know any of that.

"How…how is it you happened to come here?" Caro asked. "All together? Without even sending word?" He could hear the tremor in her voice, but whether it reflected fear or fury was less clear to him. Either way, he foresaw a disastrous scene about to play out.

Damn Laughton and his worthless brood. Maxim had enough urgent matters to manage. Somehow, he needed to persuade General Scott that the warning he had brought from France must be heeded. More important, he wanted to repair his relationship with his wife. Now Caro's family stood between him and those worthy goals.

Unless...dealing decisively with the Brents could be the first step toward repairing the trust he'd destroyed?

"May I suggest, my dear," he said, settling a hand on Caro's waist, "that we allow our guests to finish their meal, and then invite them to repair to the drawing room for this conversation? You must wish to freshen up."

She glanced up and over her shoulder at him. Beneath the sun, beside the sea, her eyes had been flecked with green and gold. But now, the strain of the moment had dulled them to an ordinary brown.

No. Not *ordinary*. Nothing was ordinary about his Caro.

"Yes?" he prompted, tightening his grip on her hip.

As he'd hoped, his reassuring squeeze restored some of the warmth to her eyes and her cheeks. "Yes. Yes, of course. Thank you." Turning back to face her family, she inclined her head, every inch a duchess in spite of windblown hair and muddy hems. "By all means, finish your breakfast. We shall join you in the drawing room in half an hour."

Maxim released her and motioned for her to precede him up the stairs. On the landing outside the door to her bedchamber, she hesitated. "There's something you should know."

He nodded for her to open the door and followed her inside. "I think I can guess what you're going to say. Your family has been begging you for money, separately and together. And because the terms of our marriage settlements made it impossible for you to help them any other way, you've sent them every cent you could spare from your pin money. More than you could spare, in fact."

Her eyes flared. "How do you know that?"

He walked past her toward the window and looked out at what had been a beautiful morning. "I found their letters in your writing desk, and I—I read them." Sheepishly, he turned back to face her, not quite meeting her gaze. "The only defense I can offer is that I've been ferreting out secrets for more than twenty years, and old habits die hard."

A frown wrinkled her forehead. "That was very wrong of you." Then her brow cleared. "But honestly, I'm glad you know. It spares me from having to explain their weaknesses—or confess my own foolishness. Besides, it would be the rankest hypocrisy for me to fault you for prying in my desk, when I quite literally pried open a crate of your private papers."

"Irrelevant," he said, stepping toward her with outstretched hands. "I had no right to do anything of the sort, and I'm s— *Bah!*" He dropped his arms to his sides. "You were clever to forbid the word, Caro. It's made me painfully aware of how many things I have to apologize for. But as I cannot *say* how sorry I am, I am determined to *show* you instead. If you will let me."

"By managing my awful family?"

"As a start."

"What do you mean to do to them?"

"What do you wish me to do? Toss them out on their rears? March them into the channel?" His attempt at a smile faltered. "Welcome them with open arms?"

"You would do that?"

Flexing his right hand, he watched the skin stretch over his knuckles. At present the sea was responsible for their battered and bruised condition, but God knew how many times in his life he'd split them open on another man's face. "My instinct is to hurt them, because they've hurt you. But if punishing them would cause you pain…"

"I don't know." Her head sank. "I'm more afraid it might give me pleasure."

Could any man alive better understand the heartsick discovery that the monster one most feared and hated might be oneself?

The difference, of course, was that Caro would never act on those monstrous impulses.

Before he could muster words of reassurance, she closed the gap between them in three rapid steps, laid her forehead against his chest, and threw her arms around his waist.

His heart stuttered. Following his childhood accident, he'd been desperate for comfort. Once his *maman* had gone, he had taught himself not to need it.

But in all his life, no one had ever sought comfort from him.

After a moment, and with slow, uncertain movements, he lightly encircled her in his arms. "*T'en fais pas, ma chérie,*" he breathed against her scalp. *It will be all right, my dear.*

Her whole body sagged against his. "When I was sick—delirious, perhaps, is the better word—I dreamed that you held me like this."

Now his heart began to thud, hard enough that she must surely hear it, feel it. "*J'y étais.*" She turned her head enough to look up at him inquisitively. "It wasn't a dream. I was by your side then. I'm here now. I'll always be here."

The corners of her mouth turned up in a gentle smile. And in that expression, he saw something he'd never thought to see again: the first glimmerings of trust.

"What should I do?" she asked.

"My first impulse is to advise you to wash your hands of the lot of them, and to let me go downstairs right this moment to tell them in no uncertain terms what will become of them if they continue to importune and harass you."

She nodded, more in understanding than agreement. "But…I don't think they're all equally guilty. I believe Papa must have persuaded the others that I had both the means and the obligation to clear away their troubles. And so they wrote. Should they be punished for their misunderstanding, for doing what he told them?"

"You have a generous, forgiving spirit—for which I can only thank God."

He felt her shoulders rise and fall in a silent huff of laughter. Then she whispered, almost to herself, "I don't know if I can forgive my father."

Maxim was quite sure she shouldn't. Then again, neither should she be ready to forgive *him*. But she had already shown herself willing to extend compassion to the undeserving. Perhaps the rest of the family, so long under Laughton's thumb, could yet be salvaged? Only time would tell. The problem was, he didn't have much of it to spare.

"Let me ring for your maid, my dear. And leave the rest to me."

Against his shoulder, her head scrubbed in a silent nod of acquiescence. Once, such a sign of her fledging faith in him, of her affection, would have prompted him to push her away—for her own good, he would have told himself.

Now, he tightened his embrace and drew her closer, determined never to leave her again.

* * * *

A quarter of an hour later, Caro stepped from her chamber wearing a fresh dress, with her hair neatly arranged, and tried not to feel disappointed that Maxim was not waiting on the landing to accompany her down to the drawing room.

A floor below, Geoffrey laid a hand on the door to open it, waiting for her nod. Muffled but familiar voices wafted from the room, and she had to lay a palm over her belly to settle her nerves. She'd been managing her family on her own for as long as she could remember. If she must, she could go on doing it. Only, he'd promised....

At the jerky, uncertain movement of her chin, Geoffrey swung open the door. At first, no one seemed to notice her arrival. Papa stood before the bow window, hands folded behind his back, staring contemplatively out to sea. Toward the middle of the long room, in the pair of chairs before the fire, Mama dozed, while Christopher slouched, idly twirling what appeared to be a guinea over and between the fingers of one hand. Beyond that, Catherine sat at Caro's desk, neither reading nor writing, while Aunt Brent... Rapidly, she scanned the large room again. Where was Aunt Brent?

"Ah, my dear, I did not hear you come in." Maxim unfolded himself from the little high-backed sofa in front of her, where he'd been sitting beside her aunt, who had surely been regaling him with stories of her supposed ill health.

"Took you long enough," muttered her father, and the sound of his voice made Mama jump, though she did not rouse. She must have taken a dose of her tonic after breakfast; travel always wreaked havoc on her nerves.

"Hartwell agrees that the sea air will do me good," Aunt Brent announced triumphantly.

"And Lady Laughton, as well," Maxim added.

At the sound of her name, Mama's eyelids fluttered. "I wasn't asleep," she insisted, pushing herself more upright in the chair and dabbing discreetly at the corner of her mouth with her handkerchief.

Christopher made a scoffing noise in the back of his throat. "No one could blame you if you were, Mama. Brighton's deadly dull." He sent a hard look at his father. "Especially this time of year. Perhaps, Hartwell, you know where there's some entertainment to be had? Cards, or the like?"

"For God's sake." Catherine tossed aside the quill with which she'd been toying. "It's not even noon, Lord Brash," she reminded him, mocking him with the contraction of his courtesy title, Viscount Brent-Ashby, by which his chums addressed him and which their father despised.

Caro's eyes shot toward Papa, awaiting a reprimand—for either of her siblings.

She waited in vain.

"How long is your visit to be?" She had to drag the inquiry from her chest, dreading the answer.

"A fortnight," a pair of voices replied in unison, a tone of delight from her aunt and one of dismay from her brother.

"I was sure we could count on your hospitality," said her father, at last turning away from the window.

Only she caught the warning flash in Maxim's eyes and, oh, how she wanted to watch him put Papa in his place, as he'd done the morning of their wedding. But of course, the effect of that set-down hadn't lasted long enough to matter. The devil was invulnerable to fire and brimstone.

"Of course you were," Maxim replied when he had composed himself, his voice quiet in a way that would have sent shivers down the spine of a man of sense. Caro noted that he promised her family nothing. "As for entertainment, here is what I propose. Brent-Ashby and I will go for a ride. Lady Catherine would no doubt enjoy a stroll with her sister along the water—"

"And to the shops?" Catherine interjected hopefully.

"Just as you wish. And Lady Laughton and Miss Brent, will you join them or stay in and rest from your journey?"

Caro expected Mama to choose the latter, but her eyes were suddenly as bright as she had ever seen them. "A walk sounds lovely." Not to be outdone, Aunt Brent nodded.

"And what do you suggest for me, Hartwell?" drawled her father.

Again, that dangerous flash in Maxim's eye. But when he spoke, he only asked with exaggerated politeness, "What would be your pleasure, Laughton?"

Caro wondered how long he intended to maintain this façade of civility, and to what end. She'd agreed to let him manage the situation, but she was still uncertain whether he could truly earn her trust.

"Is there any shooting hereabouts?" Papa had always enjoyed the pastime and frequently wrangled an invitation from friends; he had never gone to the trouble or expense of maintaining his own coveys.

Maxim's answering smile was positively wolfish. "I'm certain that could be arranged."

Caro scrambled to remember whether, among the various rumors she'd heard, there happened to be one about Maxim killing men, merely for the pleasure of watching them die? If not, he looked ready to start one.

"What a lovely day you've planned for everyone, my dear," she said with an approving nod.

In short order, the ladies had donned their pelisses and bonnets and were ready to depart through the front door, while the gentlemen, in sporting garb, prepared to leave out the back. "I've given Mrs. Horn instructions to have dinner ready at seven," Maxim announced, and they all agreed they would be ready to dine by then.

From Royal Crescent, Caro led her sister, mother, and aunt along her more usual stroll down the Marine Parade toward the center of town, though at half the pace. Still, she had the pleasure of seeing the wind and the sunshine bring some color to her mother's wan complexion.

"Brighton is a lovely spot," Mama said. "I can see now why you chose it."

"We ought to have paid her a visit sooner," said her aunt.

For the first time, Caro almost wished they had—though preferably without Papa. She'd always been lonely here. She'd told herself she wanted to be alone.

But she hadn't. Why else had she sought out a place with a constant bustle of activity? Why else had she been so quick to accept the overtures of women like Mrs. Scott and Mrs. Drummond? She didn't feel betrayed by either of them. Not exactly. She felt...foolish. Foolish for not having seen through their warm smiles. And oddly, naively hopeful that, despite the fact they'd been following General Scott's orders, there might still be something genuine in the friendship they'd offered.

Six years ago, Caro had let a fantasy of rescue, of being swept away from her problems, lure her into heartbreak. Now, however, the future that beckoned on the horizon felt different, more substantial. More real.

Had anything actually changed, though? Had Maxim changed?

Had she?

Cathy slipped her arm through Caro's. "Do you know, I have never once in my life believed that Aunt Brent was truly ill." Their father's sister stumped along ahead of them, making little use of her walking stick. For once, she was not complaining. "You seem well too. Though none of us had any notion we would find your husband in residence." Her sister's expression was sly. "In town, one hears nothing but rumors—"

"I wouldn't put much stock in those," Caro said.

They had walked along the Marine Parade to the bottom of the Steyne, still green despite the late season. Mama's and Aunt Brent's pace began to slow. "Shall we turn back?" she asked them.

Catherine's plump lips flattened into a thin line of disappointment. "I wanted to see Mrs. Fitzherbert's house. It's near here, isn't it? I've heard Prinny set her up in grand fashion—is it very scandalous?"

"It's very elegant," Caro corrected, her tone a subtle reprimand—too subtle for Catherine, she felt sure.

"I wouldn't wish to spoil your afternoon," Mama insisted. "I'm sure I can find my way back. If Hester will accompany me..." She looked toward her sister-in-law.

"The air here is fine," Aunt Brent said, as if mulling over the decision, "but one must be careful not to overdo."

"Geoffrey will accompany you both." Caro signaled to the footman who was, as always, keeping a respectful distance. "And Mrs. Horn will see to your comfort—whatever you need. Cathy and I will go on, perhaps peek into some shops. Once you have these ladies settled," she said to Geoffrey, "you may come back for us." She suspected that her sister hoped to accumulate a few purchases.

"Very good, Your Grace."

Once the two elder ladies were on their way, Caro led her sister into the narrower streets of town, expecting her to exclaim over the shop windows filled with various delights.

Cathy was oddly silent, however. At last, outside a dressmaker's, she paused to inspect a bonnet on display. Caro braced herself for the pleading to begin.

But when she spoke, she said nothing of the hat. "I thought, after you married, you might have me to stay with you. People do issue such invitations, you know."

Caro started. She and her sister had never been close, and the differences between them had only been amplified by the five-year gap in their ages. "Papa would never have allowed it," she reminded her. "Especially not given my...circumstances."

Cathy's shoulders sagged. "No. I suppose you're right. But he isn't easy to live with, you know."

Despite her annoyance, Caro felt a stirring of pity. "I know." It had not occurred to her that, in her absence, her father might transfer some of his animosity for his elder daughter onto his younger. "Has something... happened?"

That question earned her a scoffing, humorless laugh. "No. And nothing's likely to, either. I—I had an offer, Caro. Last season. A perfectly respectable offer. But Papa says he can't possibly be expected to manage on his own, with both Mama and Aunt in such poor health...as if he doesn't encourage them to carry on so," she added with another dismissive noise in her throat.

There was both petulance and pitilessness in those final words, but Caro could forgive them, for they were also honest. Papa did encourage his sister to fancy herself weak and helpless, and he had always been the first one to prompt Mama to take her tonic, until it had become quite clear she could no longer do without it. The prospect of being the spinster daughter in such a household, forever under Papa's thumb, was indeed a daunting one. Caro herself had married one of the most enigmatic and feared men in England to avoid it.

"Tell me about the gentleman," she prompted gently. "Is he kind? Is he handsome?" She marveled that her sister had said nothing of him in her letters. Had she—had she perhaps been forbidden to do so? All this time, had their father been telling her exactly what she might write?

"He's not rich enough to satisfy Papa," Catherine complained, then softened. "But yes, he is handsome. And so very sweet and gentle. Nothing like—well." Flags of color appeared on her cheeks and she cut her gaze away.

Nothing like your husband, she had been about to say. Caro felt sure of it. But for once, she didn't bristle at her sister's ignorance. Cathy's failings were not all her own fault.

"It doesn't matter, anyway," Catherine went on with a sigh. "I'm no more likely to marry Mr. Parker than…than you are to buy me that bonnet." She tossed her hand in the direction of the shop window.

Ordinarily, Caro would have dismissed those words as a transparent attempt to manipulate her. Today, however, she felt the gentle pressure of Maxim's hands, drawing her into the water, urging her to try. Urging her to open her heart.

"Come on, then," she said, curling her fingers around her sister's arm to urge her toward the shop door. "Let's have a closer look."

A bell tinkled merrily above their heads as they stepped inside. "Welcome, Your Grace," said the woman who kept the shop, dropping into a low curtsy. "I'm honored."

Word of her changed status must have raced through the streets and alleyways of Brighton; Caro could not remember ever having visited the dressmaker's shop before. Instead, Nan's clever fingers had been reworking and disguising her old dresses, the better to make Caro's pin money stretch.

But what if those pounds and pence hadn't really been what her family needed from her most?

Cathy asked to see the bonnet in the window, and Caro occupied herself by looking around at the display of ribbons and trimmings. On the counter, she spied a finished gown of bronze-colored silk, the skirts covered by a delicate overlay of gold lace. It lay half in, half out of a large box; evidently the woman who ran the shop had been preparing it to be sent to a customer when they'd entered.

"Your Grace has excellent taste," said the proprietress, stepping closer. Cathy was studying her reflection—or rather, the bonnet's reflection—in a large mirror.

"It is a beautiful gown," Caro said.

"Alas, the lady for whom it was made decided it did not suit."

"Perhaps you should buy it, Caroline," Cathy said, still preening.

The shopkeeper's brows rose in a hopeful arc as she looked between the sisters. Lifting the dress from the box, she shook out the creases, sending sparks from the gold trim. "Very few adjustments," she said, passing a critical eye over Caro's figure. "Only a moment's work for my seamstress."

And before she knew what she was about, Caro found herself trying on the gown.

"Oh," Cathy breathed when Caro stepped out of the curtained dressing room. "You must have it. I'll—why, I'll forgo the bonnet," she insisted, untying its ribbons as she spoke. "Mr. Parker says a poke brim gets in the way of—well." A blush lit her cheeks, and Caro caught a glimmering of who her sister might be, if she too could have a chance at love and happiness.

And in her sister's gaze, she glimpsed her own reflection. She let herself imagine, just for the moment, walking into the dining room this evening wearing the bronze silk gown. The look in Maxim's eyes...

She'd let happiness slip through her fingers once before. This time, she meant to hold on with both hands. Tightly enough that even her grasping father could not steal a drop. From anyone.

"I'll take it," she declared, with a twirl. "And the bonnet for my sister too. You may send the bill to the Duke of Hartwell."

After the seamstress had made a few quick alterations to the gown, they left the shop, all smiles, their packages in Geoffrey's capable arms. Caro fancied he looked pleased to at last be bearing such a burden for his mistress.

As they walked back in the direction of Royal Crescent, she tilted her head toward her sister. "I'm not yet sure how, but I believe things will work out," she whispered. "I predict the brim on that bonnet will be the last obstacle to Mr. Parker's affections."

Chapter 17

Maxim brushed away Leclerc's hands. Inheriting a dukedom had not, so far as he knew, impaired his ability to tie his own cravat.

After a little hum of disapproval, Leclerc turned his back and stepped toward the washbasin, as if unwilling to watch the unfolding—or perhaps, in this case, folding—disaster. "Will the arrival of the duchess's family mean another delay in setting out for London?" he asked in French, speaking over his shoulder as he began to clean Maxim's razor.

"Not a long one," Maxim answered. A quirk of confusion darted over Leclerc's brow, alerting Maxim to the fact that he'd spoken unthinkingly, automatically, in English. Quickly he switched to French. "I for one cannot bear to spend many more hours in her father's company."

There had been a moment, before their riding party had reached even as far as Hove, when Laughton's inability to control his mount had promised a cliff's-edge disaster, and Maxim had found himself envisioning the spectacular fall with barely disguised relish. In the end, of course, he'd intervened. Mostly to spare a tragic end for the poor horse.

It had, by all measures, been a torturous afternoon. But he had no expectation that the route to securing his wife's heart would be an easy one. By the time they'd returned to Brighton, with barely an hour to spare before dinner, he'd improved his understanding of the Brent family's situation and begun to formulate a plan.

Caro's brother, despite actually choosing to style himself "Lord Brash," was less an imbecile than Maxim had always assumed. In fact, he rather thought the young man's misbehavior might better be attributed to boredom. But gambling had turned into more than an amusement. Now, as his twenty-first year approached, and with it control over previously untouchable funds, he must be broken of the habit, before he lost more than money.

At first, Maxim had thought Laughton oblivious to the problem, blinded by misplaced paternal pride. But the more Brent-Ashby had rattled, the more Maxim had understood: Laughton wanted his son and heir indebted, prey to self-doubt, weak. Whether he hoped to go on controlling the young man's inheritance, or simply controlling the young man, was less clear.

He had similar confirmation of the root of the family's problem in a discreet report from the footman, Geoffrey, who said that the elder ladies had returned in high spirits, looking much improved by their hour in the sunshine and fresh air. And, as Maxim had retired to his own chamber, he'd heard Caro and her sister laughing—no, *giggling*—together. In each incident, he saw the possibility that away from Laughton himself, the members of the Brent family might be less miserable, and therefore not entirely worthless.

Now came the matter of determining whether they could be brought up to snuff.

In the dining room yet another large bow window overlooked the channel, this one presently covered by draperies to shield occupants from the curious gazes of passersby. The room's furnishings were elegant but not ostentatious and, as everywhere else in the house, reflected Caro's delicate tastes. Maxim hoped the spindly chairs would hold him. As he approached the groaning table, he marveled once again at Mrs. Horn's ability to marshal her staff and serve an elaborate meal on very little notice, particularly given what must be a lean household budget.

Laughton noticed too. "Do you recall once telling me, Hartwell," he asked, a triumphant laugh in his voice as he scanned the repast, "that for all you cared, I might starve? Yet here I am."

Maxim walked slowly to his seat, feeling both the servants' and his guests' eyes upon him. If someone had chosen that moment to drop a fork, it would have been audible in spite of the plush carpet. *Remove the china and silver from Lord Laughton's place,* he wanted to growl to the footman.

But this morning's conversation with Caro had reminded him of those childhood pains he had struggled all his life to dull and bury, among them the vivid and vicious pangs of hunger.

"Deprivation, starvation—those were my grandfather's methods, Laughton. Intended to keep me weak and under his control." He paused as he passed behind the other man, who was a full head shorter, at least. "I shall leave you to draw your own conclusions as to how well they worked."

He wouldn't stoop to his grandfather's tactics, wouldn't let himself be dragged down into that darkness again—not today, not when he'd finally been given a glimpse of the light.

The thought itself must have summoned Caro, who appeared in the doorway just as he stepped to the head of the table at the opposite end of the room. Beneath the candlelight, the silk of her gown rippled like molten metal, its hues reflected in the gold of her eyes and in the deep russet brown of her hair. He'd waited six years to see her attired in something truly becoming, something befitting her beauty and her station.

And right now, his devilish mind was busily picturing how she would look out of it.

Somewhere among the Grant family treasures would be gems to do that gown justice: gleaming, polished topazes to drip from her throat and disappear into her décolletage. But for now, he was more than satisfied with the bare expanse of skin, the curve of her bosom, and just the hint of a flush.

"How lovely you look, my dear," Lady Laughton murmured, and even Brent-Ashby made a gruff noise of approval in the back of his throat.

Before Maxim could begin to stump his way toward her, the footman had pulled out her chair and helped her to sit down. Once seated, she glanced up from beneath her lashes at Maxim, as if apprehensive of his reaction.

He was glowering at her. If he hadn't been able to tell by the tautness of his own jaw, he would have known by the look of alarm in her eye. His expression felt as if it were carved of increasingly heavy stones: the afternoon's annoyances, that sudden flare of lust, and the thunderous realization of just how great a fool he'd been.

He'd walked away from this woman. Away from her conversation and companionship. Away from their shared passion.

Away from love.

Snatching up his goblet, he raised it in a salute so abrupt, the wine threatened to overspill the brim. "To the Duchess of Hartwell," he managed to grind out and, without waiting for the others to echo the toast, downed half the glass in one gulp.

She blushed and dipped her head in her acknowledgment of the gesture, but she did not raise her eyes to him again.

The conversation over soup consisted of a minute description of the ladies' stroll, narrated in turns by Lady Catherine and Miss Brent. Shopping, yes. Sea air, yes. Lady Laughton's cheeks still glowed with sunshine and exertion—or perhaps from a recent dose of laudanum. Still, Caro listened and nodded and gave every indication that she had spent a pleasant afternoon.

Over the next course, young Brent-Ashby regaled the company with an exaggerated account of the gentlemen's adventures, in which, Maxim noted, the man painted himself as the one to have single-handedly staved off his father's disaster, despite never slackening his breakneck pace.

Maxim sharply cleared his throat.

"Got a bone, Hartwell?" Laughton asked, gesturing toward the fish with the tines of his fork. "Best be careful."

With a glare, Maxim took a sip of wine. Brent-Ashby hurriedly finished his story, with far fewer embellishments this time.

When Geoffrey laid the next plate before the earl—tender fillets of beef in a delicate cream sauce—Laughton grinned and patted his belly. "With hospitality such as this, daughter, I will be tempted to extend our visit. A month, at least."

Caro's shoulders sagged, and Maxim knew it was time for him to speak.

"I recommend waiting for an invitation, Laughton," he said, leaning back in his chair as he toyed with the stem of his glass with one hand. "And if I were you, I would be prepared to wait a good long time."

Laughton's brow wrinkled, either in confusion or disbelief. "Are you insinuating that I'm not welcome, Hartwell?"

"I am insinuating nothing. I believe my words were perfectly clear. You are *not* welcome here. Will never be welcome here, or in any home where the Duchess of Hartwell resides."

"How dare you speak to me thus, sir? I demand—"

"What was it you advised, Laughton?" Maxim spoke across him, his voice hardly above a whisper. "'Be careful'? I'll say the same to you—but only once. Don't cross me. Don't try to defend your abhorrent conduct. Or this lovely meal shall be your last."

In a surprising show of wisdom, Laughton snapped his mouth shut.

"Six years ago," Maxim went on, with a hasty glance toward Caro, "I met a young woman so eager to defy her father's ridiculous edicts, she was willing to sit for hours in an unheated library just to read a book. So desperate to escape his petty tyranny, she was willing to marry me."

"I don't have to listen to this attack on my character," Laughton whined.

Maxim struck the table with his palm forcefully enough to make the silver jump and rattle. "Indeed you do. You know full well it was my intention to see her well provided for—*her*, not you. You contravened my wishes, Laughton. I hoped to set her free, while you deliberately ensnared her. You"—and here he sent a look around the table, pausing at each member of the family—"and you, and you—you all took advantage of her kind heart and her generous spirit."

"I cannot fault them for doing as he bid." Caro's voice was soft but clear.

Those words did not surprise Maxim. Neither did they appease his anger. "Were they not free to resist him, as you did?" He understood now, in a way he hadn't when he was a boy, that men like Laughton and his grandfather were weak but needed others to be weaker still. If Maxim's upbringing had done nothing else, it had taught him the importance of strength.

Caro's eyes gleamed. "Ah, but you see, he gave them less reason to fight him."

And fighting him had made her strong.

He understood what she was trying to tell him without her having to speak the words. "Well, then. It seems I must thank you after all, Laughton." If Caro had not needed to defy her father, they surely would not be married. "Without you, who knows what might have been?"

The earl straightened and gave a self-satisfied smirk.

"And here," Maxim went on, sliding his palm across the tablecloth, smoothing the wrinkles he'd made, "is how I propose to show my gratitude. I will clear Brent-Ashby's gaming debts. I will settle a suitable dowry on Lady Catherine if she wishes to marry, and a stipend if she does not. And I will ensure that both Lady Laughton and Miss Brent receive whatever care is required to restore their good health."

Wide eyes greeted that announcement, Caro's widest of all.

"On two conditions. First, each of you seeks and is granted the forgiveness of my wife for your deplorable conduct to her—and I warn you, a simple apology will not do."

Gazes began to drop to the table, accompanied by sheepish murmurs.

Laughton gave a choked laugh of disbelief. "What of *your* deplorable conduct?"

"The difference, Papa," Caro interjected softly, "is that my husband did not set out to hurt me. And upon discovering that he had, he expressed regret and vowed to atone." She shifted her eyes to Maxim, and they glowed with warmth. "Over the past few days, he has shown more care for me than you ever have."

"Why, you ungrateful little—" Laughton snarled.

Maxim pushed to his feet. "I warned you."

"And the second condition?" Brent-Ashby ventured, not daring to glance toward either his sister or his father. The young man's debts must be hefty indeed.

"I will not have my efforts undercut at every turn. If you agree to accept my help, you must sever ties with him." Maxim jabbed a finger toward Laughton.

A collective gasp rose around the table and then fell to a murmur.

Had he gone too far? What he asked would be difficult, especially for the countess. But Laughton was a cancer that must be excised completely if there was to be any chance at health and happiness.

"You have no right," said Laughton, "no right to interfere with another man's wife and children." Silence followed that proclamation

To Maxim's shock, Brent-Ashby was the first to break it. "Are we not free to choose?"

"Choose?" sputtered his father. A vein bulged on his forehead as his face began to redden.

"Understand me," Maxim cautioned the younger man, sensing what might hang in the balance. "If you ever return to the tables, you will also return to your father."

Brent-Ashby gave a curt but solemn nod. "Understood."

Three people rose at once. Laughton surged across the table toward his son. Maxim grabbed him by the collar to prevent it. And Caro smoothed a hand over her lovely gown and said in a perfectly calm voice, "Ladies, I believe it is time for us to withdraw."

Lady Catherine followed her sister without hesitation. The two elder ladies naturally moved more slowly, but the look Lady Laughton cast over her shoulder at her husband was not as regretful as Maxim had expected.

"Do you really think we should—?" the countess began in what might have been intended as a whisper.

Miss Brent slipped an arm through her sister-in-law's. "I do."

"Absolutely not," Laughton roared—or tried to. The words strangled in his throat when Maxim reached up his other hand and got hold of the man's cravat. "Help me," he squeaked, his eyes rolling in the direction of his son. Not a plea, but a demand.

Brent-Ashby stayed firmly in his seat.

"Out," Maxim said, dragging Laughton away from the table as soon as the ladies had ascended the stairs, his voice as soft as his movements were harsh.

"Where will I go?" The reality of his predicament seemed to be beginning to dawn on the man. His feet stumbled over the carpet as he clawed fruitlessly at Maxim's grasp.

"An inn?" Maxim suggested, moving toward the entry hall.

Desperation flared in his eyes. "B-b-but I spent my last ready coin to get us here."

"That was Caro's coin you spent," Maxim corrected hotly. "You'll certainly not get another from me."

At that final sign of Maxim's remorselessness, Laughton's more usual demeanor returned to him. One final attempt to get the upper hand. "A brawling duke," he scoffed. "Little more than a brute. Your grandfather was right about you."

Maxim only laughed. Nodding to Geoffrey to open the front door, he pushed the older man backward, sending him stumbling down the stairs and into the chill evening air. "Go to hell, Laughton."

When he looked back over his shoulder, the dining room was empty. Brent-Ashby must have decided to join the ladies. But when Maxim reached the drawing room on the floor above, he found it empty of all but his wife.

"Have they all left, then?" The words felt heavy in his chest. He'd failed.

Slowly, she stepped toward him, the candlelight setting her gown aglow, the shadows making her eyes unreadable.

God, but he was tempted to drop to his knees before her. His pleas for mercy would put Laughton's to shame. "Did I do the wrong thing, Caro?"

She stopped with less than an arm's length between them. "You certainly didn't do the easy thing."

And then she reached up and laid her palm against his chest. A sob of relief rose in his throat, and he made no effort to disguise it.

"They're upstairs," she explained. "My brother and sister were more than willing to make do with the small rooms in the attic. Christopher has just gone up to help Mrs. Horn arrange things. And Mama is…resolved." He heard both surprise and relief in her voice. "But understandably distressed. I sent her to lie down in the back bedchamber, and my aunt offered to sit up with her tonight. She needs something to fuss over. I've long thought that focusing on my mother's health might make her less concerned for her own."

"And how are *you* feeling?"

Her fingers curled against his waistcoat. "Sad to think that things have come to this. Relieved to be free of him at last. Afraid he'll find some way—"

"He won't." Maxim settled his palm over hers, pinning her hand against his heart. "I'll make certain of it."

"But my family…"

"It will not be easy," he acknowledged. "Just as you said. But much can be learned in the struggle."

"I fear you were too generous with them."

"I learned that from you, my dear."

"And not just the money," she went on, ignoring him. "You'll be giving up your time, your peace...."

"I would give anything for your happiness, Caro. But tell me, can it ever be enough? Do I stand any chance of winning your heart?"

For answer, she took the tiniest step closer to him, so that her breasts brushed his arm when she drew a breath and dipped her chin in a careful nod.

As it had that morning, his heart began to pound. "If I'm not mistaken about the arrangements," he said, tumbling over her earlier words in his mind, "I've also given up my bed. Just where am I to sleep tonight?"

She rose up on her toes and pressed her lips once to his. "With your wife."

Chapter 18

Caro stood alone in her bedchamber, waiting. Maxim had indicated that he would follow her upstairs in a few minutes. She supposed he meant to give her time to compose herself. Prepare herself.

Though it was unlikely to be the sort of preparation he'd had in mind, she had dismissed Nan without undressing and gone to the window to watch the waves roll toward the shore, timing her breath with their steady movements.

She had not considered that Maxim would try to capture her heart in such a dramatic fashion. Her father banished. Her mother and siblings saved. In stories, men made grand speeches. They groveled. And there was, she supposed, a certain triumphant pleasure to be found in a man who was willing to abase himself to atone for the wrong he'd done. A strong man made weak by love.

Personally, she much preferred Maxim's determination to use his strength to lift others up. To lift *her* up.

In his words, his deeds, his eyes, she had seen how much he needed her. Wanted her. And she knew now how difficult it was for him to confess that desire, what it cost him to make himself vulnerable, after having been hardened by a lifetime of abuse, abandonment, and scorn.

He'd left her, he'd revealed that morning, because he'd been equally alarmed by the prospect of her needing him. And she—unwilling to betray her own weaknesses, determined to make a show of strength—had come to Brighton to prove to the world that she didn't.

But oh, she did. And he deserved to know how much.

Her breath left her in a shivery sigh as she turned away from the window, away from her contemplation of the star-speckled sky, and settled her gaze on the bed. No matter how she'd tried, she'd never forgotten those long-ago nights after her wedding, their passionate encounters in the dark. Then, Maxim had insisted on shrouding himself in the night. Now, the light of the rising moon set the linens aglow. She made no move to draw the drapes.

No more hiding their scars from one another.

A tap on the door at last signaled his arrival. Before she could open it, or even call for him to enter, the door swung inward to reveal her husband, still clad in his dinner clothes, though his cravat had worked loose. In one hand he carried two half-full wineglasses, the stems threaded between his fingers, while on that same forearm, he balanced a plate of food. Once he released the doorknob, he retrieved the plate from its precarious position, stepped inside, and toed the door shut behind him.

"I wasn't sure whether you actually ate anything at dinner," he explained.

She smiled. It reminded her of the books he'd bought her for a wedding gift, to atone for having interrupted her reading at Lord Earnshaw's. "And you didn't want the wine to go to my head." She hurried forward to relieve him of the plate and one of the glasses and carried both to the little table by the window, still positioned as it had been a few nights past. By the time she turned back, he'd drained the other glass. She cocked a brow in a teasing scold. "Have *you* eaten?"

"I'm not hungry."

But he was. His hunger was etched into the harsh lines of his face. It glimmered in the depths of his eyes.

She lifted her face to his and closed her eyes. "Kiss me, Maxim."

Instead of his lips on hers, she felt the weight of his hands on her shoulders, settling her back on her heels. She hadn't even realized she'd risen onto the balls of her feet. "I have to ask you something first."

"Yes?" Reluctantly, she raised her eyelids.

"If…" She couldn't recall seeing him nervous before. He dropped his hands to his sides. "If your father hadn't behaved so badly, would you have taken me back?"

She reached for her own wineglass and took a careful sip. "I suppose the honest answer is that, if my father hadn't behaved so badly, I would never have married you in the first place." His jaw set with an audible click, though from his expression it appeared as if he'd expected her to say as much. "But what a mistake that would have been," she insisted, laying her free hand against his chest.

"A mistake," he echoed, clearly having heard only half of what she'd said.

"Yes, a mistake." She curled her fingers around his lapel, drawing him closer. "I might eventually have been persuaded to marry a dull, so-called respectable gentleman who wouldn't have said a word against my father. Or I might have been still living in my father's house, miserable and alone. Either way, I would have spent my nights reading Robin Ratliff novels and weaving fantasies about some dark, dangerous man who could take me away from all that. Instead, I have the real thing."

"The real…?"

"You. I have you. I thought you read the end of *The Highwayman's Hostage*?"

"Yes, yes." He rolled his eyes. "The scarred villain who fancies himself a hero."

She gave a prim frown. "I presume you are referring to the strong, intelligent man who's brave enough to show the heroine how much he—" Once more on the precipice of a dangerous word, she caught herself. "How much he cares for her."

Lifting a hand, he plucked the wineglass from her fingers and took a drink before meeting her eyes. "How much he loves her, I think you mean."

Her heart leaped into her throat, and she had to swallow twice to speak past it. "Yes. So then"—she flicked her gaze to the nearly empty wineglass and back to his face—"you must also realize how much she loves him in return."

He stepped closer, ostensibly to return the glass to the table behind her. "I might have skimmed over that part." His body pressed against hers. "Care to refresh my memory?"

"I won't claim it was love at first sight," she warned teasingly. "But I did rather like the man I found myself married to. And I'm falling in love with the man I see before me now, the man you've become."

"Caro." Her name was the merest breath of sound. This time, when she rose up on her toes to kiss him, he didn't protest but lowered his mouth to hers.

Ah, but she'd forgotten—well, forbidden herself from thinking about— how marvelous his kisses were. How those wryly curved lips and sometimes cruel tongue could turn soft and wicked all at once. His large hands came up on either side of her head, his fingertips driving into her coiffure, scattering her hairpins. Perhaps he imagined himself holding her prisoner to his kiss, but she had no intention of trying to escape.

When she parted her lips, his tongue surged to fill her, and she tasted the wine, bold and earthy. An answering pang of desire throbbed at the joining of her thighs. Pressing her breasts against his chest, straining her calves to lift herself to his mouth, she gave herself over entirely to the kiss, to the passion that had flared between them from the start, and now to the promise of something more besides.

He devoured her, moving across her mouth to her cheek, her jaw, her throat. Aware that her touch might discomfit him, she was careful to do nothing more than steady herself with the hand on his coat. He must choose when, or even whether, to remove the remaining layers between them—wool and silk and linen, yes, but not only those.

At last, her knees grew so wobbly she had no choice but to sink back onto the soles of her feet if she hoped to stay upright. "I'd forgotten how tall you are." Her self-deprecating laugh was breathless, made more so by his lips pressing against the hollow beneath her ear. "And...before, we—we weren't standing up when we kissed."

"We weren't," he agreed. His hot breath striking her skin made her shiver. Dropping his hands to her hips, he turned her away from him—to undress her, she assumed. But he merely lowered his mouth to the top of her shoulder and began to kiss her there, moving up her neck in a nibbling progression that had her squeezing shut her eyes and scrabbling to grasp the table's edge for support.

Then his left arm came around her, his hand at her breast. With the pad of his thumb, he slid the silk back and forth across her nipple, barely concealed by the low neckline of her gown. When it peaked insistently against his touch, he rewarded her with a light pinch, and even that slight compression made her whimper with need.

At that sound, his right hand, which had been resting on her hip, drew her more snugly against him, his arousal nestled against the small of her back. The heat of his palm seeped through her skirts and petticoats as his hand moved to cup her sex, teasing her through the fabric, urging her to part her legs. Fisting his hand in her skirts, he inched them higher, and the cool air whispered daringly over her calves, her knees, her thighs.

"Look," he demanded, and she blinked open her eyes to discover that the moonlight, both inside the chamber and without, had silvered the window, transforming the glass into a sort of translucent mirror. The reflection of their bodies was superimposed over the view of the water, an image at once ethereal and erotic. Beneath, behind, around them, waves rolled and crashed as the tide neared its highest point.

His questing hand at last bared her mound. She caught no more than a shadowy glimpse of her private curls before her skirts slipped forward around his wrist and hid everything from view again. At the same moment, his fingertips slid over her damp flesh, between her folds, and into her. She looked like a wild, wanton thing, riding his hand, her hair tumbling loose, her heaving breasts threatening every moment to spill over the top of her bodice. And he was the devil himself at her shoulder, his dark head bent over her as he kissed her neck.

"Yes," he urged against her ear as a low keen rose in her throat. "Come for me. Just like this."

In those words, however commanding, she heard a plea for her to trust him, this time with her heart as well as her body—as if those were easily separable things.

"If you'll watch," she said, though in truth she hadn't the strength to resist either his touch or his voice.

Raising his eyes to the window, he met her reflected gaze just as she surrendered to him and shattered.

Boneless, she slumped forward over the table when he released her, her skirts swishing down into their usual place. The hand that had been at her breast now skated soothingly over her back. Trembling fingers fumbled with the fastenings of her gown. "Let me take you to bed, Caro."

With the merest shrug of her shoulders, the silk slithered to a pile at her feet, and she went willingly as he led her away from the window. The bed linens still glowed pale in the moonlight, though not as brightly as they had done, for the moon had risen higher, casting the corners of the room in shadow.

As they approached the side of the bed, he fell behind her. She listened to his footsteps, their slight unevenness muffled by the carpet, and heard the soft *whump* of his coat settling to the floor. When his touch came again—the press of his lips against the nape of her neck, the curl of his fingers in her shift, preparing to strip it from her—she drew a sharp breath.

"Maxim," she whispered, "do you trust me?"

He said nothing, but his sudden release of her shift freed her to turn and face him. Even in the dim light, she could read the panic in his eyes. Not an unwillingness to trust, per se. More an uncertainty, as if no one had ever asked such a thing of him before.

"I want to see you," she said.

"You saw me yesterday." His voice was cool, careful. "In the bath."

"I did. But I don't mean…" In spite of what they'd just done—standing in front of the bow window, no less, putting themselves on display for all of Brighton—embarrassment flared up her chest and across her cheekbones. "Before, when we first married and you came to me, it was always dark and you were…" She twisted her hips slightly, turning her bottom half toward him. "You positioned yourself…behind me."

He grew increasingly stone faced as she spoke. "As I remember, you enjoyed it well enough."

"I did. I will again, I'm sure. It's just that tonight I...I want..." She sucked in another breath and pushed the words out in a rush. "Tonight, when you're inside me, I want to be able to look in your eyes."

"Ah." If she'd thought her explanation would allow him to relax a bit, she'd been wrong. "But that would also involve seeing..."

"Seeing the rest of you, yes. Which, as you just pointed out, I've already done. It's all right, my dear. And I won't—I promise I won't touch you, if you don't wish me to. I'm sorry if my doing so this morning caused you pain." He'd been hurt enough already.

He caught her hands, which had begun to flutter nervously as she spoke, and stroked his thumbs over her palms, skating around the nearly healed scrapes. "It doesn't hurt me to be touched," he said, laying her hands against his chest and covering them with his own. The silk of his waistcoat was cool, and beneath it she could feel the steady thrum of his heartbeat. "At least, not in the way I suppose you imagine. It's more that I...I fear you'll be repulsed."

"I'm not repulsed by you. Does it help for me to say that aloud? Because I hope, deep down, you already know."

"I don't understand how you can't be," he confessed, "but I believe you."

"Is that all?"

He shook his head. "The thing is... It *used* to hurt to be touched. Quite a lot. And I can't—" His chin sank slightly, and she thought he might be looking down at his leg. "Even after all these years, I can't quite rid myself of the memory of how much."

She tried to imagine the agony of being probed and prodded by doctors, of someone changing the dressings or working some stinging liniment or salve into his injuries. Hands that had wanted him to heal, yes, but also— she had not forgotten what he'd said of his grandfather and his so-called caretakers—hands that had wanted to harm.

"Oh, my darling." She would have gladly stepped closer, kissed him, wrapped her arms around him. But he pinned her hands in such a way that all those means of offering comfort were denied to her, and she could do nothing more than press her fingertips lightly into the hollow beneath his collarbone. "Forget I asked. I don't want to—"

"I do. Trust you, that is." With his fingers, he pried up her hands enough to squeeze them and then lifted them higher, to his cheeks.

She held his face between her palms as she rose up on her toes and kissed him, her eyes never leaving his. "There's no rush," she reminded him. "We have a lifetime together."

"And thanks to my foolishness, years to make up for." He released her hands to once more clutch the hem of her shift, lifting it over her raised arms and tossing it aside, so that she stood before him in nothing but her stockings. "My God, Caro. You're beautiful." The moonlight painted her in a silvery glow, cooler than candlelight. His sun-browned hands were comparatively dark as his fingertips swept down her body before settling at her waist. "More beautiful than even my most heated fantasies."

"Heated fantasies?" she echoed teasingly—though it was surely more accurate to say he was teasing her, with his voice and with his thumbs, which at the moment were sweeping lazily along the undersides of her breasts.

"Scorching." Tightening his grip, he lifted her and tossed her crossways onto the bed, his eyes raking over her before settling hungrily on what lay between her slightly parted legs.

"You—you look like you want to devour me." She hardly knew whether the stutter in her voice was hesitation or eagerness.

"I do," he growled as he began to strip off his clothes. Every inch he revealed was tautly muscled. More quickly than seemed possible, he was down to nothing but his drawers, loosely tied with a drawstring and hanging temptingly from his—well, his hip bones, she supposed, though the prominent bulge between them surely played its part in holding up the garment. From there, her eyes could trace a line of dark hair that ran up his abdomen to spread thickly across his chest and down his forearms.

Once upon a time, she'd called him a beast.

Now, she knew it was true.

He set his good knee to the bed and crawled ever closer, dragging calloused fingertips over her body. "I'm going to kiss you here and here and here," he rasped, and this time, she understood that *she* was the cause of his sudden hoarseness, as he traced along her inner leg, raked his fingers though the forest of dark curls at the apex of her thighs, and then traveled lightly over her belly and up her breastbone. "But first I need to—" He settled his pelvis into the V of her legs, nothing separating them but a layer of fine linen.

"Yes," she hissed. She would hold him to the promised, wicked kisses... later. She canted her hips beneath him in blatant invitation. "I need you."

Distracting her with a hungry kiss, he fumbled between them to untie his drawers and shuck them over his hips. At the entrance to her body, she felt him, hot and hard. She was still slick from earlier, still eager, and without hesitation, he plunged deep inside on a single, perfect stroke that drove a moan from her lips.

"I'm so sorry, Caro," he groaned, even as he began to thrust. She wasn't sure whether he feared that he'd hurt her (far from it) or whether he was apologizing for his hunger (which she shared). Before she could reassure him, he had settled a forearm on either side of her head and levered himself upward just enough that he could look down, into her eyes. His hair fell forward in a curtain around their faces. "Sorry for all the time I've wasted, when I could have been doing this."

"Then make it up to me." She set her stockinged feet against the mattress and spread her legs wider, as far as she comfortably could, so that she would not inadvertently brush against his scarred leg and distress him, and so that nothing interfered with his pistoning hips.

"I. Intend. To."

Oh God. Had she really thought she could survive this? He held her prisoner to the exquisite pleasure of their joining with both the weight of his body and the heat of his gaze. It was an effort to keep her eyes open, not to surrender to sensation, not to try—however futilely—to cling to some small fragment of her soul. She grabbed a fistful of bedding in each hand, her nails scraping across the silken sheets.

"Put your arms around me," he ordered.

"Y-you're sure?"

Strain corded his neck. "Do it."

She lifted her arms and wrapped them lightly, carefully around his upper back. His skin was scorching, yet he shivered slightly beneath her touch, like a horse accustoming himself to the feel of a rider.

"All right?"

"Good," he grunted, shifting his body a degree or two higher, changing the angle between them from exquisite to perfection. The climax that had been hovering somewhere near the base of her spine rushed forward. On a groan, he drove deep and held himself there, and she felt the heat of his seed flooding her in spurts as she clenched tight around him.

For a moment, all between and around them fell still, quiet. The sea and the shore, the moon and the earth were in perfect harmony, neither pushing nor pulling, the tide neither rising nor ebbing. Peace.

Then a rasping breath sawed from his chest. His eyes fluttered closed, and his forehead dropped to rest against hers. She realized his arms were quivering with the strain of holding himself up, and she almost wished he would let go and press her into the bed with his full weight.

Instead, after another moment, he rolled away, onto his back, somehow bringing her pliant body with him, as if she weighed nothing at all. She found herself sprawled atop him, his arms wrapped tightly around her, her hands pinned to the mattress behind his broad shoulders, her legs still spread around his hips. She panted against his neck, relishing the way the hair on his chest tickled and teased her sensitive nipples.

He smoothed one palm down her body, his fingertips skating along the cleft in her bottom, not quite dipping into the hollow between her thighs. "I like you like this," he murmured, and she realized that though their bodies were no longer joined in this position, they could be.

She squirmed against him in anticipatory pleasure. "Oh. I never imagined." And to think, they had a lifetime together in which to discover even more.

His deep laugh stirred her hair and vibrated beneath her. "You should go back to reading Robin Ratliff novels. They'll give you ideas."

Somehow, she managed to lift herself up enough that she could kiss him. "*You* give me ideas," she whispered against his lips. Which was perfectly true…his naughty fingers were doing so, right at this very moment. But then she remembered a question she had been waiting years to ask him, made newly urgent by his revelations about his work for General Scott. "Speaking of that night, in Lord Earnshaw's library… Did you ever find what you were looking for?"

"I'm not sure what it was I expected to find," he admitted with a rueful shake of his head. "But I found what I needed." She gasped as he cinched her more tightly against his body. "I found you."

Chapter 19

Fitz had thought himself inured to frustration. But never had he known frustrations to accumulate in quite such a spectacular fashion.

The problem had started yesterday, when he'd risen from Fanny's side—hard enough to hammer nails, while she lay beneath him, sweet and soft and eager for more—and gone as promised to deliver her message of apology and concern to the Duchess of Hartwell.

When he'd returned to German Place, intending to keep quite another sort of promise, he had found waiting for him not sweet, soft, eager Fanny, but cool, reserved, proper Mrs. Drummond. If she'd brought one of those high-necked black gowns with her to Brighton, she would surely have been wearing it. She'd nodded at news of the duke's expected recovery and refused to discuss anything with Fitz but the Hartwell case.

One might have imagined that the ensuing lengthy discussion of who was trying to kill the Duke of Hartwell would have been enough to cool his ardor too, but no.

Because his cock—and not only his cock—had leaped at this morning's summons from her…only to discover that the matter of urgency once more involved a message from the duchess.

"She *is* my assignment," Fanny had reminded him, a little testily.

And you're mine, he'd wanted to growl.

Not just his assignment. *His.*

He'd left without saying anything.

He really wasn't a selfish sort. He'd meant what he'd said about pleasing her a dozen more times at least before even thinking of his own satisfaction. The fact of the matter was, he'd found pleasing her wildly satisfying in its own right.

Perhaps he hadn't done quite as grand a job of it as he'd imagined, though, if after all those years with a lout of a husband who cared not at all for her pleasure, she could sit in one of those straight-backed wooden chairs with her hands folded in her lap, not a hair out of place, not a hint of a blush on her cheeks, and address him as *Lieutenant Hopkins*.

Fanny had spent the afternoon discreetly following the duchess and her unexpected guests—evidently her family—through Brighton. And so Fitz had spent his afternoon even more discreetly trailing Fanny.

Now, the end of the day found him lurking in the shadows behind Royal Crescent, while she stood farther off, watching—for what, he couldn't be sure. He wanted to be closer to her. Much closer.

And she didn't want him at all.

If he'd been a drinking man, he might have taken recourse to his flask to drown his sorrow. But his father had been a drinking man, whose behavior had left Fitz determined never to become one. Absent the traditional consolations of whisky or woman, he contemplated alternative methods for warming his blood. The October evening had grown chilly.

But in the end, he simply thrust his balled fists into the pockets of his greatcoat, hunched his shoulders, and waited for one of the servants belonging to Number 2, Royal Crescent to appear. As long as the person who opened the back door was not the housekeeper, he might at least have an opportunity to ask a few probing questions. Mrs. Horn was nearly as impervious to his charms as Mrs. Drummond.

The first person he saw was Tilly, the younger of the two housemaids, carrying a bucket of something that she splashed into the alleyway. She paused to turn her face toward the stars and might have stayed in that posture for some time if Nan, the other housemaid, hadn't stepped out a moment later.

"Oh, there you be, Tilly. Mrs. Horn was looking for you. The duchess's sister wants hot water, and Mrs. Horn says the two old dames are like to run her ragged."

Tilly sighed. "But who's to do the dishes once Geoffrey clears the table? If the kitchen's not set to rights, I'll catch it."

"I'll do them," Nan offered. "Her Grace dismissed me for the night."

With a shrug of her shoulders, Tilly handed off the bucket and went inside. Another moment later, Geoffrey the footman appeared, a glass of wine in either hand. "There's more where this came from," he told Nan, holding one out to her. "As distracted as folks are, I don't think they'll miss it."

"From downstairs, it sounded like a row." Nan set down the empty bucket to take the goblet from him. "Was it as bad as all that, then?"

"Worse. The duke meant to kill the duchess's father, I'm certain of it. Tossed him out the front door like a pail o' slops and then charged upstairs after everyone else. Left all these half-full glasses behind. And while the cat's away..." he finished with a suggestive grin and clinked his goblet against hers.

"Mrs. Horn will have our heads if she catches us stealing from the upper table," she cautioned. But Geoffrey merely grinned and began to drink, and after a moment's hesitation, Nan followed suit.

Fitz sorted through what the fragments of their conversation had revealed. So, the unexpected visitors *had* been the duchess's family, most of whom were spending the night in Royal Crescent—also unexpectedly, if the servants' hustle and bustle was anything to go by. And as he'd overheard on the day of the visit to the circulating library, the duchess didn't get on well with her father, which might explain Hartwell's dismissal of the man.

Unfortunately, tossing him out the front door meant thrusting him into Fanny's path.

Fitz turned and hurried from the alleyway on silent feet. But when he reached the front of the house, he saw no sign of her. The black-tiled edifice glittered, an echo of the starry sky above. Moonlight cast eerie shadows, any one of which might disguise a man—or a woman. At the center of the crescent stood a poorly executed statue of the Prince of Wales—one armed, thanks to the corrosive salt air, and looking ghastlier than ever. Fitz's steps slowed as he crept from one spot to another, all the while trying to persuade himself that she would not have been so foolish as to have followed the man.

Except, of course, that she'd been precisely that foolish—no, *determined*—all day long. Determined to handle matters on her own.

"*Damn,*" he muttered beneath his breath.

From a nearby hedge he heard a quiet, but clearly disapproving, gasp. "Lieutenant Hopkins?"

Crouching, he slipped between two bushes and saw her. The moonlight silvered her hair—she'd shed her bonnet, apparently, or lost it to some wayward branch—and lent her eyes and cheeks a ghostly pallor. He had the sudden, strange sense that if he reached out a hand to grasp her, it might pass right through.

"What are you doing here?" she demanded in a fierce whisper.

"I might ask you the same thing."

"I'm here to protect the duchess."

"And just how do you propose to do that from behind this shrubbery?" She lifted a finger to point at herself. "I—"

For one glorious moment, he thought she was at a loss for words. Then her eyes widened, and she turned her finger to point at him. No, *behind* him. He tried to twist around in silence, but leaves rustled beneath the balls of his feet.

The duke's manservant, who had been descending the front steps of the house, paused to look about him. He was a slender, graceful fellow, the sort who moved on cat's feet under the most ordinary of circumstances. Difficult to determine whether he was trying to be sneaky at present. After all, if the duchess had dismissed her maid for the night, certainly the duke might also have dismissed his valet.

Apparently deciding that the noise from the shrubbery was nothing to alarm him, he moved along the path the duchess ordinarily took on her morning strolls. Fitz caught the scent of peppermint before he realized Fanny had shuffled closer to him.

"What do you suppose he's doing?" she whispered, gripping his arm as if to steady herself.

Fitz shrugged. Perhaps the fellow only wanted a bit of fresh air.

Once the man had traveled some yards down the Marine Parade, Fitz stood. Fanny, still holding his arm, rose up with him. The little noise of protest in her throat suggested that her muscles had grown stiff from crouching in the cold. "Time for you to head back to German Place, I think," he said, curving a hand beneath her elbow with the intention of directing her steps westward.

Her hair sparked like diamonds as she shook her head. "I want to know where he's headed," she insisted, walking toward the iron paling that edged the cliff.

From this vantage point, they could watch as Monsieur Leclerc descended to the beach. As he approached the row of bathing machines, he began to move more quickly, weaving among their jagged shadows so that his path became difficult to track. Perhaps ten minutes later, he reappeared and began to walk back toward the Marine Parade, his stride once more leisurely. Fitz took Fanny's arm and led her into the shadows. Not long after that, Leclerc passed in front of them and returned to the house. Within a quarter of an hour, the entire interlude was over.

"Surely, now you can return home," Fitz declared.

Once more, Fanny shook her head. "I want to know what he was doing down there, among the bathing machines."

Probably taking a piss, Fitz thought. "Why?"

"Don't you find his behavior the slightest bit suspicious?"

He'd been trained to regard everyone with suspicion. Still, he shook his head. If it took a lie to get Fanny home safe, so be it.

"Well, I do," she said. Slipping free of his hand, she set off in the direction of the bathing machines.

After a mostly silent string of epithets, Fitz followed.

The hour was not late enough to ensure they would not encounter anyone. The grand houses edging the Steyne were still brightly lit. A fine time for respectable Mrs. Drummond to be wandering about without a bonnet to disguise her distinctive hair. For a moment, he could almost regret that she'd abandoned those hideous wigs Colonel Millrose had once insisted she wear.

Thankfully, they descended to the beach without being seen. The row of bathing machines looked perfectly unremarkable, drawn up into the shelter of the cliff face. High tide left only a narrow strip of pebbled strand between them and the water. Fanny picked her way across it with surprising dexterity.

"If you wish to give the duchess a full report on her servants' after-hours activities," Fitz said, catching up to her when she paused to examine the fourth bathing machine from the end, "you should also mention that her footman and her upper housemaid are carrying on beneath her nose." Fanny sent him a skeptical, sidelong glance. "I watched Geoffrey try to win Nan over with a glass of wine lifted from the duke's dinner table. It seems the family abandoned their meal in the furor over the duchess's father," he explained.

"Yes, I know. I heard the duke tell him to..." Her gaze darted away and her voice dipped to a whisper. "Go to hell."

"Good for him," Fitz declared, earning a wide-eyed flare of surprise from Fanny. "From what she told you the other day about her father, Hartwell was in the right to do it. It's a gentleman's duty to protect his lady."

Fanny sighed and moved on to the next bathing machine, and he remembered too late her ambivalence toward protective men. But just as her hand reached for the door, she paused. "Did you say...did you say that Geoffrey was drinking the duchess's wine?"

"I'm not sure whose particular glass he'd snatched, but yes."

"And is that...common behavior among servants, do you suppose?"

He shrugged, stepping carefully over the iron tongue of one of the contraptions, the means by which it was hauled into the water. "Must be hard to see it all go to waste."

She nodded, thoughtful. "But if it were a habit..."

"What are you getting at?"

"The morning the duchess was taken ill," she said, turning toward him so abruptly they nearly collided, "Geoffrey was too. And the only explanation anyone ever gave was something they'd both eaten. But Mrs. Horn was adamant that the duchess never eats before her walks. So what if…" Though her gaze was far away, she stood close enough that he could soak in her sweetly spicy scent. "What if it was something they both drank? Wasn't there…?" She screwed her eyes shut for a moment, then opened them wide again, latching onto his. "When the duke carried her upstairs, there was a coffeepot sitting on the table on the landing. Outside her bedchamber door."

"Are you suggesting the duchess's servants were trying to poison her?"

Doubt flickered into her eyes and she turned away again, laying her hand not on his chest, as he'd hoped, but onto the painted wood of the bathing machine. "No. No, of course not. That would be…that would be ludicrous. Because everyone knew she took nothing before she went out…" He could practically hear the gears turning in her head. When she spoke again, excitement once more raised her voice. "So that coffee must have been left there for the duke."

"You think the duchess's servants were trying to poison the duke?"

"No. Look." Her fingertips were tracing a mark carved into the door of the bathing machine. No mere incidental scratch. An X, small but definite. And recent too. The wood beneath was pale, unweathered. "What if the duke's valet intended to poison him? What if he—he—?"

"Don't get ahead of yourself," Fitz cautioned, raising his own hand to follow hers over the wood. "Hartwell would have taken every precaution to make sure such an intimate associate was trustworthy. He brought him back to England, for God's sake."

"I hope you don't mean to suggest that General Scott's men are incapable of misjudging?"

In spite of the seriousness of the moment, Fitz narrowed his eyes at that direct hit. "I wouldn't dare, Mrs. Drummond."

She ignored him. "It makes perfect sense. You know it does. Leclerc left the coffee, intending for the duke to drink it. Instead, the duchess did—and passed her not quite empty cup to the footman as she left the house. And…and Leclerc was also the one who arranged for the boat that sank. Now he's…" Her hand slapped the wood in frustration. "He's what? What was he doing down here?"

"This could have been a rendezvous point. Or a place where a message had been left." He opened the little door and climbed the slatted wooden steps.

He'd never been inside a bathing machine before. All was dark. The piney scent of cedar mingled with brine and a vaguely musty dampness. Even with his head bent, he was conscious of the low ceiling. When he took a step forward, his shin collided with a bench built along the back. Ladies willingly undressed inside these rickety little boxes and let themselves be dragged out to sea? With outstretched hands, he felt all around the walls for a crack, a niche, a loose board: anywhere a note might be hidden.

When his questing fingertips encountered Fanny—specifically, Fanny's bosom—he froze. "I—I didn't realize you'd come inside."

"Aren't you going to move your hand, Lieutenant Hopkins?" Some of the primness in her voice had been replaced by a trembling note.

He grazed the pad of his thumb over her nipple, feeling a surge of triumph as it peaked beneath his touch. "Like this, Fanny?"

"Fitz." Hardly more than a breath of sound. Certainly not a scold. And then, "We can't."

"We already did," he reminded her. "And I had been very much looking forward to doing it again."

"*I* can't," she insisted, even as she stepped closer, her breast filling his hand. "I *can't*." In the darkness, her lips sought and found his. She tasted of peppermint drops. "I can't."

He dragged his mouth across hers and wrapped his other arm around her, the search for a hidden message momentarily forgotten. "Why not?"

"Because." Her hands came to rest on his chest, her fingertips curling into his coat at first, then flattening to push him ever so slightly away. "Because it would ruin everything."

It took all his strength to release her, and the cramped quarters made it impossible for them to get far enough apart not to touch. "How so?"

She pushed open the door, which let in a gust of fresh sea air and the faintest trace of moonlight, enough that he could pick out her delicate profile. "What you did to me yesterday was...extraordinary. I never knew—" Her head sank. "In some ways, I wish I still didn't. That's the sort of knowledge that could ruin a woman."

"But what a way to go, eh?" he tried to tease.

"It's no joking matter, Fitz. Not to me. Don't you see? I...I can't let myself need you. All my life I've been defined by my relation to a man: a daughter, a wife, a widow. I've done what's expected, what's proper. I've stayed in. I've kept house. But now? Now I'm a spy." She breathed excitement into the word, the promise of adventure. "And I don't want to go back to what I was before."

"I see. And you think that if we—"

"Do more of *that*—"

"You'll have to—"

"Give it all up. Colonel Millrose will know how weak I am, how womanish. General Scott will insist we marry."

Given the general's propensity for matchmaking, Fitz rather thought he might try to insist on it, regardless. "And you don't want that?"

"I...don't. It's nothing to do with you," she quickly added, reaching for him in the darkness.

Until his sister's recent, and unexpected, decision to wed, he had not given much thought to his own matrimonial prospects. He liked his work well enough not to be in any hurry to settle down, and General Scott seemed to expect men to choose domesticity over danger and leave his service when they married, though there had been a few notable exceptions to that rule.

"Oh, it's *something* to do with me, I'd say. After all, you're deciding my future too."

He felt as much as heard her swift intake of breath. "You mean, you thought of pr-proposing?"

Had he? Truth be told, his thoughts regarding Fanny had been neither coherent nor gentlemanly. He only knew he wanted her. Desperately.

Enough to want her to be happy.

"This is hardly the place for a discussion about it," he said, dipping his head to brush a silencing kiss across her lips before ducking through the low door and descending the three wooden steps.

"Nor the time," she agreed as he reached up to help her down. "We've got to—"

"Warn the duke and duchess? Not just yet." He peered into the bathing machine behind her. The blade of moonlight slicing through the doorway revealed no sign of a hidden message. Though of course Leclerc might just as easily have been retrieving as leaving one. "I'd like a little more than raw speculation about thirsty servants and tainted coffee before revealing myself to a possible double agent. I've given enough of myself to the French already."

She cut her gaze away, her lips parted on an inaudible gasp. "How could I have forgotten what you went through?"

"Don't get me wrong, Fan," he said, reaching out a hand, careful not to touch her, but to wait until she laid her fingers in his. "But I'd rather you didn't spend your time thinking of it too."

She'd been there, of course, when he'd returned to the Underground, weak and battered, both body and spirit bearing the marks of the tortures he'd endured. She'd covered him with blankets, for the Underground was cool despite the hot summer weather. She'd brought him strained soups and mashed vegetables, until his teeth had decided whether to stay in his gums.

No surprise, he supposed, that he had fallen a little bit in love with her. And no wonder that she did not regard him with the same passion. He'd been captured. He couldn't even say he'd been strong enough not to give up any secrets, because the truth was, he hadn't been important enough to know any. He'd found the codebook quite by happenstance, passed it to a stranger on the street when it became clear he was being followed, and prayed his fellow spies would be able to find it—and him—again. Hardly the stuff of heroes.

"I've been so excited about the possibility," she said, her voice almost too quiet to be heard over the rumble of the tide, "I pushed aside all my fears of the reality. The dangers..."

He squeezed her hand, trying to offer reassurance. "You'll make an excellent secret agent, then. Because that's what you have to do, carry on despite the risks."

Her fingers curled around his in an implacable grip. "Despite the risks," she echoed. Her expression suggested she was about to say something more.

But at just that moment, a low, terrible groan came from a neighboring bathing machine.

Fitz cursed under his breath, wishing he were armed. Fanny strained toward the sound. "I think someone must be hurt," she whispered. He nodded and motioned her back, to indicate he would investigate. Her eyes rolled—to her credit, the motion was slight; it might not have been visible if not for the moonlight sparkling in them—and she reached for his hand. "Together," she mouthed.

They stepped toward the next bathing machine in line, almost identical to the one they'd been examining. The door, Fitz realized belatedly, hung open a fraction of an inch, as if impeded by something. Had they misjudged which bathing machine Leclerc had visited? After another squeeze of Fanny's fingers, Fitz freed his right hand and formed it into a fist as he reached for the door with his left.

A man's head lolled out into the opening, and even in the moonlight it was easy enough to guess that the dark smear at the corner of his brow was blood. His hair was matted with it, in fact. With unseeing eyes, he stared up at them, silent now. Fitz wondered whether the groan they had heard had been the man's last.

"It's Caro's father," Fanny breathed. "Is he—?"

"I'm not sure." After a quick look inside the bathing machine, to make certain the attacker no longer lay in wait, Fitz bent and laid his ear against

the man's chest. After a moment, he found a faint pulse. "Not yet. But…"
Grabbing the duchess's father under his arms, he dragged him almost from
the bathing machine. "Catch his feet." Fanny nodded, taking a booted heel
in each hand. "We'll have to carry him. Can you manage?"

"I'm not as frail as some people think." And indeed, she had not quailed
at the sight of blood. She bore her share of the man's weight without
complaint as they made their way back along the beach.

"Trefrey's house isn't far."

"Who would do such a thing?" Fanny asked as they approached the
physician's establishment.

But wasn't it obvious? Fanny herself had said the duke was dangerous.
He'd forcibly expelled the duchess's father from his house, and all but wished
him dead. He must have sent his supposed manservant to finish the job.

The question was why—and would the duchess be next?

Chapter 20

At the first gray light of dawn, Maxim awoke to find his wife snuggled against his chest. Sweeping a few strands of hair from her face, he fought the temptation to rouse her with kisses. He still couldn't get enough of her. But after the night they'd passed, she surely needed her sleep.

The mere memory curved his lips in a wicked smile, but he slid his arm from beneath her neck and eased himself from the bed before he could act on the impulse. After gathering up last night's wrinkled clothes from the floor, he put them on again. He did not think his mother-in-law would appreciate him barging back into his former bedchamber at this hour for fresh ones.

On restless, silent feet, and with only two backward glances at Caro's sleeping form, he left the room. All was silent; even the servants seemed not yet to be about their daily tasks. A chill had settled over the house. Well, he could wait to ring for coffee or a fire. He did not want to incommode Mrs. Horn. An excellent housekeeper was worth her weight in gold, and he did not intend to give her any excuse to leave.

He would occupy the time writing letters, arranging certain matters of business. Sellers would be surprised—and not so secretly pleased—by his benevolent turn. But Maxim wanted information first. Details about Brent-Ashby's debts. Some sense of the character of the man with whom Lady Catherine fancied herself in love, according to Caro. Lady Laughton's history with her laudanum-laced "tonic." So he steered his steps toward the drawing room and Caro's ridiculous little writing desk.

When he saw the faint seam of light beneath the rear door to the drawing room, his first foolish thought was that he had misjudged the hour after all, and one of the maids had already laid a fire. But why start here? He supposed it might have been light from the windows that made the room comparatively bright. Its warmth suggested a flame, though. Perhaps some member of the Brent family had already risen, come down, and lit a candle?

Beside the door that gave on to the forward part of the drawing room, he paused with caution and listened. Not a sound came from within. When he laid a hand on the door, he half expected to find it locked. But the knob turned easily, silently in his hand. Peering through the narrow opening, he focused first on the desk on the far side of the room, where he supposed Lady Catherine might be penning a letter to her gentleman friend.

What he saw instead made so little sense he at first distrusted his eyes. "*Qu'est-ce que tu fais?*" he demanded of Leclerc as he burst into the room. The man was seated cross-legged on the floor, surrounded by neat piles of papers from the crate Sellers had sent and Caro had opened. A single wax taper in a candlestick illuminated the circle.

Leclerc looked up, unperturbed, almost unsurprised. "Organizing, sir," he answered in French, as he laid a letter atop a pile with one hand while reaching into the crate with the other. He made no motion to rise. "Is it not my job to assist you?" He peered at the document he'd fished from the box before deciding where to put it.

Maxim answered by shutting the door behind him and stepping closer. "*Mais oui.* And yet I would not have thought of giving you such a task."

"*Porquoi?*" Leclerc gave a thin smile as he reached into the crate again.

"Because those papers are written in English."

The young man glanced around him, blinking as if in surprise. "So they are," he said, his English accented but flawless.

"You can speak English?"

That ridiculous question was answered with the contempt it deserved. "And read it too. Yes, Monsieur le Duc, my command of your tongue is almost as good as yours of mine. It has…how you say?...come in handy over the years."

"Handy? How so?" Maxim's mind whirled, trying both to make sense of what he saw before him and to figure out what he must do next.

Leclerc shook his head. "Really, sir, you disappoint me. You were cleverer before you let yourself grow besotted by your wife."

The joke was on Leclerc—Maxim had been besotted by Caro long before he'd met the man. "You read my papers. You know the real reason I was in France," he said. "You figured out what I managed to uncover of the French plans and shared it with those who could use it to anticipate the English response." He took another step closer. "You're the reason I'm suspected of being a double agent."

"Oh, very good," he replied with a nod, though his eyes narrowed. "Although you never made it easy. You are a man who likes to keep his secrets."

"Is that what you expect to find in there?" Maxim jerked his chin toward the crate. "My secrets?"

"Quite honestly, I assumed the box was merely a—a decoy. Until you made such a fuss when the duchess and her friend peeked inside."

Maxim muttered a curse beneath his breath. "Why did you insist on coming with me to England?"

"Never before had you delivered your message to your superiors in person, so I could guess that you had discovered something *très important*. My assignment was to slow your progress, give my fellow agents a chance to sow doubt about whatever story you planned to tell."

With the dispassionate clarity of a fellow spy, Maxim could sense the truth of Leclerc's story. "And you decided that the best way to keep me from reporting to London was to drown me?"

"Not at first, no."

"Not at first..." Anger simmered in Maxim's gut like a well-stoked fire as he recalled Mrs. Drummond's suspicions. "Good God. Caro's illness. You—you—"

"No, no, Monsieur le Duc. It was never my intention to harm your lovely lady wife. I left that tainted coffee for *you*...."

Maxim remembered the cold coffeepot he'd spied on the landing that terrible morning. Caro must have poured herself a cup on her way out.

"It was, I confess, a dose calculated for someone larger," he said, looking Maxim up and down. "I hoped that in the throes of illness, you might reveal something interesting. But alas." One shoulder rose and fell.

"*Alas?*" Maxim echoed, no longer quiet. "*Alas?* You might have killed her by mistake. Then there was the incident with the boat. Not an accident, I presume?" Leclerc shrugged. "And I suppose that dose of laudanum you offered me afterward..."

"It would have made you very sleepy." Leclerc made a rocking motion with his flattened hand, moving lower with each sweep. "You would have slid deeper and deeper into your tub, until your bathwater managed to do what the English Channel could not." When he reached his knee, he slapped it. "Very bad form of you to break the glass."

"Drowning me would seem to make it more difficult to discover all my secrets." He sent another glance toward the crate.

Leclerc lifted his brows. "*Oui.* But perhaps I no longer care about those. An agent's orders are subject to change, as you well know."

The sun had risen high enough that the light of the candle was no longer needed to see the other man's expression clearly, though the sky itself could hardly be called bright. How long before someone else in the house rose and interrupted this cozy tête-à-tête? What did Leclerc mean to do then?

Maxim folded his arms over his chest. "What now?" he asked, trying to sound as if the answer were inconsequential.

"Now?" Leclerc unfolded his legs and pushed to standing. The hand that had been dangling inside the crate reappeared, clutching a small pistol. "Now I mean to keep you quiet forever. No more playing Frenchman, Monsieur le Duc. You will die as an Englishman, wet with your own piss and tears."

In spite of himself and the grim situation, Maxim laughed, a mere gust of sound, dry with irony. Once, he would have begged for a bullet to be rid of his pain. Now that such a remedy was at last on offer, he had every reason to live. "I would not be so sure, Leclerc," he answered, shifting back to French. Had he not already proved himself a fighter?

Leclerc's delicate mien ought to have been incompatible with the pistol, but he handled it with assurance. "Perhaps you would prefer to watch your pretty little wife die first?"

Maxim would have laughed off that remark as well, merely another empty threat, if he had not at that moment heard Caro's delicate tread descending the stairs.

She was going for her usual walk, he supposed, and he might have been glad to have her out of the house if she did not have to pass by the doors of this very room on her way. Had she heard their voices? Had she wondered at his rising early? Would she stop to speak with him?

He tried to take a step backward, in order to block the closest door, but his bad leg wobbled beneath the unequal distribution of his weight. Leclerc shook his head, at once a pitying gesture and a warning. "No, no, monsieur. It is not for you to choose who dies first."

Sweat broke out on Maxim's brow when her footsteps paused on the landing. He heard a creak of hesitation, but both doors remained closed, and in another moment, she had gone on her way. In the entry hall, he heard her speak—to Geoffrey, he presumed—and finally the front door of the house closed with a thud.

Leclerc shrugged and lifted the pistol to sight along its barrel. "It seems Fate has spoken."

"Wait."

One brow arced; the pistol did not move a fraction of an inch. "*Porquoi?*"

Why, indeed? Better to let the man get on with it now, while Caro was out of the house. Leclerc would be gone before she returned and before any of her family came downstairs and found themselves caught in the crossfire.

But that damned instinct for survival would not let him surrender so easily.

"If you looked at the papers in that crate, you must have some idea how wealthy I am now. Surely there must be something that would tempt you to reconsider your plans?"

"Oh, monsieur." He chuckled. "I have long suspected *your* motives for spying. You have no home, no family. No loyalty. But *my* heart belongs to France. I cannot be bought with your English pounds and pence." He laughed again, derisively. "You are as pathetic as your father-in-law when you beg."

"My father-in-law?"

"Lord Laughton, eh? When you threw him out so unceremoniously, he made his way down to the beach. I believe he meant to make his bed in one of those silly contraptions, the huts with wheels...."

"A bathing machine?" Maxim suggested, incredulous.

"Just so. Alas for him, I had arranged to pick up a message from a colleague in that very spot. When I realized he had seen me, I knew I couldn't let him get away. He offered me anything I wished to secure his freedom. I knew already he had nothing of value—*you* had made that clear. So—" He mimed striking someone with the butt of his pistol, and then tipped his head to the side, tongue lolling, to show the result of the blow. "A pity."

Maxim sucked in a breath, feeling not guilt over Laughton's fate, exactly, but concern for Caro, who was too tenderhearted to wish her father dead. Once more, the burden of caring for her family would fall on her shoulders. And if Leclerc succeeded where so many had failed, she would have to bear that burden alone. A wealthy widow, just as he'd said.

"A message, you say?" What did he hope to gain by stalling? The footman had surely accompanied Caro. Brent-Ashby was the last man in the house, not precisely reliable, and probably sound asleep. "About me?"

"You think always of yourself. But when you are gone, the war will continue—for a little while. I am to go to London, however, and see to it that your General Scott has given his last order."

Maxim's skeptical reaction to those words was not feigned. "And how do you propose to get to him?"

"Oh, monsieur. I am but a humble valet, dragged to foreign shores by my employer. When I explain to your general how great your suffering had been, how you took your own life when the laudanum no longer kept the pain at bay… How, near the end, the opium loosed your lips…" Another artful shrug. "He will want to know what I know. And I will tell him just enough to persuade him to trust me, just as I once persuaded you."

"*Bâtard*," Maxim spat.

"*À toi de même.*" He gestured with the pistol as if it were a wineglass. "From one bastard to another."

Blood thundered in Maxim's ears, loud enough to drown out the constant swish and sway of the tide outside the window. But long practice made it possible to drive back the slur's sting. For years the image that he had called to mind in such moments had been that of his sainted mother. Now, however, he could think of no one but Caro, for whom he had to remain calm and in control. He had survived far worse than this. He had survived.

Leclerc cocked his head in a listening posture and made a clicking noise with his mouth. "How unfortunate. It would seem the duchess has already returned. And I have hardly decided which will give me the greater satisfaction: to kill you first, or to watch the hope drain from your eyes as the life drains from her body."

Maxim strained to hear the footsteps. *Not Caro's,* he thought. At least, not hers alone. Then whose?

"Open the door, Monsieur le Duc, and welcome our guest. But do not think of stepping through it. I would not hesitate to shoot you in the back."

Reluctantly, Maxim turned, bracing every moment for the searing pain of the bullet, uncertain even for whose intercession he ought to pray. Laying his hand on the doorknob, he counted to three, drew a deep breath, and opened the door a crack. Pale blue eyes met his.

"Mrs. Drummond?!"

"Good morning, Your Grace." Despite his effort to keep her from entering the room, she slipped past and sailed inside, slicing through the tension in the air. "I hope I'm not interrupting. I had hoped to speak with the duchess before she went out, but the housemaid who answered the door told me I missed her. If it's not too great an inconvenience, I will simply wait here until she returns."

"I think, ma'am, it would be best…" He glanced toward Leclerc, whose face was etched in a scowl, and who was gesturing with tiny movements of his shoulders and jaw for Maxim to order her from the room. The gun had, for the moment, disappeared from view. "It would be best if you made yourself comfortable," he finished, realizing the benefit of her presence. "I cannot say how long Caro will be gone. Shall I ring for some refreshment?"

"Not necessary, thank you." She moved deeper into the front portion of the room, wending her way among the various groupings of chairs and sofas, though she did not sit down. With each step she took, Leclerc was forced to turn to keep his pistol hidden, until his back was to the wall, opposite the fireplace.

She knew. She must know—no one could be so lucky with her movements. And, after all, she had been sent to Brighton by the foremost expert in British intelligence, a man who did not suffer fools. Scott had seen this ability in her, had known that ice water ran through her veins.

"Is your manservant below, Mrs. Drummond?" Maxim asked, stepping away from the door and putting enough distance between himself and Mrs. Drummond that Leclerc could not track both of them easily. "I'd like his assistance in the removal of that crate. It's too heavy for Leclerc alone."

The supposed valet cleared his throat reprovingly, but Mrs. Drummond ignored both him and the contents of the crate, strewn across the floor behind him. "I'm afraid he is not, Your Grace. The moment we arrived in Royal Crescent, I dispatched him on another errand."

Her expression was so impassive, he could not determine what those words might mean. He prayed the young man was fetching reinforcements or leading the others in the household to safety. He could not like the idea of keeping a woman in danger, but right now, the distraction she had provided was the only thing standing between him and Leclerc's bullet, the only thing standing between Caro and a wardrobe of unrelieved black.

He was going to have to trust that the agents Scott had sent to keep an eye on him were capable of doing their job.

"Are you always out and about this early, Mrs. Drummond?" he asked. He had noticed, finally, how disheveled she looked. The hems of her gown and pelisse were dirty, she wore no gloves, and her hair was tumbled, far worse than it would be from the mere removal of a bonnet. And she was fatigued, too—her light eyes were underlined by shadows so dark they might have been bruises.

"Your good lady has taught me the benefit of a morning constitutional along the strand, and now I wouldn't miss it for the world." She gestured toward the view out the bow window but did not turn toward it. "The air here in Brighton is so fresh and clear. Of course, anything would be, in comparison to town."

Maxim watched Leclerc fidget, still trying to pass himself off as a servant, though a true servant would have left the room when Mrs. Drummond entered. He had crossed both arms behind his back, so as not to draw attention to his attempt to hide his weapon.

"Ah, yes. You said you came from London. I had forgotten." Maxim could feel his desperation rising, straining to listen for some sound—Caro's return, a rescue attempt—and hardly daring to hope. Despite being knocked off balance, Leclerc still had the upper hand, and any move Maxim might make would further endanger Mrs. Drummond.

"What can you tell me about this painting, Your Grace?" She stepped toward the far wall and nodded at a framed print of a watercolor. "I have often wondered about it."

Maxim had never even noticed it before. It depicted a stretch of the strand below, though under stormier conditions. He wondered who had purchased it for the house. His wife?

Understanding that the question had been intended to draw him across the room, he moved closer, albeit reluctantly. Mrs. Drummond might have a strategy in mind, but so did Leclerc, and lining up the man's targets would seem to forward his plan, rather than hers.

As he had predicted, Leclerc turned too, pleased to be able to watch the pair of them more easily. The set of his shoulders relaxed, and one of his arms came forward almost to hang at his side, though his hand—the one holding the pistol—was still hidden behind his leg.

"A thrilling scene, is it not?" Maxim asked, flicking his eyes to the painting and back to Leclerc, his gaze crossing Mrs. Drummond's in the process.

She appeared cool and collected, more so than she had since entering the room. Good God, had her assignment been to draw him into the line of fire?

"Yes, indeed," she answered, her voice rising. "One can almost hear the crashing waves. See how the lone figure of the woman creates an oasis of calm amid the storm?"

Those words drew Maxim's notice firmly to the painting in spite of himself. Since he had never paid it any mind before, it certainly was no surprise he had never noticed the woman, tiny against the backdrop of a wild sea, her dress and veil whipped by the wind. He thought of what Caro had told him the day before, about how she had forced herself to face the remorseless water, though it frightened her, because she had imagined it would prepare her to face him again one day. Some local artist must have managed to capture one of those moments in which she had stood, buffeted by the storm but not backing down. Her fierceness stole his breath.

He loved her. He'd foreseen himself falling in love with her six years ago, and he'd expected the emotion to bring with it nothing but pain and a terrifying loss of control. But now the realization suffused him with

warm and strength. He loved her. And if he had to die today, he would
not do so without telling her.

With a new determination he turned back to face Leclerc. Mrs.
Drummond had positioned them so Leclerc's back was to the room's far
door, and now Maxim understood why. Fortunately, Mrs. Horn made
certain all the door hinges did not squeak, for Mr. Hopkins and Caro's
brother had entered the room behind him, any noise they made muffled
by Mrs. Drummond's enthusiasm over the painting.

The pair crept toward an unknowing Leclerc, Brent-Ashby in his
nightclothes and Hopkins in the lead, his rumpled breeches streaked with
dirt. Though the pair appeared to be unarmed, they had the advantage
of surprise. Maxim only narrowly managed to keep his expression from
revealing his relief and giving away the game. Instead he forced himself to
turn back toward the painting and Mrs. Drummond, positioning himself so
that he was between her and Leclerc as the man slowly raised his weapon
and sighted along it.

Out of the corner of his eye, Maxim saw Hopkins lunge, catching Leclerc
behind the knees and driving him forward. The pistol discharged as the
man hit the floor with a shouted oath. Glass shattered, and the ordinarily
calm and collected Mrs. Drummond shrieked.

But the bullet had not struck her, or anyone else. Only the beautiful bow
window at the front of the house, which now let in a rush of cool morning
air through a broken pane. After ascertaining that Mrs. Drummond was
unharmed, Maxim hurried toward the scuffle in the center of the room.

Leclerc was prone on the floor, spewing a steady string of epithets in
French. Hopkins had one knee in the middle of his back, pinning his arms
with one hand while gesturing with the other for something to tie them.
After a flustered moment of searching, Brent-Ashby untied his dressing
gown and offered him the sash. "I say, that was rather thrilling, wasn't it?"

"A little too thrilling, I'd say."

The reply came from near the door. His ears still ringing from the
gunshot, Maxim hadn't heard it open. But his wife stood there now, pale
faced and wide eyed as she looked from the struggling Leclerc sprawled in
front of the empty hearth to Mrs. Drummond near the shattered window.

Maxim hurried toward her, kicking aside the pistol as he went. "Caro.
Thank God you're safe." Heedless of the company, he gathered her into
his arms, not sure this time whether she or he trembled most. "I love you,
Caro. I love you."

When she looked up, he could see that her cheeks were flushed with pink
and golden sparks twinkled in her eyes. "After last night," she answered in

a whisper that must nonetheless have been audible to the other occupants of the room, "I did have some inkling of it."

He was gratified to hear that he had succeeded in showing her what he felt, both through his offer to care for her family and, he hoped, in the hours he had spent worshipping her body. He had every intention of continuing to show her how much he loved her. But...

"I wanted you to hear the words."

The glittering brightness of her eyes was dimmed by a sudden rush of tears. She nodded, the movement wobbly. "Yes." And then she said something he could hardly remember ever having heard before, and never in English. "I love you too, Maxim." Palms against his chest, she pushed up onto her toes and brushed her lips against his. "Always."

Mrs. Drummond's sob and Brent-Ashby's gruff clearing of his throat reminded Maxim they were not alone in the room. Reluctantly, he set his wife on her feet and turned to face the others. Hopkins grinned as he stood, having secured Leclerc's hands and taken advantage of the length of the dressing gown's sash to tie the man's ankles as well. "Sorry about your window, Your Grace."

Leclerc continued to swear in words likely Maxim alone could make out—he didn't know about Brent-Ashby's or Hopkins's education, but Caro's English governess had never taught her those particular French phrases, he felt certain. Nevertheless, Maxim unwound his cravat from his neck, stepped toward the prisoner, and stuffed the wadded length of linen in the man's mouth, effectively stoppering the string of invective.

"I'm grateful to you," he said to Hopkins, then turned to incorporate Mrs. Drummond into his gratitude. "To both of you." He'd been thinking of their presence in Brighton as an annoyance, an interference. Now he saw them for what they were: fellow agents and, more importantly, allies. "But how did you know?"

Hopkins nodded toward Caro. "The duchess overheard enough of your conversation with this fellow"—he paused to press the sole of his boot into Leclerc's back, forcing him to emit a muffled groan—"to guess that something was awry. She came to find us."

"I did," Caro agreed, stepping close enough to slip her hand into Maxim's. "As you once remarked, this house isn't much for privacy. I'm glad Mrs. Drummond and Lieutenant Hopkins's plan was successful. But if no one here was hurt,"—she gestured with their twined fingers toward the smears of what Maxim had taken for dirt on Hopkins's clothes—"won't someone explain whose blood that is?"

Chapter 21

"If I may, Your Grace," Fanny said, stepping forward before Fitz could speak. The look in the duchess's eyes was less cool and distant than Fanny had expected, which only made it more difficult to say what had to be said. "Lieutenant Hopkins and I saw the duke's manservant leave the house last night. We followed him down to the strand and discovered a badly injured man in one of the bathing machines—your father."

"Is he—?" The duchess gasped, and the sound drove a dagger into Fanny's breast.

"He's in the care of Dr. Trefrey," Fitz explained gently. The Duke of Hartwell made a skeptical noise in the back of his throat. "He'd suffered a blow to the head and hasn't regained consciousness, but Trefrey believes there's every chance he still may...."

The breath that the duchess had sucked in left her now in a shaky rush. "Oh." Fanny saw the duke grip his wife's fingers more tightly.

Fanny understood, perhaps better than most, the welter of emotions that struck upon hearing such news about a man one had wanted to love but found oneself despising instead. Shock. Sorrow. Relief. Guilt.

The other young man, who bore such a resemblance to the duchess he could only be her brother, stepped forward, gathering the sides of his dressing gown to cover his nightshirt. "With your permission, Your Grace," he said, addressing the duke, "I'll dress and go to him."

Hartwell nodded once, grimly. A shiver passed through his wife, and she stiffened against it, as if gathering her resolve. "I should go tell Mama and Aunt Brent," she said.

The duke lifted her fingers to his lips and kissed them. "Yes, my love. And Mrs. Drummond and Lieutenant Hopkins must prepare to return to

London and report what's happened. I'll stay with Leclerc until Geoffrey can fetch the constable."

Vaguely, Fanny wondered whether Leclerc would still be alive when the constable arrived if left in the duke's, er, *care*. But she couldn't muster much sympathy for him, particularly not with Fitz at her side, urging her toward the door.

She stepped toward them, toward the duchess, and reached out a hand. "I'm sorry, Your Grace. Sorry for deceiving you. Mrs. Scott only wanted to ensure that you were safe, and the general—well." She would not presume to speak for General Scott. "But please believe I did not lie about my esteem for you. If I may be so bold, I think we could have been true friends, under different circumstances."

"Dear Fanny," Caro said, releasing her husband's hand to take the one she had extended to her. "You never hid your heart. I believe we *will* be true friends. As soon as I return to London, we shall visit all the best bookshops together, yes?"

"That would be lovely, C-Caro," Fanny managed to say around the lump that had formed in her throat. Of all the adventures and excitement she had imagined would surround her first mission, she had certainly never imagined finding a friend.

Or a lover. Fitz's fingertips resting lightly against her waist were warm, even through the layers of her dress and pelisse. With a bow of his head to the duke and duchess, he directed Fanny out the door and down the stairs, pausing to speak with Geoffrey to relay the duke's instructions before escorting her from the house. Whatever fragments of a servant's demeanor he had managed to piece together, he had now shed entirely, as he walked beside her, with his hand beneath her elbow. Once it would have seemed to her a sign of possessiveness. Now she understood it could also be a gesture of support.

He would have pointed their steps toward German Place, but Fanny paused beside the iron paling that separated them from the strand and stood looking over the water. She couldn't honestly say she would miss the seaside, but she was more than a little apprehensive about what awaited her in London, Caro's offer notwithstanding. Would she be expected to return to the Underground and resume the dull, matronly part she'd been playing for the past year? Was another future even possible?

She glanced over her shoulder and found Fitz with his eyes closed and his face tipped toward the weak sunlight. He put her in mind of a lion, his posture of drowsy ease disguising something dangerous.

But that wasn't really fair to him. The greatest danger lay within her, in her attraction to him. Because just as she'd told him, if she gave in to it, she feared she would find herself trapped for sure.

"Did you mean it?" she began abruptly. "Last night, when you hinted that you might propose to me?"

His eyes popped open, but he didn't immediately look down at her. "Honestly? I'm not sure."

Why did those words make her chest ache? She hadn't wanted a proposal from him. And yet...

"I understand why you would be reluctant to rush into marriage again." He wrapped one hand around a fence post. "And I—well, I didn't exactly grow up with an excellent model for how to be a husband." When his knuckles whitened, she reached out to lay her fingers over them. "Or a father."

"I can't have children." She pushed the whispered words past her lips in a rush, not even sure why she needed him to know.

"Can't?" he echoed, sounding dubious. "If you did not conceive during your marriage, the problem might just as easily have been Drummond's."

"Oh." Heat rushed into her cheeks. "I...I hadn't considered that."

"Not that it matters, either way," he insisted, at last turning his face to hers. "I like children well enough, but it can't have escaped your notice that I haven't a fancy title to pass along, like Hartwell. I only have a pretty little stone manor house that I inherited when my father died." His gaze drifted past her. "I really ought to sell it. I don't see myself settling down in the country."

With her first finger, she began to connect the scattering of freckles on the back of his hand. "Never?"

He shrugged. "I like my work."

"I like your work too," she confessed after a moment. "That's strange, isn't it? For a woman?"

"Why?" He frowned. "Why shouldn't you like a bit of excitement? Why shouldn't you want to use your talents to help defeat the French? You've got the makings of a first-rate agent, Fanny. You can get people to open up to you, tell you their secrets. You're quick thinking and tenacious. You're brave."

"Thank you. But I doubt General Scott or Colonel Millrose will see it that way."

"You do them a disservice, Fan. Neither of them is what you might call conventional. If they were, what sort of intelligence operation would we have? If they were, you wouldn't be here now."

"These were extraordinary circumstances. That doesn't mean they'll be willing to send a woman—me—out into the field again."

Fitz fell silent for a moment. The air around them was punctuated by birdsong, snippets of conversation from the people walking along the Marine Parade, the clop of horses' hooves. Those sharper notes were rounded out by a deeper tone, the constant, low rumble of the water. "I predict they will see the value of having a lady spy," he said at last. "But it's true that I don't think they will want you going about on assignment all on your own."

"You mean, they would send an officer to accompany me?" She tried to tamp down the hope that rose into her chest. "Disguised as my manservant, or perhaps my cousin?" she asked, echoing General Scott's suggestion.

"Maybe even your betrothed." Fitz had said as much once before, and though he smiled as he spoke, there was something else hidden in his expression.

She slid her hand over his, up his arm to his shoulder, where she made a project of pretending to dust away some imaginary lint. "Would I get to choose my partner, do you suppose?"

At the word *partner*, he turned his whole body toward her, so that her palm came to rest against his chest, an increasingly familiar posture—caught between warning him away and drawing him close.

"I don't know what to do, Fitz. I meant what I said last night—I can't go back to who I was before. I want something else, something more out of life. But I also want you." Heat prickled in her cheeks, but she made herself hold his gaze. "I want you to keep that promise you made the other day. A dozen more times, wasn't it? And I want—I want you to teach me how to return the favor."

She felt rather than heard the growl that rumbled through him. "God, Fanny. If we were back in German Place, I'd—"

"I know. That's why I wanted to have this conversation here." Though, given the molten steel of his eyes, she wasn't sure even this place was quite public enough to keep him from kissing her senseless. "If General Scott finds out we're lovers, you know what he'll do."

"I suspect he'd make another tally mark on his list of matches, don't you? But maybe he won't figure it out."

She cocked a skeptical brow. "Be serious. And if anyone else finds out, there'll be a scandal."

"So?"

"Spoken like a man," she tossed back with a sigh of exasperation.

"If there's a scandal, I know a pretty little stone manor house in the country where we could escape until things blew over."

His enthusiasm was both boyish and contagious. Still, she hesitated. "We'd be deceiving everyone."

"Darling, we're spies. Deception is part of the job. All that matters is that we aren't deceiving ourselves or each other, about what we want, or how we feel."

"You might change your mind, decide you do want to settle down after all. You're young—"

"If you bring up my age one more time, Fanny Drummond, so help me I'll…"

"You'll what?" she demanded, lifting her chin.

Wickedness sparked in his eyes as he leaned toward her and whispered something in her ear, something so very wanton she wasn't even sure it was possible.

Her heart began to pound, and she clenched her thighs against the echo of its erratic pulse in her sex. "That, um…that doesn't exactly sound like a punishment."

If she'd thought his eyes wicked before, they were nothing to his smile. "Then imagine how I'd like to reward you for being good."

She swallowed, suddenly fearful she might melt into a puddle on the spot and trickle away over the edge of the cliff. "All right. I won't mention that you're only four and twenty." One remarkably, enticingly stern brow arced skyward in warning. "I'll simply ask what will happen if you should grow weary of me, or decide you want something different from our arrangement?"

"If I'm willing to trust you with my life as my partner in espionage, don't you think you can trust me to tell you how I feel? How's this, for starters?" He took both of her hands in his, giving her no opportunity to hide from his steady regard. "I've known and admired you for some months. I find you amusing and clever and beautiful. And I would like nothing better than a chance to know you even better—and not only in the carnal sense," he added with a wink.

Nervousness and excitement and uncertainty and joy mingled inside her, rushing out in a trembling laugh. "Oh. That sounds an awful lot like a proposal." Though admittedly, nothing like the one she'd received almost a decade ago.

"Well, it's not," he insisted. "Because experience has taught you that marriage is the opposite of freedom, Fan. And I want no part of making you feel like a prisoner. In fact…" He dropped to one knee in front of her and brought their clasped hands to his heart. "I vow on my honor never to ask you to marry me."

She laughed again and flushed and tried to tug him to his feet, certain that the scattering of passersby must imagine they were witnessing quite the opposite of what was actually taking place.

"That way," he went on, rising at her urging and stepping somehow closer still, "if you should one day say, 'Fitz, will you marry me?' I'll know for certain your feelings about the matter have changed. But a proposal of marriage has nothing to do with my feelings for you."

No one had ever said such marvelous things to her before. Which was to say, no one had ever troubled himself to listen to her before, or to think what it was she would like to hear.

"All right," she agreed with a breathless nod. "Let's try."

He beamed as he looped her arm through his. "Have you a great deal of packing to do?" She could guess by the tone of the question that he hoped to spend the rest of the morning, and perhaps some of the afternoon, in quite another fashion.

"No. But I would dearly love to take a bath."

"Mmm." Desire flared in his eyes. "How fortunate, then, that you have a footman so ready and willing to fetch your hot water."

"And wash any places I can't reach?" she teased.

"Oh, most assuredly. Along with a few places you can."

A shiver of anticipation passed through her. She was quite sure the world wasn't ready for a lady spy and her lover. There would be whispers and probably far worse. At times it might feel as if they were drowning, swimming against the current of society's rules.

But as together they turned their backs on the channel and began to walk toward their future, she fully believed that love would prove more powerful than the tide.

Chapter 22

Maxim had been to General Zebadiah Scott's office in the Horse Guards many times in his younger days. But very little had changed in the intervening years. The view of the parade ground from the window did not alter much with the season. Unless Scott's aide had recently made a clean sweep of things, the desk was always buried beneath a mountain of books and papers. Scott himself still looked like an absentminded grandfather, with his spectacles perched on his forehead and a smear of ink on one sleeve.

Behind that disguise hid the brightest mind Maxim had ever known.

Perhaps the only notable difference to either the room or the man was that no tobacco smoke wreathed his head, though its warm scent still clung to the dark blue drapes. A cursory glance revealed the pipestem peeking from beneath a stack of important-looking documents. Maxim hoped the pipe was unlit.

"I gave it up," Scott explained, as if he could guess what Maxim had been thinking. "Mrs. Scott took the notion I should just before we left for Brighton, as a matter of fact. I don't miss it…much. Mostly when I'm trying to think." And with that, he rescued the pipe from its near burial and clamped the stem between his teeth.

Certainly, over the course of several conversations since his return to London, Maxim had given him plenty to think about: the intelligence he had brought from France about Napoleon's plans in Spain, which could send the war in a new and terrible direction; the information he had managed to extract from Leclerc about the network of French spies operating in Britain; and now Maxim's decision to travel into Northumberland before the weather turned and take up the mantle of Duke of Hartwell, to reclaim the title from its associations with his grandfather's cruelties.

Scott looked neither surprised nor especially disappointed. "I shall miss your insights. No other of my men knows France and the French the way you do. But," he concluded with a sly smile, "I suspect your duchess is happy to have you home to stay."

Maxim still could hardly convince himself it was true. Caro's trust and love were unexpected and precious gifts he would happily spend the rest of his life trying to earn—and to repay.

Setting aside his pipe, Scott reached down to open a desk drawer and withdrew a decanter and two glasses. After pouring a splash of amber liquid in each, he handed one across the desk to Maxim. "A toast. To your lady's health."

"And to yours. *Santé*," Maxim replied with a nod before tossing back the contents of his glass, a surprisingly mellow Scotch whisky.

The general took a more careful sip, savoring the brew. "I had it from one of my men, now stationed—er, settled in the Highlands."

"Settled, eh?" Maxim twisted the tumbler in his fingers. "I wonder, sir, whether there isn't some truth to the rumors about your matchmaking. Six years ago, I was certain you must have sent me to Earnshaw's because of some suspicion you had about the man." He watched a droplet of liquid skate across the bottom of the glass. "Was it in fact Lady Caroline Brent you wanted me to meet?"

"Oh-ho-ho!" The exclamation was drawn out with a sort of laugh that, to Maxim's ear, did not sound much like a denial, though it was followed by the general saying, "I would have thought you, of all people, unlikely to put much faith in rumors." He winked. "Besides, how was I to know which of the seven eligible young ladies invited to Earnshaw's party would best suit?"

It was surely the closest to a confirmation of Scott's machinations that Maxim would ever get. Still, he found unexpected comfort in the knowledge that the general had imagined him worth saving—and not just for his ability to speak fluent French.

He rose and bowed. "I should go and help my wife finish our preparations for the journey northward."

Scott too got to his feet. "I wish you and your duchess safe travels, Hartwell, and much happiness. And may I extend the same on behalf of Mrs. Scott? Our wives became great friends during our visit to Brighton, you know—and *not* at my instigation, lest you were wondering. Though when I later explained the situation, Helen had her doubts about—well…"

"Me?" Maxim suggested.

"And me," Scott answered with a shrug. "She called the match a fiasco. But I encouraged her to have a little faith."

"Then sent Mrs. Drummond and Lieutenant Hopkins to the seaside to keep an eye on us. Just in case."

The general appeared not the slightest bit chagrined. "You know the old saying. All's fair..."

"In love and war. Yes." Maxim tried—and failed—to muster one of his terrible scowls. "Did you and Mrs. Scott lay a wager about whether I would come to my senses?"

"Not in any formal terms, you understand. Let us simply say that tobacco was not the only habit Mrs. Scott was inclined to have me forgo. I am relieved not to have to give up another." Aimlessly, he fingered some papers on the desk, no longer meeting Maxim's eye. "Before you go, I do have one more favor to ask."

"Twenty years of spying for you isn't enough to even the balance sheet?" he asked, the words themselves mild, but underlined by the sharpness with which he set his tumbler on the corner of the desk.

The general folded his hands behind his back, perfectly unperturbed. "You tell me."

No. Of course not. Nothing could repay Scott for having put in motion the plans that had led him to Caro. "Go on."

"I know you'll be busy with your new life. But there may come a time when you see, or hear, something you think I might find of interest. I hope if that happens you will keep in touch?"

Suddenly, Maxim understood just how Scott knew what often seemed impossible for one man to know: the network of supposedly retired secret agents he'd managed to install throughout the country and abroad, under the guise of seeing his men happily married.

But that was a cynical interpretation of the situation. Outside the windows of this office, a storm loomed—one that had nothing to do with the steely late October sky. It was impossible to forget that the British forces' ability to stop Napoleon depended in large measure on the brave men—and women; one must not overlook Mrs. Drummond—who reported to this man.

It was also impossible to doubt that Scott was a romantic at heart, someone who wanted everyone, especially those who risked so much and served so loyally, to be as genuinely happy as he and Mrs. Scott. So he had somehow managed to bring together two disparate worlds, military intelligence and romance, more successfully than anyone would have guessed.

"Love and let spy, as it were?" Maxim's lips quirked.

Scott's blue eyes twinkled. "Precisely."

Maxim bowed. "You have my word, sir."

* * * *

Inside the grand, high-ceilinged entry hall of Hartwell House, near Hanover Square, Maxim conferred with the butler.

"The package has arrived? And you've had it put in the duchess's bedchamber?"

"Yes, Your Grace."

"And not breathed a word of it to her?"

The man looked affronted. "Certainly not, sir."

"Where is she now?"

"In the library, sir. Looking over the letters that came in this afternoon's post."

"Very good."

Maxim took himself to the library on the first floor, which adjoined the drawing room, though at present the doors between the two rooms were shut. Both rooms were darkly furnished, heavy and austere. He had intended to strip out every trace of his grandfather immediately, until his wife had pointed out that the man had rarely visited London, and the style of the rooms actually reflected tastes popular long before his grandfather's day.

"What does it matter?" she had told him with a dismissive wave of one hand as she began to examine the impressive collection of books. "When we return from Chesleigh Court, we can decide whether or not to redecorate."

Now he found her at the enormous mahogany desk—the furniture here was much better sized for him than the spindly legged chairs and tables of Royal Crescent, he had to admit. Her head was bent over a letter, just as the butler had indicated. When he cleared his throat, she looked up and Maxim could see she had been worrying her lower lip.

"Distressing news, my love?" He crossed the room in a half dozen strides, no longer determined to disguise the unevenness of his gait, no longer convinced his limp was a sign of weakness.

"Oh, no. Quite the opposite, in fact. Aunt Brent writes that Mama is doing as well as can be expected, and the doctor expects further improvement still, though it will be gradual. The sea air has been a blessing to them both."

They had left the two older ladies firmly ensconced in the house in Royal Crescent, with Mrs. Horn and the other servants and under the care of a physician—not Trefry, whom Maxim could never again persuade himself to trust. Lady Laughton's cravings for her "tonic" were slowly abating, though not without pain and difficulty. Miss Brent had shown herself a surprisingly able nurse as well as a steadfast friend to her sister-in-law, and in taking care of Lady Laughton had nearly forgotten all her own aches and pains, just as Caro had once predicted.

Maxim took up the delicate hand that lay atop the letter and squeezed it. "Excellent news, I'd say. And what of Lady Catherine?"

"Her engagement to Mr. Parker has been announced." Caro's eyes were that rare luminous golden shade, the one that warmed him to his core. "Thanks to you. My aunt says they will wait to wed until spring, so that Mama may enjoy the celebration. I wondered whether we might not invite them to be married from this house?"

"Whatever you wish, my love," Maxim assured her, turning the letter with his free hand to scan Miss Brent's sloping handwriting. He saw no mention of Laughton's condition.

When the earl had recovered enough to be moved from Trefrey's establishment, Brent-Ashby had taken his father to Springhallow, the family estate in Hampshire. The man had no recollection of Maxim throwing him bodily from the house, no memory of the attack that had rendered him speechless, listless, a shadow of his former self.

Brent-Ashby's true mettle had been shown in his ability to take up his father's affairs and manage them more effectively than Laughton had ever done. Repairs on both the house and the tenants' cottages had begun, along with plans to improve the produce of the farms come spring.

Nevertheless, Caro's guilt over her father's condition had been heavy, as Maxim had expected. He had been nearly at the point of relenting and suggesting that she go to him, rather than come to London. But the strength shown by her siblings, mother, and aunt had persuaded her to join her husband.

"Come with me," he said, tugging gently on her fingers to coax her to rise.

She laid aside the letter and came to her feet, slipping her hand along his arm. "What is it?"

"You'll see."

Together they climbed the stairs to the ducal suite: a pair of sitting rooms and dressing rooms to match two bedchambers, all joined by a pair of ornate doors that were never locked. One of Caro's delicate brows arched. "Ah. I think I have some idea what you have in mind...."

"Do you?" He smiled down at her, the curve of his lips deliberately wicked. "And you may be right. But first..." He swung open the door to her sitting room. Atop a low, curved-leg table sat a large wooden crate, remarkably like the one Fitz Hopkins had brought back to Brighton, the one that had been the cause of great distress and greater understanding.

Now both of Caro's brows rose.

"Something to help you through the cold northern winter," he said, nodding toward it to urge her forward.

"Furs? Velvets?" Her fingertips curved more tightly against his forearm, and she fixed him with a seductive gaze. "I already have everything I need to keep me warm."

"I'm flattered, my love. But why don't you open it and see?"

At last she took a cautious step toward the crate, the top of which had already been loosened, according to Maxim's instructions. Laying it aside, she dug through the packing straw to reveal stacks of leatherbound books, trios of volumes bundled together with twine. She traced the cover of the set that lay uppermost and glanced at him with a curious expression. "Novels?"

"The complete works of Robin Ratliff, as a matter of fact."

"Maxim..."

"Oh, I know. Both you and Mrs. Horn were kind enough to inform me that ladies are better off not reading such silly, romantic books. But when I met you, you were reading one, and I—I can't help but think that if you hadn't been, you might never have seen anything in me worth having." She favored him with an expression of mild annoyance and disbelief, but he went on speaking before she could correct him. "We can't go back to the beginning, I know, but I want you to have everything you were denied, or denied yourself. All the things that bring you pleasure."

She pressed her lips together and shook her head, then stretched up on her tiptoes and kissed him lightly. "Are you not worried they will distract me from my wifely duties?" she teased.

"Not in the slightest," he replied, bending toward her for a more thorough kiss. Her arms came up around his neck. "I'll even read them aloud to you, if you'd like."

"Oh, my love," she said a few moments later, breathless and pink cheeked. "Thank you. I predict this is a gift we will both enjoy."

"Only a fraction of what you deserve, Caro. And nothing compared to the gift you've given me." Reaching behind his head, he caught her hands and brought them forward, planting a kiss on her knuckles. "My grandfather told me I was unworthy of being the Duke of Hartwell, because I would never be whole and could never be contented."

The answering shake of her head was almost pitying. "Some people have no imagination."

"But I fear he would have been proved right—I could never be those things, without you."

"And some people want to leap to all sorts of ridiculous conclusions without waiting for the end of the story," she chided.

"The end of the story?" He turned her hand in his and pressed his lips to the delicate skin of her inner wrist, relishing the leap of her pulse.

Anticipation—of his further touch, of their future—trembled in her voice. "The happily ever after, of course."

Epilogue

July 1815

Helen Scott had long been a novel reader, the more spine tingling and hair raising the better. But she could not ever remember feeling such a rush of excitement at the prospect of starting a new chapter.

Not, of course, that Zebadiah's retirement would mean completely setting aside his duties in favor of a life of relaxation. He would always be General Scott, someone with knowledge and experience to be consulted on matters of grave importance to the nation. Nevertheless, the end of the war—the true end, this time, not the brief peace of '02 or that silly business of trying to contain Napoleon to Elba—had opened a door and her husband had stepped through it. No more long days at Whitehall or visitors to their home on Audley Street that she was supposed to pretend to know nothing about. Just the two of them, together, with time and leisure they had never had in almost forty years of marriage.

Even now, nearly a month after he had told her his plans, the thought of it still made her heart beat with anticipation.

Today's celebration, a garden party at the Richmond home of Sir Langley and Lady Stanhope, was the last and least public event marking the occasion of Zebadiah's retirement. The majority of the guests were intelligence officers—*former* intelligence officers, Zebby had corrected her more than once. She had never met most of them, but she knew them, knew the work they had done to keep the nation safe.

She was not *supposed* to know them, however. Or their work. Zebby had made such a point of shielding her from it. He had never spoken of such matters over dinner or in the privacy of their bedchamber, had not confided in her in times of either triumph or trouble. But she had always known, all the same.

Particularly about the matchmaking.

Behind the Stanhopes' charming stone manor house, a lush lawn descended in broad, easy steps to the banks of the Thames. Every level was dotted with couples, brought together by her husband's machinations. And though she was proud of all her husband had accomplished in his years in military intelligence, it was this—his determination that love would win in the end—that made her heart threaten to burst.

She knew also that most of these men, though no longer serving in any official capacity, had continued to provide vital information to the Crown. Most interesting of all, some of their wives were not just aware of their husbands' work as shadow intelligence agents, but fully involved themselves.

Take Lady Stanhope, for instance. Helen turned toward the tent beneath which her host and hostess stood together, surveying the scene with satisfaction. Lean and stern-featured Sir Langley still had the erect posture of an officer; his wife was softer, more willowy. Some might describe her as flighty. When the former Lady Kingston had married Major Sir Langley Stanhope, the reserved knight and the reclusive widow had stunned society by making something of a career of hosting lavish house parties. Given their experience, Helen had been confident everything would be elegantly arranged today.

But she had also long ago guessed that the Stanhopes' house parties were not mere entertainments. After all, such gatherings would also be excellent opportunities for overhearing things, important things. And for all Lady Stanhope's supposed propensity for chatter, Helen guessed she was more than capable of listening.

Just as she stepped toward the Stanhopes, she spied Zebby moving through the crowd in the same direction. When she looked at him, she saw both the distinguished general in his midsixties and the young man she had married. His hair had been red then, and his rank considerably lower; silver hair had come early, well before the promotions. Always clever, he had used the premature appearance of an absentminded old man to his advantage, playing the part to great effect with certain of his officers, and once, with the king himself.

Of course, she wasn't to know any of that, either.

"Mrs. Scott," he exclaimed as he drew closer. With a familiar twinkle in his blue eyes, he extended an arm to her. "Can I tempt you to take some refreshment?"

"I should like very much to thank our host and hostess," she replied, linking her arm with his, tamping down her nervousness. She was about to do the unthinkable in a gathering of spies. But it was time to have everything out in the open.

Sir Langley bowed and Lady Stanhope curtsied as they approached.

"You've managed everything to perfection, Lady Stanhope," Helen said. "Even the weather." A playful breeze made the warm sunshine pleasant, sending puffs of white clouds scurrying across a blue sky.

Lady Stanhope acknowledged the praise with a dip of her head. "It has been our sincere pleasure, ma'am. Everyone was eager to gather together to honor the general."

Zebadiah's chest puffed, just a little, and Helen smiled. "Well," she said, with a determined look at the other three, "it makes a fitting end, given all the other parties you've hosted on his behalf."

The breath left her husband's lungs in a sputtering cough. Lady Stanhope glanced uncertainly toward her husband, whose eyes glittered behind his silver-rimmed spectacles. "Why, Mrs. Scott," he said mildly, amusement tugging at the corner of his mouth, "I haven't the faintest notion what you mean."

"I'd be shocked if you did." Helen plucked up a glass of crisp white wine from a nearby table and handed it to Zebby. "Otherwise, you would not be one of my husband's best agents." She turned toward Lady Stanhope. "Your sons are both at Cambridge, are they not? I hope now that the war is over, you will be able to enjoy having the house more to yourself."

One of Lady Stanhope's slender hands fluttered up to rest over her husband's heart. "I think we will, yes. Thank you, Mrs. Scott."

Once he had recovered, Zebby nodded to the Stanhopes and tightened his hold on Helen's arm to draw her on. He'd been sipping carefully at the glass of wine, but once they were apart from the others, he tossed back the remainder as if in need of fortification. "About the Stanhopes' house parties, my dear. What on earth made you imagine—?"

"That you were behind them?" she supplied lightly. "Oh, it was really a matter of simple observation. The gossip pages were always the most rumpled parts of the newspaper, and as I had never paid them much mind, I realized it must have been you who was carefully poring over the latest on-dits. Once I started reading them regularly, I began to notice a pattern: an arrest for sedition or something like it inevitably followed one of Lady Stanhope's grand house parties."

"Why, that could be mere coincidence."

"If one believed in such things," she agreed with a teasing laugh, knowing that her husband held no stock in chance.

He opened his mouth to retort, but before he could speak, they were divided by a brown-and-white spaniel racing between their legs, its leash trailing behind. They sprang apart just in time to make room for the little boy of about four who came next, a piece of cake clutched in one hand, not so much running after the dog as running away from his elder sister, who was just a few steps behind, shouting, "Thomas Eleazor Sutherland, when I catch you, I'll—"

"Ah. A perfectly timed interruption," Zebby said when the trio had passed. A hand on Helen's elbow, he made a beeline for a plump, brown-haired woman seated beside a tree with another spaniel in her lap. "I know you will wish to make the acquaintance of Lady Magnus, my dear. It is she whom you must thank for the early copies of all those Robin Ratliff books you so enjoy."

"How lovely to meet you, ma'am," the woman said, tucking the dog under one arm as she rose and extended ink-stained fingers to Helen. "But a few books can never make up for the debt of gratitude I owe your husband. He was kind enough to send Lord Magnus to me in Scotland, where I was working as Mr. Ratliff's secretary."

They were joined by a gentleman with curling brown hair and laughing wrinkles at the corners of his hazel eyes. "You make it sound as if I arrived gift wrapped, my dear." He had the runaway dog's leash in one hand, and the shoulder of the cake-besmeared boy in the other. The girl, perhaps six, looked on triumphantly.

"Magnus was one of mine, before he inherited his title," Zebadiah explained. "Of course I had no way of knowing—"

"Yes, yes. Another of your remarkable coincidences, I'm sure," the gentleman said, "insisting I return to Balisaig where the woman I'd loved and lost just happened to have taken up residence." He bowed. "A pleasure to meet you, Mrs. Scott."

"Likewise."

"I'm Tommy," piped up the boy, which earned him another frown from his sister.

"You were supposed to be keeping an eye on the dogs," the girl announced. "I found him hiding beneath the cake table, Mama."

"Don't tattle, Theodora," Lady Magnus told her. "As for you, young man, no more sweets—for you or the dogs." Hardly had that edict left her lips when the spaniel in her arms squirmed free to lick cake crumbs from the boy's face, making them all laugh.

Lord Magnus handed both leashes to his daughter, who dutifully took her brother's sticky palm in her own and led the three troublemakers away. Zebadiah shook Lord Magnus's hand. "I'm honored you would come all this way."

"We wouldn't have missed it. And the trip gave Lady Magnus a chance to take care of some business at Persephone Press."

"So you still work for Mr. Ratliff, then?" Helen asked.

Lord Magnus answered in a pleasant Scottish burr, "Indeed, Ratliff would be nothing without her." Helen thought she saw him wink at his wife out of the corner of one eye.

Just then a tinkling chime sounded, and they all turned to discover Sir Langley tapping a goblet with a silver spoon to call them all together beneath the shade of a canopy.

With a nod to Lord and Lady Magnus, Helen gently steered her husband back in the direction from whence they'd come.

"A ceremony, my dear? Really?"

"Only a toast."

As they walked to join the others and the crowd of former intelligence officers parted to make way for them to pass, he said to her in a low voice, "Do you honestly fancy that all these men are somehow still in my service?"

"In their own ways, yes. And some of their wives too."

"Now really, I must protest—"

Helen tipped her chin toward another couple, a woman with short golden locks and a handsome, dark-haired man. "I also took note that tales of the scandalous thief Lady Sterling disappeared from those same gossip columns around the same time our butler informed me that Lord Sterling—Captain Addison, that is—paid a late-night visit to our house with the young woman who is now his wife."

Zebadiah glanced toward the man and woman in question, who stood fortunately out of earshot. Lady Sterling's head was at present tipped upward, looking into the laughing face of the little girl seated easily on Lord Sterling's shoulders.

"And Everham Estates always receives a sizable donation shortly after some shockingly dissolute nobleman gets his comeuppance." The Sterlings managed one of Britain's foremost charitable institutions on behalf of injured soldiers and exploited domestics.

"The Crown has ways of showing its gratitude for valuable information," Zebadiah acknowledged. "But that hardly means—"

For just a moment, she thought he meant to go on denying his influence, and she sighed.

But in the end, it seemed he too was tired of keeping secrets. His shoulders sank a notch. "How long have you known?"

"Why, my dear, I've always known you had a soft spot for your men—for keeping them safe, for seeing them happy. The sheer number of wedding invitations over the years would have told me that. And if some of their gifts of gratitude—a lovely bottle of Scotch whisky, for instance—arrived with a thick letter that sent you back to the office late in the evening, well…"

Zebadiah hummed. "Painstaking work, piecing together all those bits of evidence. If you were one of my men, I'd recommend a promotion."

She arched one brow and sent him a mischievous glance. "Can't you think of any other suitable reward, Zebadiah?"

"Several, actually. To start, I'd like to—"

She laid a staying hand on his arm as Captain Fitz Hopkins approached them, one of the few gentlemen present clad in his scarlet uniform, which clashed magnificently with his coppery hair. Helen could not help but be reminded of a young Zebadiah. "Good afternoon, sir," he said. "May I take the liberty of wishing you well?"

"Captain Hopkins. Thank you. I suppose Colonel Millrose sent you in his place? I thought perhaps, given the peace, he'd be more willing to abandon the shop."

The young man's gray eyes flared in surprise. "I, er, I assumed you'd already heard—"

"Heard what?"

"The very morning that the peace was declared, Colonel Millrose decided to…" Another pause sent Zebby's bushy white eyebrows a notch higher, making them visible above the top rim of his spectacles. "He's on his honeymoon," Captain Hopkins finished weakly. "Apparently he'd been nursing a tendre for that missionary lady who hangs about the neighborhood—"

"Miss Davis," Zebby supplied easily. "So, she finally said yes?"

"So it would seem. Not five minutes after the news of Napoleon's defeat had arrived, Colonel Millrose walked up from his office and out the door of the tobacco shop, crossed the street to Miss Davis's usual post, took her in his arms, and"—he glanced toward Helen, then paused to swallow hard—"kissed her. They were married three days ago."

"How romantic," Helen declared.

"Yes, ma'am," agreed the flustered young man. "We're all happy for him."

"You must take good care of the Underground in his absence, Hopkins."

The captain straightened, suddenly every inch the officer accepting his charge. "Yes, sir." And then he bowed his gratitude three times before hurrying away.

When he was gone, Helen asked, "What was it, do you suppose, that finally convinced Miss Davis to accept Colonel Millrose: the peace or the kiss?"

"Mrs. Scott," Zebby scolded her teasingly. "I'm astonished at you. Smiling at such scandalous conduct from one of my officers."

"Oh, don't pretend with me. You knew about the wedding. Of course you must have known. Why, I daresay you had some hand in the lady's choice of that particular neighborhood for her mission field."

"Certainly not!" he protested. "I will confess to knowing something of his interest in her, but beyond that, I am innocent. This time, at any rate." His blue eyes twinkled, but as the crowd gathered and grew, some of their sparkle dimmed. "You promised there wouldn't be a fuss."

"I said there wouldn't be a *great* fuss," she countered. "You must allow us to fuss over you a little." At his resigned sigh, she added reassuringly, "I have asked the Duke of Hartwell to make a toast. He is hardly an effusive, sentimental sort of man."

"He *was* not, I'll allow. But since his reunion with his wife..."

"All your doing," she reminded him. "Come, my dear. It's time for a taste of your own medicine."

In the crowd, she spotted the Duke of Hartwell limping forward, his steps impeded not by his injuries, but by a pair of little girls of perhaps two and three, their arms wrapped around his legs as he trudged along, pretending to search for them as they laughed and squealed in protest. The duchess walked beside them, smiling indulgently at her husband and daughters. When she turned and held out a hand to the young Marquess of Chesleigh, a lad of not quite six, her high-waisted gown clung to her figure to reveal the impending arrival of another blessing.

"After so many years apart, it would seem the duke and duchess have made good use of their time together," Helen said in a low voice. It was marvelous, after what seemed a lifetime of war, to find oneself surrounded by so much love. And even better to think that her husband had played such a prominent role in ending the one and forwarding the other.

"Always knew they would be well suited, if Hartwell would let down his guard. All it took was a little prompting. Though when I think back on those days, I do wish Hopkins and Mrs. Drummond had made a go of things too. They've spoiled a perfect record," he confided with a self-deprecating laugh.

Her eyes found Frances Drummond at the edge of the crowd, still coolly beautiful with her pale eyes and blond hair. Captain Hopkins stood near, but not beside her. Through a little spy work of her own, Helen had worked out that Zebby had paired the two for several more assignments after the Hartwell case. But she'd never found any evidence of the love affair Zebadiah had hoped for. Their careful, professional regard for one another, reserved when everyone around them was merry, cast the slightest shadow over an otherwise glorious day.

"I hope you can forgive me, my dear," Zebby said, snatching two glasses of champagne from the tray proffered by a passing footman and handing one to her.

"For what?"

"I might have known I could have trusted you, confided in you. But I wanted—"

"To protect me." She tipped her head to his shoulder. "I understand—I understood. It kept me from feeling anything like resentment. I could not bring myself to take you to task for wanting our home to be free of talk of espionage and war. Besides, don't I bear some share of blame for the deception? I might have revealed what I'd worked out. But I never wanted to be the cause of more worry—you had enough to manage."

Just then the Duke of Hartwell began to speak in his deep, compelling voice and they were obliged to turn and listen.

"Ladies and gentlemen, it is my very great honor to offer a few words of praise and gratitude to a man who has meant so much to all of us. But what can I say that will not already have occurred to every person here?

"So instead, I ask you to raise your glass if you ever doubted his orders, followed them grudgingly, and were glad you did." A laugh rippled through the crowd, and a few bold men lifted their glasses shoulder high, among them Lord Magnus. "Raise your glass if he sent you on a mission for which you were not qualified, and during which you discovered a side of yourself you never knew existed." A glass shot skyward. Helen craned her neck to see whose hand held it and discovered Lord Sterling, color staining his cheeks as he sent his wife a chagrined glance. "Raise your glass if you owe him your life," Hartwell continued, more somber. Several glasses went up then, including the duke's, but Sir Langley Stanhope's rose highest. "And finally, raise a glass if you once thought yourself immune to his matchmaking and have never been so grateful to be proved wrong." More laughter, a nodding murmur rippling like a wave through the crowd, and then almost every glass was in the air, the ladies' as well as the gentlemen's.

Out of the corner of her eye, she saw Captain Hopkins's arm move, almost involuntarily, and Mrs. Drummond's reach out to steady it. He laid his free hand over hers and nodded once, conspiratorially.

Perhaps Zebby's matchmaking record was unblemished after all?

He had been thinking in terms of a marriage announcement, of course. How would he respond to the possibility that Captain Hopkins and Mrs. Drummond *were* in love and happy, just as he'd hoped—but preferred to keep their affair secret?

Helen gasped and turned eagerly toward her husband. "What is it, my dear?" he asked, glancing down at her, tears glittering in his smiling eyes.

Pressing her lips together, she shook her head. Of all people, Zebby could appreciate that some matters were best left unspoken. Some secrets weren't hers to tell. "It's just all so…so perfect." Then she raised her own glass to join the others glinting beneath the summer sun.

"To Zebadiah Scott," the Duke of Hartwell finished, and the crowd echoed their response as a single booming voice.

Helen had thought this day might never come. She had imagined the occasion marred by regret. But now she could only laugh at how wrong she had been. This was a celebration of love, of the future.

After her husband had dipped his head in acknowledgment and everyone had drunk their toast to him, he cleared his throat to speak. "Thank you all for coming. It has been the honor of a lifetime to work with you. And now, I will go into my retirement content in the knowledge that I did all I could to secure the peace, both abroad and"—he nodded knowingly at the couples nearest him—"closer to home. But it would be remiss of me not to acknowledge that, of all the matches I've made, my first was clearly the wisest and the best. To beginnings."

Around them, she heard sniffles and sighs of approval. But her eyes were only for her husband, the spymaster who loved her.

With a mischievous smile, she tipped their glasses together. "And happy endings."

ABOUT THE AUTHOR

Almost as soon as she could hold a pencil, **Susanna Craig** began writing stories. Today, she pens award-winning Regency-era romance novels that blend history and heart with a dash of heat. An English professor, wife, and mom, she's currently finding her happily ever after in Kentucky while holding onto her Midwestern roots. Find her online at www.susannacraig.com.

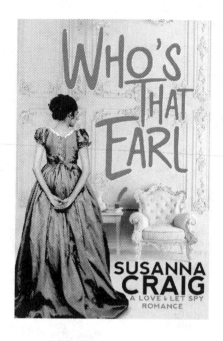

WHO'S THAT EARL
Love & Let Spy Series
Will scandalous secrets stand in the way of a second chance at love?

Miss Jane Quayle excels at invention. How else could the sheltered daughter of an English gentleman create lurid gothic novels so infamous someone wants their author silenced forever? Fortunately, Jane has taken steps to protect herself, first by assuming a pen name, and second, by taking up residence at remote Dunnock Castle, surrounded by rugged scenery that might have been ripped from the pages of one of her books.
Her true identity remains a secret, until one dark and stormy night . . .

After years of spying for the British army, Thomas Sutherland doubts the Highlands will ever feel like home again. Nevertheless, thanks to a quirk of Scottish inheritance law, he's now the Earl of Magnus, complete with a crumbling castle currently inhabited by a notorious novelist. When the writer turns out to be the woman Thomas once wooed, suspicions rise even as mutual sparks reignite. As danger closes in, can Jane and Thomas overcome their pasts to forge a future together?

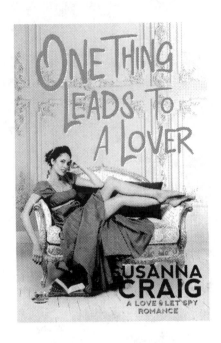

ONE THING LEADS TO A LOVER
Love & Let Spy Series
***Opposites attract more than trouble in the latest captivating Regency
romance from Susanna Craig.***

Amanda Bartlett, widowed Countess of Kingston, is a woman beyond
reproach. Married at nineteen, she dutifully provided the Earl with an
heir and a spare before his death three years ago. Since then, Amanda
has lived a simple, quiet life. A life that, if she were honest, has become
more than a trifle dull. So when an adventure literally drops into her lap,
in the shape of a mysterious book, she intends to make the most of it—
especially if it brings her closer to a charismatic stranger. . . .

Major Langley Stanhope, an intelligence officer and master mimic known
as the Magpie, needs to retrieve the code book that has fallen into Amanda's
hands. The mistaken delivery has put them both in grave danger and in
a desperate race to unearth a traitor. It's also stirred an intense, reckless
attraction. Langley believes the life he leads is not suitable for a delicate
widow, but it seems he may have underestimated the lady's daring . . . and
the depths of their mutual desire. . . .

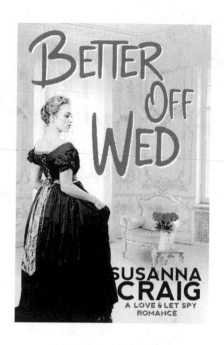

BETTER OFF WED
Love & Let Spy series
She's an avenging angel . . . who tempts him like the devil . . .

If Miss Laura Hopkins desired a husband, her beauty, brains, and fortune would make it easy to acquire one. Instead, Laura prefers to put her charms to another purpose entirely. Using the alias Lady Sterling, Laura helps young women who have been mistreated or compromised by their employers. Some might see it as theft and blackmail. For Laura, it is a small measure of justice. But while in pursuit of her latest target, Laura is unexpectedly aided by a gentleman who announces that he is *Lord* Sterling.

As a spy for the Crown, Captain Jeremy Addison, Viscount Sterling, has been assigned all manner of dangerous missions, though none as complicated as investigating the beguiling Lady Sterling. Forced to pose as newlyweds at the home of a disreputable earl, Laura and Jeremy forge an unexpected alliance . . . and a passionate connection. But can such a dangerous masquerade possibly lead to a real, lasting love?

Printed in the United States
by Baker & Taylor Publisher Services